Hell or High Water

Jerrie Alexander

Copyright © 2013 Jerrie Alexander
Cover Art: Meredith Blair © Author's Angels
www.AuthorsAngels.com
Formatting: Marissa Dobson – Sizzling PR

All rights reserved. No part of this book may be used or reproduced in any manner whatsoever without written permission of the author except in the case of brief quotations embodied in critical articles or reviews.

This is a work of fiction. Names, characters, places, and incidents are either the product of the author's imagination or are used fictitiously, and the resemblance to actual persons living or dead, business establishments, events, or locales is entirely coincidental.

Printed in the United States of America

ACKNOWLEDGEMENTS:

I would be remiss if I didn't acknowledge the following people. Their support, advice, and enthusiasm were invaluable.

To my editor, Joyce Lamb, your guidance helped me polish this story until it shone. For that, you have my sincere appreciation.

To Barb Han and Jackie Pressley, who critiqued my words, poked and prodded me when the story stalled, listened while I complained and pressured me to work through the rough spots. My thanks and gratitude for your support.

To my advisor on all firearms and tactical matters, a real American hero who prefers to remain nameless, thanks for sharing your knowledge and for your service to our country. Any mistakes are my own!

To my husband, who has always said I could do anything I set my mind to, and our daughter, who believed in this book from the beginning, thank you for your unwavering love and support.

Last but not least, thanks to my readers. I hope you enjoy this story as much as I loved writing it.

Contents

CHAPTER ONE	7
CHAPTER TWO	15
CHAPTER THREE	21
CHAPTER FOUR	27
CHAPTER FIVE	33
CHAPTER SIX	39
CHAPTER SEVEN	49
CHAPTER EIGHT	58
CHAPTER NINE	65
CHAPTER TEN	73
CHAPTER ELEVEN	79
CHAPTER TWELVE	87
CHAPTER THIRTEEN	95
CHAPTER FOURTEEN	102
CHAPTER FIFTEEN	109
CHAPTER SIXTEEN	116
CHAPTER SEVENTEEN	122
CHAPTER EIGHTEEN	127
CHAPTER NINETEEN	133
CHAPTER TWENTY	141
CHAPTER TWENTY ONE	148

CHAPTER TWENTY TWO	154
CHAPTER TWENTY THREE	162
CHAPTER TWENTY FOUR	168
CHAPTER TWENTY FIVE	175
CHAPTER TWENTY SIX	182
CHAPTER TWENTY SEVEN	189
CHAPTER TWENTY EIGHT	197
CHAPTER TWENTY NINE	203
CHAPTER THIRTY	212
CHAPTER THIRTY ONE	217
CHAPTER THIRTY TWO	224
CHAPTER THIRTY THREE	230
CHAPTER THIRTY FOUR	238
READ COLD DAY IN HELL	249
ABOUT THE AUTHOR	257

Chapter One

The desire to surrender, to slip into a painless, deep sleep tugged hard at Kay Taylor. A voice inside her head warned not to sink into the beckoning void. Danger lurked in the darkness.

She forced her eyes open.

A thin stream of light shone through a slightly ajar door. Kay blinked in hopes of clearing her blurred vision. The slight movement set off an explosion inside her head. She bit back the scream gurgling up the back of her throat. My God. Her wrists were bound.

Her thoughts splintered. She remembered walking across her apartment's parking lot. Someone had attacked her from behind.

Why? Where was she? The empty room with its pale, windowless walls and cool cement floor provided no answers. She pushed up on one elbow. A wave of nausea forced her to lie back down. Pain surged over her right ear. Her stomach roiled at the acrid scent of blood.

Her blood.

Cool air chilled her midriff. That her blouse was torn sent a new tremor through her. Her shoes were gone, but her slacks were intact and still zipped. Relief washed over her.

She ignored the white-hot headache and pushed her churning, queasy stomach from her mind. Panic simmered just under the surface, waiting to claw to the outside. This was the time to make smart decisions. Survival took precedence.

Her feet weren't bound, so she maneuvered herself to a sitting position against the wall. The movement brought another round of explosions in her head. Voices from outside the room seemed to move closer. Kay's skin crawled. Beads of sweat formed above her lips. She hurriedly raised her wrists to her mouth and tore at the tape with her teeth.

"I don't get it. Why'd we take her?" a deep gravelly voice asked.

Kay's fight-or-flight response launched to hyper-drive. Her heart pounded against her rib cage, and her feet demanded she run.

"We're not paid to 'get it.' Boss said snatch her. He's got some questions for her. You better hope you didn't hit that woman too hard." The second voice sounded closer.

"I didn't hurt the bitch. I tapped her upside the head to stop her from fighting."

"And ripped her clothes," Gravelly Voice commented.

"Just checking out the merchandise." The man's chuckle sent Kay into a full-body shiver. A jolt of adrenaline flooded her system. The voices got louder, which meant her kidnappers were coming closer.

The last of the tape ripped, freeing her hands.

She'd heard all the horror stories about women being kidnapped and raped. No way. She wouldn't let that happen without one hell of a fight.

Nothing good came from waiting for evil to come to you. Kay pulled her legs under her, and after a couple of tries, pushed herself to her feet. She braced against the wall for a second to gather strength. Blanking out the rockets going off in her brain, she widened her stance, prepared to kick the first person to enter the room.

The sound of the voices peaked then faded. Had they passed by?

Issuing a silent prayer, she inched down the wall toward the slightly open door. She sidestepped closer, straining to listen. A male voice shouted, threatening consequences if the woman was dead. Was he talking about her?

Escape was now or never. With her captors' attention elsewhere, Kay stepped through the opening then headed toward a red exit light in the opposite direction of the voices.

She braced her hands against an outside door. Decision time. If the alarm was armed, sirens would blast the second she pressed the bar. A dry swallow, and then she wrapped her fingers around the cool, hard metal. She pushed slowly, relief washing over her when the only sound was the snick of the lock opening. She stepped out into the night. Her sweaty skin chilled in the warm air.

Too soon to celebrate freedom. She put one foot in front of the other and kept moving.

A few overhead lights illuminated the area. Smells of gasoline and exhaust fumes assaulted her senses. She'd exited into a parking lot full of tractor-trailer rigs with Texas license plates. At least they hadn't taken her across state lines, or worse, the Mexican border.

Kay ran toward a chain-link fence. She darted behind a row of parked trailers. Her breath came in gasps, and her lungs burned like a wildfire raging out of control. Sweat dripped down her back. She couldn't give in to the pain. This might be her one shot at freedom.

Her bare feet slapped against the pavement, echoing through the darkness. Kay stumbled on a loose piece of asphalt and had to wave her arms to regain her balance. She swiped a hand over her eyes as if she could wipe away her blurred vision. Her injury was more serious than she'd hoped. She needed help. Soon. Very soon.

Voices from behind drifted through the night air. The gravelly voice seemed to be getting closer. She fought the urge to look over her shoulder.

"Run faster," she whispered the brave words, hoping to counteract the icy fingers wrapped around her spine, chilling her bones. Her thoughts grew fuzzy. She had to stay focused.

At the end of the fence line, she spotted a long building with floodlights blazing. Thank God. The warehouse had hundreds of trailers lined up like sentries outside unloading docks. Somebody was working a late shift. Could she reach the structure without exposing herself to the voices chasing her? Help was within reach. If she hid in the shadows, she might get across the street into the industrial park undetected. She pulled in a deep breath, and used her last burst of energy.

Black dots formed in front of her eyes. Again, she shook her head, holding back the dark tunnel closing off her vision.

A loud buzzer sounded, ratcheting her heart rate higher. Seconds later, giant overhead doors opened. One after another, they went up, flooding the area with more light. Life saving light. Workers would be there to unload freight at any moment. She stayed pressed to the wall and crept to where two men stood with their backs to her. They were just inside the building.

"Help," she called out, but the darkness pulled at her.

Her legs buckled, unable to support her any longer. Strong

hands grabbed her arms from behind. She struggled to stay out of the black hole.

A losing battle.

****

"You think she's dead?" A warm breath brushed across Kay's cheek.

Half asleep and drowsy, Kay didn't have to open her eyes to recognize the voice. The aroma of stale coffee and donuts reminded her of days spent in the patrol car. Another odor weighed in stronger. Sterile. Bleach?

"Nah. She's got too much color in her cheeks. The dried spittle is a giveaway. Dead people don't drool."

She wiped her mouth in case Tomas wasn't lying and opened her eyes to find herself flanked by her two favorite detectives.

Memories slammed into Kay with the force of a tsunami, snapping her wide awake. She moved her mouth, but no sound came out.

"Take it easy. You're safe." Wayne's slow drawl eased her tension.

She scanned her stark, white surroundings. The medicinal scent seemed to grow stronger, and she recognized her room as being in the Dallas Memorial Hospital.

Dallas Police Department detectives Tomas Mendez and Wayne Kern dragged chairs close to her bed then stretched their legs out in front of them. They appeared to be staying. She was glad the chief of police had sent these two men. In the past, the three of them had investigated and resolved some serious child-abuse cases. The expressions on their faces made her tense.

"How and when did I get here?"

"Almost forty-eight hours. Warehouse foreman called 911," a solemn-faced Wayne spoke. "The report of your attack made it back to the chief. He assigned the case to us."

"I'm glad. Either of you talk with my doctor?"

"We did. He assured us your injuries aren't serious."

Kay tried to wet her lips and failed. She spotted the water jug next to a brochure advertising the hospital. "Good to know." Her voice cracked.

"You've been mumbling," Wayne continued. "We couldn't make

out many words. But kidnap came through loud and clear. Any idea why somebody would snatch you?"

"None." The safety of Dallas Memorial didn't stop the shiver of fear racing through her system.

Her mother stepped into the room followed closely by Kay's best friend, Holly. Their wrinkled clothes and disheveled appearance tugged at Kay's heart. The frowns on their faces and circles under their eyes indicated neither had slept last night.

"I knew we shouldn't have gone for coffee." Kay's mother rushed to her side.

"Have you met my mother, Beth Taylor, and my friend, Holly Hoffman?" Kay didn't ask about her father. He wasn't coming.

"Sure did," Wayne said. "They're welcome to stay while we talk. If that's okay with you."

"More than okay." She clung to her mother's hand.

"Mind if I record our conversation?" Wayne's red hair and freckles gave his features a boyish quality. Probably fifty, he looked closer to thirty.

"Not at all."

He placed a small recorder on the roll-around table and glanced over at Tomas. His nod was barely noticeable.

Her mother held a straw to Kay's lips, and she drew the cool water into her mouth, letting it soothe her parched throat. As always, Mom knew what Kay needed.

"Thanks. You guys look like you're at a funeral." Kay mustered a smile for the small group. "You said I'm fine."

"And you are," Tomas agreed. "We're more concerned about what brought you here. Any pissed-off parents mad enough at you to seek revenge?"

Kay's brain filtered through her last few cases. In the past, she'd dealt with lots of unhappy moms and dads. In her line of work as investigator for Dallas Child Protective Services, the kids' needs and welfare were her focus.

"Nothing lately. Most of my attention has been on working the Vaughn abduction with you two."

"You visited Leann Vaughn in this hospital yesterday, right?" Wayne asked.

"I did. How'd you know?"

Wayne raised one eyebrow. "Well, your name is on the card. What time did you leave the girl's room?"

"I don't remember exactly." Kay reached into her memory again. "They'd just delivered her dinner tray. Why?"

"A nurse discovered her dead shortly after you left. Slashed her left wrist deep enough to bleed out pretty quick."

"No." Kay bolted upright. The sudden burst of lightning in her head and the surge of nausea sent her right back down to her pillow. "It's not true."

"The girl had the weapon in her right hand. You know as well as I, suicides rarely cut both wrists. Any idea how Leann might've gotten her hands on a knife?" Wayne was in full-out cop mode.

"No. You don't think I gave something that dangerous to a teenager. Do you?" Kay glared at Wayne.

"Of course not. Leann mention any other visitors?"

"Only that I'd just missed her mother. And no way was Leann suicidal yesterday."

"The autopsy will tell us more. What do you remember about your conversation?"

"I was on a mission. Chief Compton sent me to convince her to testify against Hank Walsh." A blast of guilt hit her chest.

"What?"

"She didn't want to testify. I pushed her too hard."

"You did your job." Tomas moved to stand beside her bed. His hand gripped her arm reassuringly.

"Leann was lucid and showed no signs of depression. She didn't want to testify. All she wanted was to move on."

Tomas continued. "What happened when you left Leann's room?"

Kay took a deep breath, pushed her guilt aside, and described how she'd been attacked from behind. She presented the facts not as a victim but an outside, unaffected party, exactly like her previous police work had trained her to do.

Victim? She recoiled at the word. As an investigator, she worked with victims. Comforted them. Protected them. Hell, she'd transferred from Dallas Police Department to work with children.

Her two years spent on patrol had given her a taste of what some of these kids went through. She'd never been through the trauma they had.

"The two incidents must be related." She tried to remember more, anything to help.

"Not necessarily," Wayne interjected. "Anybody you can think of who'd hate you bad enough to snatch you?"

Kay didn't hesitate with her answer. "You both know who. Hank Walsh. And that makes Leann's death and my kidnapping related." Damn, sometimes Tomas and Wayne were thickheaded.

"You need to take a break?" Tomas patted her wrist.

"No, thank you." Kay withdrew her trembling hand. "Let's get this over with."

"We're almost finished," Wayne chimed in his support.

Tomas leaned forward. "If I show you an aerial shot of the industrial park where you were found, could you point out the building where you were held?"

"I doubt it." She closed her eyes for a moment. "I'm sorry, Tomas. I can't remember anything else. I can't tell you whether the moon was out or not."

"*Está bien.*" He glanced at her mother. "It's all good. We'll figure it out."

"Drive me around the area and let me look. Maybe something will come back."

"When you're better. Anything else?" Wayne asked.

"No." A memory of the gravelly voice flashed. "One of the voices said I was too old."

"What if they snatched the wrong person?" Holly piped up. She stood and approached Kay's bed. Her long blond ponytail swished from side to side.

"Shh." Kay's mother cast a stern glance at Holly.

"Actually, that's a good question." Wayne gave Holly a don't-worry-about-it headshake. "Maybe after they got a better look at you, they realized you were older than their intended target." He shut off the recorder. "Get some rest. Call us if you remember anything."

"Who's gonna stay with you?" Tomas pocketed the recorder.

"That would be me." Tyrell Castillo's tone left no room for

dispute. His broad shoulders and hulking frame filled the doorway.

"Come in." Kay held her hand out for him to take.

Wayne and Tomas got to their feet. Tyrell crossed to her bed without cracking a smile. Kay introduced him to Tomas and Wayne, puzzling at the rigidity of their body language as they shook hands. Tyrell leaned down and dropped a kiss on Kay's forehead before turning to face her mother.

"Mrs. Taylor you're looking well."

"Liar." Kay's mother stood for a hug.

"Holly." Tyrell ruffled her hair as if she were a kid.

Standing next to the detectives, Tyrell's six-foot-two-inch linebacker frame dwarfed both of them. His caramel-colored skin, a gift from his black father and Hispanic mother, stood out against the white shirt he wore.

Kay almost laughed at the sparks shooting from the three men. They looked like dogs circling each other to see which one backed down first.

Her money was on her longtime friend. His black eyes and bald head gave him a menacing aura. Tyrell wouldn't blink.

Tomas rolled his eyes and cast a glance at Wayne. "Let's ride, hillbilly."

Chapter Two

"The doctor said take it easy. He didn't say I had to stay at home." Kay defended her decision for the third time. "Besides, it's important I get to the morgue."

Holly's sea-blue gaze narrowed. "This isn't a good idea. Tyrell will be mad when he finds out you left the apartment alone."

"I'm not. You're with me. Besides, the cops will never find my purse. It would be naïve of me to hope it turns up intact."

"I still don't think he'll like it."

"He's not the one without a cell, a license or credit cards. And his opinion isn't as important to me as it is to you."

"Maybe we should take his advice and get away. Use our two-week vacation and go somewhere nobody knows us. Then you'll be safe."

"I'm not stupid. I intend to be careful." Kay kept her old Camaro's speed level. Getting a traffic ticket wasn't on the agenda. She'd take care of her personal stuff first, but her main reason for this little outing was the trip to the morgue.

"I like Tyrell's idea of us spending a week on Padre Island. A butt crack full of sand, half-naked men and an order of hot sex on the side sounds good to me. Our vacations always fall victim to you chasing a case."

"Damn it, Holly. Leann Vaughn is dead." Speaking the words started a tremor deep inside that spread until Kay's hands vibrated on the steering wheel.

"Excuse me for trying to cheer you up." Holly's gaze shifted. She stared out the window.

"I'm sorry," Kay quickly said, applying a mental slap to her head. "I'm upset at the system and myself. We're why the girl is dead."

"Don't start that crap." Holly's wounded tone had vanished.

"You're an investigator. You did your job."

"My job was to protect her." She pressed harder on the gas pedal. The surge of power from her car mirrored the flood of anger pumping through her system. "I don't buy into this crap she committed suicide. The entire thing bugs me. Leann's state of mind was good. Nothing she said makes me believe she'd take her own life."

"Believing somebody killed her might be your way of easing this unreasonable guilt you're feeling."

"Think what you want. I'm not convinced it's a suicide." Kay exhaled a shuddering breath. "Leann outsmarted the bastards who kidnapped her, raped her and sold her to be a sex slave. She wanted to live. Something's not right, and I need to figure it out."

"Then maybe you should slow down. I've never fancied myself in a pileup on Interstate 75."

Kay lowered her speed. Holly, with her eclectic looks and humor usually lightened a somber mood. Not today. She simply didn't get it. Regardless of how Leann died, Kay was at fault.

"You worry me," Holly announced.

"Why? Because I care?"

"No. Because you get too close." Holly emitted an audible sigh. "Promise me you won't do anything stupid."

"You can help by dropping me off at the morgue's side door. Run by work and bring me Leann's file. I'll call you when I'm ready to leave." Kay laughed at Holly's raised eyebrow. "Sheesh, we're talking ten blocks. You'll be back before I'm ready to leave."

****

Kay signed in and made her way down the stark white halls of the medical examiner's building. She paused for one last breath before pushing her way through the double doors to where the air was frigid, dank and produced a sweetish scent.

Her grandfather sat at a small, weathered metal desk. A bronze name plate that read Doctor Wendell Taylor had been shoved to the side. His half-glasses were perched on the end of his nose, and he was staring at a computer screen as if any second it would speak. His disheveled silver hair and a pocket protector full of odd items, which caused down one side of his white smock to sag, gave him an absentminded professor appearance. He spoke with the assurance of a man who'd been medical examiner for thirty-plus years. If anyone had doubts about his qualifications, their questions quickly vanished. The morgue was his domain.

The urge to run into his arms for comfort gripped her heart and squeezed. She'd made her mother promise not to mention the kidnapping to him. No need to worry him. She cleared her throat to avoid startling him.

He swiveled his chair in her direction. A smile lit his face. "Kaycie."

"Hey, Papa." Hearing her full name had her reaching for the small medallion hanging around her neck. Papa, her seventy-two-year-old grandfather, and Nathan Wolfe, the ass who'd broken her heart, were the only men who'd always called her by her given name. She jerked her hand away from the reminder of Nate and pushed him from her thoughts.

"It's been awhile since you dropped by." His grin broadened and deepened the wrinkles around his warm, brown eyes. He rose to his feet and dragged her in for a hug.

"Sorry. I'll do better." She kissed his forehead before pulling a roll-around stool over to sit next to him.

"Not to worry. I know you're busy." He shoved his glasses to the top of his head, forming a makeshift headband. The move left his hair standing on end. "What can I do for you?"

"I'm looking for information on Leann Vaughn. She probably came in last night or this morning."

"She's here." He waved a hand in the general direction of the back of the building. "Not one I'm scheduled to work." His gaze zeroed in on Kay. "Is she one of your cases?"

"Yes, sir. Will you personally do the autopsy? Please. I'm not slamming the other MEs. This girl needs your expertise, deserves your knowledge. I don't believe she killed herself." Kay counted on him believing in her instincts.

"She's important to you?"

"Very." Kay trusted him beyond questioning. If the truth would help Holly, he'd find it.

His bushy, silver eyebrows rose high on his forehead. "And if I rule suicide?"

"I will never question one of your decisions." And she wouldn't. When others his age were parked in their La-z- Boy rockers watching TV or out playing golf, Papa had stayed on the job. His mind was sharper than most of his younger peers'.

"Then I'll move her to the top of the waiting list. Do the autopsy myself." He lowered his glasses, one-fingered them in place, and then turned to his computer. His thin fingers raced across the keys, pulling up what Kay assumed to be Leann's preliminary information.

Kay didn't speak. He'd slipped into his world of analysis. She gave him a minute then asked, "When can I ..."

A frown deepened the wrinkles on his forehead, ending her question. "I'll call in a few markers and get the tox results moved along. You'll hear as soon as I know something."

"You're the best."

"For a while longer." His words fell hard and sharp, a direct result of forced retirement at the end of the year. He'd yet to complain to her, but his tone spoke volumes.

"I'll bet when the word gets around you're available for consultation, you'll be busier than you are now." Kay stood and returned the stool to where it belonged before he reminded her everything in his morgue had a place. "I hate to beg and run. I'm a phone call away."

She'd removed her cell from its holder and had made it to the double doors when his booming voice delivered the message she'd dreaded since entering his domain.

"Stop by and say hello to your folks."

"Sure thing. Love you." Getting more than a hello from her father would require a miracle, but Papa never gave up hope. She stopped and called Holly. "I'll meet you at the door."

"See you in ten." Holly's summery lilt made Kay wonder if she ever really got angry.

Kay started pacing at fifteen minutes. At twenty, she hit redial and got Holly's voice mail. After thirty minutes, Kay was getting uneasy.

Had Holly misunderstood? Was she waiting outside in the heat? Kay walked to the side exit, opened the door, and cautiously stepped outside. An hour ago, the side parking had been jammed full. Now the place looked like a barren oasis. Friday afternoon in Dallas meant almost everybody was at happy hour.

She looked both ways and then stepped a few feet down the drive.

A man wearing a ski mask came out of nowhere. He grabbed her just as a white van drove up and stopped. Kay twisted out of his grip and ran back to the door. Her heart dropped to her feet. It had locked behind her. The man in the vehicle had jumped out and was bearing down on her.

Adrenaline spiked, and her mind scrambled. She screamed long and loud while banging on the door. Strong hands gripped her arms, shoving her knees onto the hot pavement. She twisted free, and sprang to her feet, ready to defend herself, but the largest one blocked her punch while the other grabbed her, dragging her as if she weighed nothing.

"Hurry up." A voice came from inside the van. "Somebody's coming."

Thank God. Somebody responded to her cry for help. She turned her head toward the sound of an engine. Kay's eyes almost popped out. A motorcycle barreled straight at her. This maniac was going to kill them all.

Even at the high rate of speed, the rider expertly laid the bike down on its side. He stepped off with precise timing, never losing his footing. Sparks shot through the air as the out-of-control hunk of metal slid across the pavement. Dressed in black, wearing a black helmet with darkened visor shielding his face, he sprinted toward the van.

The stranger's arrival turned her attacker's attention away from her. Air gushed from Kay's lungs as the tension on her arms relaxed.

"Run," the motorcyclist growled, shoving her out of his way. She stumbled forward almost falling facedown onto the pavement again.

His right foot lashed out and connected with one of her attackers' kneecaps. The snap of breaking bone echoed like a shotgun blast. Fists, feet, and elbows moved at mesmerizing speeds. Ski Mask Jerk number one hit the cement, moaning. Holy shit, a ninja had dropped out of the sky to rescue her. Kay's jaw dropped at the display of raw power.

"Run, Goddamn it." Her rescuer's growl had turned into a roar.

His attention had been on her attackers—how did he know she hadn't run? Didn't matter. He was right. Kay bolted toward the front of the building. Heaving, gasping for air, she ran into the lobby. The girl at the front desk called out that she had 911 on the phone.

"The operator says cops are on the way."

Kay knew the drill. She should stay put until the squad car showed up. But how could she leave the stranger behind? What if her attackers overpowered him? If he'd been killed, she'd be responsible for another death.

The sounds of sirens in the distance were enough to give her the confidence to run back outside to check on her savior.

Gone? How could that be? The men, the van, and the ninja were gone.

She had nothing to validate her story except her skinned knees and the scars on the pavement where the motorcycle had dug grooves during its slide.

Through all that had happened, one thing stayed at the top of her mind. Holly was missing.

Chapter Three

Nate Wolfe leaned against a cement pillar, his gaze never straying from Kaycie and the cops taking down her information. The third floor of the garage across from the morgue offered a clear view and allowed Nate to stay out of sight.

His mind raced over the events in the parking lot. Christ, what if he'd arrived five minutes later?

The sight of the two assholes dragging Kaycie toward the van had sent him straight to combat mode. Damn, he'd wanted to kill both of those bastards.

He spit the taste of disgust from his mouth. One of the first lessons he'd learned in hand-to-hand combat was to eliminate the threat, never allow the dickheads to escape. Glancing away to ensure Kaycie had run as he'd instructed had allowed one of the assholes to clock him from behind. Stupid new recruit mistake. Distractions could get him killed.

A gust of wind ruffled Kaycie's disheveled, chocolate-brown hair. Whatever hairdo she'd set out with was long gone, which was understandable since she'd been knocked to the ground and then dragged a few feet. He watched as she no doubt described the attempted abduction to the law. That she couldn't talk without making elaborate gestures brought a smile to his face and a stirring down deep he refused to recognize.

He twisted the Saint Jude medallion hanging under his shirt then jerked his hand back as if burned. He should've taken it off years ago. The small charm, which never left his person, warmed against his skin, reminding him of an earlier time. An innocent time when youth, love and sex were plentiful.

From what he could see, the pretty twenty-two-year-old criminal justice student had matured into a beautiful woman in the last decade.

She'd made her opinion of him and his choices perfectly clear when they'd parted company. Still, the sun reflecting off her hair brought back images of long, silky, chocolate-colored waves spread across a white pillowcase, and her cinnamon-flecked brown eyes darkening to black when she climaxed.

He needed his head examined for agreeing to get this near her. Now he was in it for real. No fucking way would he step back and let harm come to her. Even if she hated him. Which in all likelihood, she did.

Nate whirled at the sound of footsteps.

"A mite jumpy, aren't you, Bro?" Tyrell Castillo stroked a small patch of whiskers on his chin as he sauntered a circle around the banged-up Harley. He made a tsking noise and then plopped himself down on the ledge, effectively blocking Nate's view.

"Paying attention has kept me alive." Nate moved to the other side of the cement pillar where he could keep Kaycie in his line of view.

"No shit." Tyrell nodded slightly. Having spent a few years in Iraq and Afghanistan, he would understand the importance of staying alert. "What's the emergency?"

"How'd you know Kaycie needed protection?"

"Somebody snatched her Monday. She got away, but until the cops figure this shit out, I felt she needed a bodyguard."

"You should've told me that when you called." Nate ground out the words. Had he known about the previous attempt, he'd have glued himself to her ass and not watched from afar.

"I only had a second or I would have. Why?"

Nate watched Tyrell's expression change when his gaze shifted and caught a glimpse of Kaycie in the parking lot across the street with the cops.

"What happened?"

"You want my help? Answer my questions first."

"I'm telling you straight. She's been working this case, supposed to be done with it, but they found the girl dead Monday. Kay was the last person to see the kid alive. Maybe an hour later Kay got snatched."

"Who told you all this?"

"She did."

Tyrell pointed at a small blonde who'd parked, and then launched herself like a rocket and ran toward Kaycie.

"Holly Hoffman." Tyrell ran a hand over his smooth head. "What's going on down there?"

"Finish your story."

"Holly called me from the hospital, said Kay had been hurt. I stopped by, and she told me what happened."

"Then you called me."

"Right." Tyrell stroked the small patch of hair under his bottom lip, craning his neck toward the cops talking with Kaycie. "I had a commitment and couldn't tail her."

"Go on." Nate cocked his head. Waiting.

"Kay's an investigator for Dallas Child Protective Services. Worked with DPD on this case—a seventeen-year-old girl who'd been kidnapped and raped. The kid had been sold and was in Virginia when she outsmarted the truck driver and escaped. No telling where he was taking her. She picked out the pervert who'd violated her from a photo array. Tagged the son of a prominent businessman."

Nate's stomach rolled over. "What's the correlation between the dead girl and Kaycie being snatched?"

"I don't know."

"And the news keeps getting better."

"Now that you're back and have a PI license, you can have the job of protecting her." Tyrell glanced down at the parking lot. "Kay's the only one who knows the facts. What if the asshole doesn't go to prison? Maybe she needs you."

"That's a big maybe." Nate's blood flash-heated to boiling. Had Kaycie gotten herself ass-deep in human trafficking and murder? If so, Tyrell was right. She could be in a world of shit. "So the girl was killed to shut her up?"

"Word is she slashed a wrist."

"None of this makes any sense." Nate paused. "One thing's for sure, Kaycie has pissed off somebody bad enough to try to kidnap her twice."

Tyrell blasted off the ledge. "Somebody tried to snatch her again?"

Tyrell had always claimed he was faster than a speeding bullet. Might be some truth to that since he'd made it through Iraq and Afghanistan without a scratch.

"Yeah. If I hadn't been here, who knows where she'd be right now."

"She all right?" Tyrell leaned further over the ledge trying to get a better look.

"She's fine. The two bastards who put their hands on her have a couple of broken bones, but she's okay. If I'd used my head, I could've hung onto them for the cops." Nate rubbed the back of his neck, refusing to recognize the nagging headache.

Tyrell's eyes went wide. "How'd you let them get away? Never mind." He grinned, flashing white teeth and shrugging his shoulders. "She get a look at you?"

"Hell no. Been a lot easier to fight without the helmet, but I kept it on. You haven't talked to her?"

Nate's skin chilled even though the temperature had easily reached the century mark. He'd planned on inserting himself into her life at some point. This trouble pushed the schedule ahead.

"Gonna have to soon. Kay's leaving me phone messages. Shit, man." Tyrell's eyebrows pinched. "How'd these bastards know she'd be at the morgue?"

"Good question. You understand protecting her just became a twenty-four-seven assignment."

"Yeah." Tyrell removed his buzzing cell and checked the caller ID. "It's her, again."

Nate moved closer to the ledge. She and the short blonde had headed for the car. Unprotected.

"Remember our agreement. She'll learn I'm involved when I'm ready."

Tyrell tilted his head forward and answered the call. The hair on the back of Nate's neck tingled when Tyrell answered, calling Kaycie "Little Mama."

Nate rolled the two words around on his tongue. A knot formed and wedged in the bottom of his gut. Tyrell and Kaycie? Together?

Nate balled his fists, choking back the urge to pounce on his old friend. Somewhere in the recesses of his brain, he overheard Tyrell say he'd meet her at the police station.

"Call me when you need me to take over." Nate stalked to his Harley and threw a leg over. He coiled his hands around the handlebar controls. His fingers itched and bad things went down when that happened.

"Hold up a minute." Tyrell's hands formed the timeout sign. "Let's discuss this. You've been back in Dallas six months. Grow some balls, you got to face her sooner or later."

"I'll take later." Nate brushed aside that idea. No way would Kaycie welcome a reunion with him. "Get out of here. Without you, she's vulnerable, unprotected."

"She's following the patrol car to the station. I'll meet her there after she fills out her statement."

Nate dug around in the saddlebags until he found something to write on and a pen. He had Tyrell give him the name and a brief background on the bastard who Kaycie believed killed the young girl.

Nate needed to think. To sort through everything he'd just heard. While he was at it, he'd rein in his out-of-control libido. He hadn't expected such a strong physical reaction to her after all these years.

"Why don't you let me set up a place for us to meet? Be good to have us back together again. All we need is Marcus and Jake."

Tyrell's voice trailed off at the mention of Jake Donovan, the fifth member of Wolfe's Pack as Kaycie had dubbed them. The fact Jake had died in a fire while deployed in Afghanistan wasn't a topic to discuss.

"No."

"Seriously? Bro, you gotta come out of the shadows. Tell her you saved her life. You should've heard her on the phone. Christ. Going on about this badass ninja appearing out of nowhere and then vanishing."

Nate started and revved up the engine to drown out Tyrell and his advice. The best tight end the University of Texas ever produced had turned down a professional career in football to join the Army. Maybe becoming a Ranger and wearing that tan beret made Tyrell think he could tell people what they should and shouldn't do. Rangers didn't *tell* SEALs shit.

"If you change your mind," Tyrell yelled over the roar.

"Tell me what time I need to be at her place."

"I'll call you." Tyrell's expression hardened, his eyes full of concern. "She needs more than a shadow."

"She has *more*. She has me."

Chapter Four

Johnny Darling leaned back in his office chair and ran the blade of his new KA-BAR up his forearm. The razor-sharp edge shaved off a strip of hair, leaving behind smooth skin. The new knife was a beauty. Odd how the feel and weight of the big knife gave him a sense of being with an old friend.

Johnny knew killing. How he knew was a mystery he'd given up on solving. No more poking and prodding his brain searching for the past. He had a new name. New job. New life. And after killing the girl, a promotion.

He lifted the ringing phone to his ear, listened to the security guard at the front entrance to the warehouse parking lot, and then dropped the receiver on its cradle. "Mr. A just drove past the gate."

Johnny struggled to hide his complete and total disgust for the man sprawled opposite him in the chair. After this recent screw-up, he hoped to get the go-ahead to eliminate Hank. If he did, Hank would be dead by morning.

Hank grunted, pushed himself to his feet, and followed Johnny into the hall. He opened the door to the distribution center, but Hank shrugged his shoulders and sauntered the other way to his office. Spoiled rotten, rich as shit, Hank only worked because of the girls. Johnny knew he liked to sample the merchandise.

Mr. A didn't need an escort. Johnny considered meeting the boss up front a show of respect. After all, he owned the damn place. Ran all his businesses with the control of a four-star general.

Johnny tightened the knot on his tie and straightened the jacket of his fifteen-hundred-dollar suit on his way to the front of the warehouse. His footsteps echoed as his boots hit the cement floor. The warehouse was closed on Saturday, and the absence of truck engines and forklifts jockeying around pallets of freight made the trip up front quicker.

By the time he crossed the building, the boss waited inside. With his impeccable taste in clothing, he cut an imposing figure. Medium height, around one-hundred-eighty pounds with salt and pepper hair, his slate eyes reflected no emotion.

Johnny's confidence soared at the approving nod he received. He'd swapped the western footwear with extremely pointed toes for a more conservative style made from eel skin. He preferred the boot, because the knife fit perfectly next to his ankle.

Johnny smiled, showing a mouthful of white teeth. After all, his pretty-boy face, complete loyalty to the man in charge, and talent for violence were all he had to offer.

"Nice look. I knew my tailor would put you in a quality suit."

"Thank you. I appreciate you fronting me the money for these clothes." Johnny ran his hand over the Italian silk with pride and fell in step with Mr. A.

"You're welcome. Consider the clothes a gift. Your promotion comes with responsibilities. I expect my managers to dress professional."

"I won't let you down."

"Of that, I'm sure. I saw the news report on the Vaughn girl's death. You took her picture as I directed and then conducted the search personally?"

"Yes sir. Short of cutting up the furniture, I looked hard. Didn't leave a trace I'd been there."

"Good. Hank's waiting?"

"Yes, sir."

Mr. A's icy glance sent a shiver of uncertainty down Johnny's spine.

"Did you have knowledge of his plans?"

"No, sir." Thank you, baby Jesus.

Johnny could see the boss's jaw nerves jumping like a cat set on fire. His teeth were clamped shut, making his smile even more menacing.

"I thought not." He moved at a brisk pace toward the south side of the distribution center. "Everything else under control?"

"Yes, sir." With a swipe of Johnny's ID, they entered what was known as The Market.

Through a brilliant piece of redesign and construction, this area was hidden from the public eye. The warehouse functioned as a cover for the real business. A shipping manager and his supervisors, housed in the north side of the building, were responsible for the freight. Their exorbitant salaries and fear of retribution guaranteed their silence.

"You shipped the latest Market order without any problems?"

"This morning, after I confirmed the transfer of funds, the last two went out with a load of dishwashing detergent."

"Excellent."

Johnny stepped to the side and let the boss take the lead. They traveled down the hall past the soundproof rooms. Mr. A paused and looked inside one.

"I'll make sure everything is cleaned thoroughly." Johnny didn't think the cot was much in the way of furniture, but the room came with a toilet and sink. It beat sleeping on the floor.

The boss passed the conference room, complete with a small stage and collection of photography and video equipment. The walls, also soundproofed, allowed privacy for picture taking and live bidding.

Mr. A strode to Hank's office. Back rigid as if a fireplace poker had been surgically implanted up his ass, he stared for a second then silently turned away and moved down the hall.

Curious, Johnny glanced in at Hank. Fuck. He sat at his desk with his head bent over a double line of white powder. Greasy brown hair fell over his forehead. Why did the old man tolerate this shit? If Hank knew too much, there were ways to deal with him.

Johnny's heart rate ratcheted up a notch. He hoped babysitting wasn't one of his new responsibilities. Be a damn sight easier to kill the useless son of a bitch.

The boss unlocked his private office and stepped inside. His face showed no emotion when his eyes met Johnny's. Johnny's ball sack tightened, squeezing his nuts. A fucking shark's eyes reflected more warmth.

"Tell Hank I wish to speak with him."

"I'm here." Hank spoke from the doorway. He rubbed his nose

with the back of his hand and sauntered over to a chair. "I guess you heard."

"You're an imbecile." Mr. A's face flared red, yet his tone remained low and deep-freeze icy. "I'd ask what you were thinking, but the answer's apparent—you weren't."

"How else am I gonna find out if the Taylor bitch has my ring? Johnny wasted the Vaughn girl before I could make her give it back. If it wasn't in her house, she must've passed it to the Taylor woman. I would have asked before I killed her."

"Johnny followed my orders. Which is more than I can say for you."

"Wouldn't have happened if you'd waited to kill the girl." Hank sniffed and shrugged his shoulders, apparently unfazed by the boss's piercing glare.

"The Vaughn girl had escaped, forcing me to refund money to an unhappy buyer. And Hank, she identified you as her attacker. Her death was necessary."

"So the boys fucked up both tries." Hank defended the two idiots he'd sent to bring the Taylor woman to the warehouse. "If that ring gets in the wrong hands, the initials on it will lead the cops right to my door. And you don't want that to happen."

Johnny waited for an outburst from Mr. A, but instead, he sighed a long drawn-out breath, staring at Hank as if he was no more than shit on the bottom of a shoe.

Johnny headed for the door.

"Stay." The command sliced through the air with the finality of death.

Johnny returned to his place, his hands hanging loosely at his sides. If anybody else had ordered him to "stay" as if he were a dog, they'd find their guts spilled with a flick of the KA-BAR. However, he needed this job. At least until he figured things out. The money in his pocket, the new clothes on his back, and opportunities for advancement made putting up with a few indignities worthwhile.

One of these days, the boss would pull the plug on Hank. Johnny ached to be the one who got the order. Should his services be required, he was ready.

"Johnny, I'd like your thoughts on the signet ring missing. Hank was in the room with the girl, wasn't he?"

"I've seen it on his finger a lot, and now it's gone." The hell with saying more. He didn't have to like Hank to know you didn't rat out a member of the team.

"Do you have men on this woman?" The boss dragged in a jagged breath as he waited for Johnny to answer.

"Yes, sir."

"If you can't get to the Taylor woman, find someone she values." His eyes narrowed to slits. "Offer her a trade she can't refuse."

Hank opened his mouth and was cut off with a hand slashing through the air.

"Don't speak. The only thing you've done lately that showed any sign of intelligence was holding the Taylor woman at one of my empty warehouses." Mr. A leaned back in his chair, pinching the bridge of his nose. "If you'd brought her here and jeopardized the security of this building, put my operation at risk ..." The boss paused and then said, "Go get us a cup of coffee."

Johnny shoved off from the wall. "Yes sir. Be right back."

"Not you." The boss's eyebrows drew together. "Hank's happy to run an errand for me."

Johnny resumed his position, forcing a pissed-off Hank to step around him. This wasn't over. Hank didn't take orders well. Johnny waited, knowing the boss did nothing without a reason.

"Make those two idiots Hank used go away. Select a couple of men you can trust." His tense jaw seemed to relax.

"Consider it done."

"Where are the pictures of the Vaughn girl?" The man's personality had shifted from furious to casual.

"Locked in my desk." Johnny hadn't asked why the boss wanted them.

"Show them to each new girl. An example of how we reward disobedience."

"Yes, sir." Killing the girl left a bad taste in his mouth, and he couldn't figure out why. He shoved his momentary weakness aside. Now that he understood her death served a double purpose, his respect grew for the boss's tactical planning.

"Now, let's check out what you've got for the next auction."

Johnny removed the card-key to the holding rooms from his pocket and led the way down the hall. He'd picked up two more girls last night. Found them inside a mall looking to meet guys. Avoiding the cameras, luring them outside and into his car had been laughably easy. He'd drugged them, brought them to the warehouse and turned them over to the night guard before midnight. Pretty ones. They would bring a nice piece of change. Though Johnny doubted one of them would sell after Hank had finished with her earlier.

"Added two seventeen-year-olds."

"Keeping them on hand for more than a day or two is dangerous. Send out word we're moving the date up to Monday."

He stopped at the first door, leaned down and peered through the peephole, which had been installed in reverse. When he turned, his gaze bore down on Johnny hard.

"Hank tampered with the new merchandise?"

Johnny swallowed. It was bad enough Hank was an asshole and liked having a taste before the ketamine wore off, but why beat up a half-conscious girl? Johnny had no answer, but he'd caught the snick of the lock when Hank had gone inside earlier today. Oh, hell, yes, Hank had tampered with the product.

Johnny's non-answer was an answer.

"Goddamn it." The man's eyebrows dove toward the bridge of his nose. "One of these days, Hank will cause more trouble than I can tolerate."

Chapter Five

Nate shifted in the seat, stretching his legs out as best he could. His pickup had decent legroom for a regular-size person, but six-feet-four pushed the boundaries of normal out the window. He'd backed into a parking spot outside of Kaycie's apartment and then spent the night watching the opening at the top of the stairs.

His eyelids scraped like sandpaper across his eyeballs, but he could go for days without rest. He'd been without food and water for longer than overnight. It would take more than hunger, lack of sleep, or heat to get the best of him. However, his bladder had a mind of its own. If he didn't take a leak soon, he'd be scrubbing the interior of his truck this afternoon.

The layout of Kaycie's apartment complex sucked when it came to keeping an eye on her. For Christ's sake, he didn't have a clear view of her front door. He could see who went up, but once they turned the corner, any asshole could break into her apartment.

During the night, three men had climbed those stairs. Nate had shadowed each individual, ready to step in, but no one went near her door.

It pleased him that Kaycie slept alone last night. He'd tried to boot the naked image of her lying in bed from his mind. Hadn't worked. Why couldn't he forget? He'd spent hours hard as a steel rod imagining how nice it would be to slide into her bed and drag her warm body next to his.

She'd have kicked him out on his ass.

His fingers itched to run over her curves and touch those sensitive places that used to drive her over the edge. She'd melted when he kissed that spot right behind her ear, or the tender flesh under her breasts, and she completely surrendered when he nipped his way up her inner thigh getting closer and closer to heaven. His skin burned from the memory of his hands buried in her silky hair. A couple of times, he'd have sworn her scent permeated the inside of his pickup.

The passenger-side door opened and Tyrell slid in, passing over a sack containing coffee and two breakfast sandwiches.

"Figured you needed a shot of caffeine."

"You were right. I'm not sure whether to drink this or dump it and piss in the cup." Nate settled for taking a long gulp. Lukewarm or not, the jolt of energy was welcome.

"Spare me the sight. Quiet night?"

"Yep. You expected different?" Nate unwrapped a sandwich.

"I don't know what I expected." Tyrell glanced around the parking lot as if still worried.

"You talk with her this morning?"

"No, I called Holly. She lives a couple of doors down. They hang together most of the time. Holly can handle herself and is taking weekend duty. She'll make sure Kay is safe."

So Tyrell and Little Mama wouldn't be spending Saturday night together. A whisper of guilt hit Nate. No way would Tyrell mess with her. It was against the man code.

"Is this Holly a cop?"

"No. But she's a better shot than both of us. After she got her license to carry a concealed weapon, I drove her and Kay to the firing range for practice a few times."

Nate's gut rolled into a tight ball. A few trips to the practice range didn't mean this Holly could protect Kaycie from the bastards who'd tried to snatch her. He couldn't cover her twenty-four hours a day. Tyrell would have to step up, but they'd need more manpower.

"Where's Marcus Ricci? Last news I have on him was after his stint in the Marines, he'd bought a place on some lake here in Texas."

"He shouldn't be hard to find. Want me to hunt him up?" Tyrell patted his cell.

"I'll do it. Maybe he's available."

"Nate, you heard his wife was killed by a drunk driver while he was deployed."

"Yeah." Marcus's loss sat heavy in the pit of Nate's stomach.

"Had to be tough. He was crazy in love with her."

"Yeah. I just wanted you to be aware. He don't discuss the accident or her."

"Might be good for him to have a project." Nate could imagine Marcus withdrawing from life. "Between the three of us we can cover Kaycie."

"Don't discount Holly. She comes across a little far out there, but she's tough."

"I'll take your word for it."

"FYI, it's Kay now. She stopped using Kaycie years ago."

A piece of useless information. She'd never be Kay to Nate. "Call my cell if you need me. I'll be in my office most of today."

"You hung a shingle?" Tyrell's head bobbed with a look of approval.

"No sign. You're my first civilian case. But there's definitely a threat to her safety. We need to assess the situation and decide how we'll protect her."

Tyrell stepped out of the pickup, looking back over his shoulder. "All pro bono. Right?"

"For now." Nate waited for Tyrell to leave, but when he cocked his head and flashed a buttload of white teeth, Nate braced for a wiseass remark. "Something else?"

Tyrell stroked the soul patch on his chin. "Just one thing. You didn't ask me for Kay's address, so how come you knew where she lived?"

"Mind your own business." Nate started his pickup and dropped it in gear, forcing his old friend to step back. "Since we're getting personal, what's 'Little Mama' to you?" He'd made no effort to hide the ice in his tone.

"If you're asking if we're doing the nasty, my answer is ... what do you care?"

"I don't." Nate clamped his teeth together to hold back the spew of cuss words boiling up from his gut.

"Which is why you already knew where she lives." Tyrell chuckled and then paused on the way to his car. He glanced over his shoulder and called out, "We're friends."

Nate was grateful when Tyrell slid behind the wheel of his car and closed the door. A few more seconds listening to that chuckle and Nate would've popped a vein. Tyrell's vehicle roared to life, and he followed Nate out of the parking lot. They parted ways at the apartment complex exit. Nate's old friend turned south while Nate hit the freeway headed the opposite direction. He was edgy. The unknown threat was always the most dangerous. He tamped down the panic edging toward the surface.

Nate parked in front of the small office space he'd rented in Richardson, a Dallas suburb. He opened the truck door and stepped out, freeing himself from the confines of his pickup.

"Damn," he muttered when his joints cracked and popped as he stretched his torso. The rapid round of fire shooting through his knee got the blood flowing to his brain.

He locked the door behind him, dropped the AC to sixty degrees, and then fired up the motel-size coffeepot.

Note to self, next time rent an office closer to a coffeehouse.

The small front lobby with an office to the side was perfect for his needs. If this place had a shower, he'd live here. Eventually, if he decided to do more than government contract work, he'd pick a name as Tyrell suggested and hang a sign out front. For now, he was content the private detective business was up and running.

After the incident in the morgue parking lot, he'd driven the Harley to his office and parked it inside. Leaving it outside unprotected wasn't an option. When he wasn't riding the Hog, he'd prop his laptop on the handlebars and use the bike for a desk chair. He'd buy more furniture one of these days.

He used the bathroom, splashed water on his face, poured a coffee, and then slung his leg over the bike. When his computer booted up, he dug out the information Tyrell had given him and ran a search on Hank Walsh. Kaycie probably had intel, but Nate didn't figure she'd be open to sharing with him. Didn't matter. He preferred to do his own fact-finding. Know your enemy better than your friends. Safer that way. He'd research the dead girl's family next.

For thirty bucks, Nate had subscribed to a service that allowed him to access the details of nearly anybody's life. It required nothing more than a few keystrokes. The Walsh name provided him with tons of financial facts. Hank's dad, being a transportation and logistics mogul, drew plenty of media attention. On the board of two major charities, a library, and a children's hospital, Anthony Walsh's wealth could buy a lot of silence. Kaycie was convinced the girl had been murdered. The old man had probably spoiled his kid to the point he believed himself to be above the law.

Hank's background read like a rap sheet. In and out of drug rehab, traffic tickets for DUI, kicked out of college for cheating. His current employment showed to be Walsh FasTrak Transportation, a division of Walsh Enterprise, Inc.

Works for Daddy. Imagine that.

The kicker was his current probation. He'd pled out on an attempted sexual assault charge three years ago, trading jail time for a healthy fine and five years probation. Anthony Walsh's baby boy would have the rest of his sentence tacked on if found guilty of rape within the next two years.

However, if found guilty of murder, Hank would hang around on death row for years while his appeals ran their course, but the state would eventually give the victim's family closure—via lethal injection. Seemed like a waste of time and money to Nate. Thirty-eight cents for a bullet was cheaper and quicker. Any man who'd hurt a woman didn't deserve more.

If Nate proved Hank had hurt Kaycie, the state might not have to pay for a trial.

Next, he read up on Leann Vaughn and her family. A hard-nosed Baptist preacher, Harold had spoken to all manner of media after his daughter's disappearance. No keeping her name a secret, her picture had been on every newspaper and TV in the state. Leann's mother stood next to her father in every picture, clinging to his arm. Eyes sunk back in her head and lips turned downward, Patricia Vaughn appeared to be on her last leg.

With all his research, Nate saw nothing to indicate Hank Walsh was anything more than a sleaze-bag rapist. Human trafficking or murder would be a hard rap to hang on him.

A dead girl. Two attempts to kidnap Kaycie. Hell, none of it made sense. If she had learned too much, why snatch her? Why not just kill her too? One well-placed shot and their problem would be solved.

Nate turned his attention to locating Marcus. Finding his phone number didn't take long. Always the quiet one of the group, Marcus hadn't changed in that regard. He wasn't forthcoming with his personal information, but he readily agreed to help out. Through the entire call, he didn't mention his dead wife and neither did Nate.

Nate rubbed sleep-deprived eyes with the heels of his hands. He hadn't planned on looking up Kaycie. The past was better left dead. Those days were gone, just as he would be when the next job came in. Until then, he was her bodyguard.

He saved everything he'd found on the Walsh family and the Vaughn case to a flash drive. Having second thoughts, he made hard copies then tossed the lot into an old leather briefcase.

He dragged his tired ass out to his pickup. He'd driven away from Kaycie's apartment worried. Now it had blossomed to full-blown concern for her life. He drove away with a gnawing foreboding in his gut.

Chapter Six

Most of Kay's neighbors had left for work, leaving the parking lot with only a few cars. So why, standing under the morning sun, did she feel like a bug under a microscope? If she whirled around, would somebody be right behind her?

She dropped her hand to her hip. The Glock 22 riding there gave her a measure of comfort.

She hurried to catch up with Holly, who waited next to her car. Holly wore blue slacks with a matching blouse. Red parrots dangled from her neck and ears. Her blond hair, tied in a ponytail, sported a red streak coordinated to match the birds. Kay glanced down at her gray slacks, ivory short-sleeve blouse and lightweight black linen blazer. The word drab came to mind. Her only jewelry, the Saint Jude medallion, rested hidden above her breasts.

"I'm not sure we should go to this funeral," Holly protested.

"I have to. Stop making me feel guilty for dragging you along with me."

"Like Tyrell said, where you go, I go."

"And I appreciate you. Really. But you shouldn't have to be my private taxi. After the funeral, I need to stop by the police station. I'll call Tomas. Ask if he can drive me."

Holly dug her car keys out of her ten-gallon purse and shook them at Kay. "Get in."

Kay almost laughed at her friend, because secretly Holly was probably getting a kick out of being the boss. "Tyrell should call you Little Mama, not me."

"Thanks, but I'd rather he called me to bed."

Normally, Kay would've laughed at the innocent blue eyes behind such a sexual innuendo. Would she ever find anything funny again?

"If you want him, do something about it."

"No need to get pissy. You want us to fall in love. I'm only interested in his body."

"I'm sorry. It's none of my business. I should never meddle in affairs of the heart." Kay didn't want to argue. Romance seemed like a really inappropriate topic today.

Her skin prickled suddenly. No doubt about it this time. Somebody's eyes were trained on her, giving her the weird sensation of being naked. Kay did another visual sweep of the parking lot. Nothing. Damn. Between Tyrell and Holly, Kay was jumping at shadows.

She'd reassessed her situation over the weekend. Admittedly, she'd been careless at the morgue. Since then, she'd been on high alert.

Kay had barely buckled her seat belt when her cell buzzed. Einstein's picture on the tiny screen smiled up at her.

"Hey, Papa. I hoped I'd hear from you today."

"Morning, Kaycie. You visit your folks this weekend?" His tone gave no hint of his ruling on Leann's death.

"I didn't. Ran out of time." She hated to lie to him. She didn't tell him about almost being kidnapped in the morgue parking lot. He would only worry himself sick.

"I think if you'd make the first move, your dad will come around."

He wanted the riff repaired between Kay and her dad, Papa's son. It was one she didn't know how to fix short of bringing her twin brother, Kevin, back to life. This conversation was repetitive and futile.

"Apparently, you worked too." She moved off the subject. "The body was released yesterday afternoon. Her funeral's at ten this morning."

"You were in a hurry for answers. I got everything I needed from the girl. Saw no need to make the family wait."

She leaned back in the seat. The quickening of her heartbeat thumped under the medallion while she waited for the news.

He continued, "Preliminary lab results confirmed your young woman had traces of ketamine in her system. Not something she'd be given by her doctor and not a drug we'd normally have tested for. I wouldn't have looked if you hadn't doubted that she'd committed suicide. Therefore, my ruling is homicide."

The stomach acid churning in her stomach rose to the back of her throat.

"It's of no comfort, but she didn't realize what was happening. Someone slashed her wrist after the drug was administered."

Kay's throat clamped shut. The ugliness and the horror of the crime flooded her with guilt and anger. "Oh, God. She was just a kid."

"I've informed the appropriate parties of my finding. Her case is with the Dallas Homicide Unit."

She shifted the elephant sitting on her chest to the side. "Thank you for working all weekend. I know exactly who killed her. After I prove it, the state of Texas will stick a needle in his arm for murder."

"Don't be ridiculous," he barked out the admonition. "This girl was murdered. Step back and let the police earn their keep."

His words sounded harsh and flat, but Kay understood he wasn't angry with her. He dealt in death every day. He honored and respected the people who unfortunately found themselves on his table. However, Papa was a realist. He had to separate himself from the pain and despair families of the deceased went through.

He was wasting his breath lecturing her. She'd never step back as he suggested. Not on this case.

"I knew this girl was too strong-willed to have killed herself." Relief washed over her. "Thank you, Papa. I owe you big time."

Kay disconnected before he told her how she could repay him.

"I'll ask one more time," Holly said. "Are you sure you want to do this?"

Kay glanced out the window and discovered they were parked in front of the church. She'd gotten so lost in her own misery she'd blocked out the drive.

****

The lush green grass and full-leafed trees gave the cemetery an eerie feel. Kay couldn't help but compare the vivid colors with the dry, brown leaves of summer seen elsewhere in the city. She stopped just outside the blue tent covering the coffin.

"Tell me again why we're here," Holly whispered. "The church services were hard enough on you. Coming to the cemetery is above the call of duty."

Holly's words barely penetrated Kay's subconscious. She'd sat in the back of the church, unable to face the lifeless body of the young girl who'd given Kay her trust. Coward.

"I didn't have the nerve to give the Vaughn family my condolences. I'll do it now." Kay stepped closer. Her hand paused at her belt. She'd locked her gun in the glove box before entering the church. Even though it was legal to carry in her position, she'd never been comfortable wearing it. Now, she missed the weight riding on her hip.

After she paid her respects, she'd casually take a look around. It wasn't uncommon for the perpetrator to show up at the cemetery to enjoy watching his kill being buried. Some sick bastards fed off the grief and loss they'd inflicted on the victim's family. Yeah, a discreet check for someone lurking, watching from the background was in order. If nothing else, she'd snap a few pictures with her cell and share them with police.

A wave of whispers drifted across the small group when a chair toppled backward and Leann's mother rushed from under the canopy toward Kay.

"How dare you show your face," Mrs. Vaughn screamed. Her expression was a study in anger. "Go away. You're not welcome here."

Stunned into silence, Kay felt her jaw drop. She'd never been this dumbfounded. Harold Vaughn rushed to his wife, gathering her in his arms just as the woman collapsed. His red-rimmed eyes and trembling chin reflected his pain.

"I'm sorry," Kay managed to whisper, welcoming Holly's arm around her shoulder. "I didn't mean to upset anyone."

"This is your fault." Mr. Vaughn held his sobbing wife closer. "Our daughter wanted to forget what happened, wanted to move on. You pressured her, convinced her to testify. You're as guilty as the bastard who took her from us."

Hate radiated from his every pore. Kay's heart caved inside her chest at the agony gushing from him. She couldn't find words to convey her feelings. Holly's grip tightened, and Kay allowed herself to be led away from the gathering crowd.

"I hope you burn in hell," Mr. Vaughn screamed.

Kay fished out her sunglasses, anything to help hide the shame. The Vaughns' anger was appropriately placed. Kay would carry the burden of the teenager's death forever.

A chill slammed into her. Again, somebody's eyes on her sent a shiver up her arms. She whirled.

A black Harley was parked down the block. She paused at the rear of the car and stared at the rider. Odd that he'd parked away from the funeral crowd and watched from a distance. Damn, the black visor didn't stop the burn as his gaze bore down on her. Her breath caught. Was this the man who'd saved her? Wearing a black leather jacket and matching helmet, the man remained motionless.

She started toward him, and the rider stepped off the bike. If this was her ninja, she'd demand answers after she thanked him. He turned his back to her and then removed the helmet. His fingers wound through shoulder-length black hair, tying the strands together with a piece of leather. There was something vaguely familiar about him. His movements. His shoulders. His hands.

He turned to face her, and her heart rate hit the ozone.

"Hello, Kaycie."

Ten years of missing Nate Wolfe boiled over. He was here. Really here. She sprang into his arms, clutched his broad shoulders and leaned into his hard-as-a-rock chest. God, his scent, a mixture of leather, woodsy cologne and virile man washed over her. Damn. Her body betrayed her by melting into him.

"Nate," she whispered into his neck. "You saved me." Her flesh heated when his large hands flexed against the small of her back and drew her closer.

"Come hell or high water," he whispered, his warm breath sending heat streaks across her skin.

A split second passed before memories of his lying tongue using that same phrase so many years ago hit her. A volcano of heartbreak erupted and spewed forth.

"Don't touch me," she spit the words at him while scrambling out of reach. "And don't you dare say that to me. Ever."

"You hugged me." His eyes went wide, and he held his hands up in surrender.

Damn him and his Cheshire cat grin. Kay plowed her right fist into his jaw. God, pain shot up her arm. His head barely moved. Still, she relished the snap of his teeth. He rubbed his scruffy jaw while that sexy little smile inched right back up his cheeks.

"Why are you following me?" Her knuckles hurt like hell, but he'd never know.

"What?" He held his hands in front of him, palms up. "No 'good to see you, Nate'? No 'how you been?' No nothing."

"I'll try this again, slower. Why. Are. You. Fol—"

"We need to talk." The fun had left his gaze. The sparkle dimmed to seriousness.

She stepped further away and sent him a glare designed to blister his flesh from head to toe. Unaffected, he picked up the cell phone earpiece she'd knocked off and reattached it to his ear while never taking his navy-blue eyes off her.

"No, we don't. Thank you for saving my life. Now do what you do best. Go away." She spun on her heel. Rubbing her now-swelling hand, Kay stalked straight to her waiting friend.

"You okay?" Holly asked over the top of the car before she slid behind the wheel.

"If I didn't break my fist on his cement jaw, I will be." Kay stabbed her seat belt a second time before fastening it properly. She cursed the tears welling. Cursed the feel his warm body imprinted on her breasts. Cursed the memories that sent her heart spinning.

Holly dropped her .380 in her purse.

"Did you take that into church this morning?"

"Hell yeah. God knows I carry. And the law gave me a permit. Glad I had it, because I didn't know what the hell was going down when you hit him. Who's the hunk?"

"Nate Wolfe."

"Holy shit. The guy from college?"

"The same. He's been watching me. I'm sure of it."

"I should've shot him." Holly punched the gas pedal, ignoring the speed bumps.

"Thanks for having my back. And for getting the concealed carry license."

"I'm never without protection. Or a gun." Holly chuckled at her own joke. "Where to?"

"Home."

****

The cemetery wasn't the place to argue, there'd be plenty of time for that later. Nate threw his leg over the Harley and let Kaycie and her blond friend drive away. Hell or high water had popped out of his mouth. First time in ten years the phrase had crossed his mind. He'd made matters worse by pulling out an old memory. Who knew she'd react violently?

Made no difference. Somebody intended her harm, and he'd be there to prevent it.

From the corner of his eye, he detected movement. The Mercedes that had followed her from the church was pulling away from the curb. No way was this bastard tagging along after the women.

Nate rode up beside the car at a stop sign and knocked on the window. He doubted the occupant would start trouble out in the open.

"You wouldn't be tailing those two women. Would you?" He spoke to the dark-tinted glass. "Why don't I tag along with you for a while?"

The driver drove backward a few hundred feet, executed a U-turn, and then drove off. Nate was right behind. After a few miles, he sped down an exit, leaving the Mercedes with no idea where Kaycie had gone. Problem was, he didn't know either. At least her blond bodyguard was with her.

His reunion with Kaycie had gone pretty much as he'd expected. She hadn't forgiven him. But, shit, ten years was a long time to hold a grudge.

Nate worked his jaw from side-to-side. A smile inched up his face. Damn, her right hand had moved faster than a gunslinger's in a John Wayne movie. Nobody did mad as sexy as she did. Her entire body hummed when she was angry.

She'd connected soundly, but not before he'd breathed in her scent. Nothing had changed. She still reminded him of green pastures, safe places, and sex. What was the old cliché? Too late to turn back now. Or was it?

He'd canceled his plan to tell Kaycie she'd picked up a tail when the woman named Holly had shifted her position, allowing the sunlight to glint off the gun she'd tried to hide against her thigh. Maybe Tyrell was right. Holly sure hadn't blinked when Nate locked eyes with her.

He called Tyrell. "My office in one hour."

"Something go down?"

"Enough. I'll call Marcus and bring him in."

Nate had to tell Kaycie someone was following her. What did they want from her? Or did they just want her?

****

Kay flipped down the sun visor on Tomas's car and studied her reflection. His mirror confirmed she'd failed to hide the dark circles under her eyes with makeup.

"You had to point that out?" She flipped the visor back into place.

"Count on me to be honest." He chuckled to himself.

She breathed a sigh of relief when he didn't grill her. Truth was, she'd spent half the night tossing, turning, and thinking about Nate. She would've bet money she would've recognized him from miles. She'd seen, mapped, and stroked every inch of his athletic body back in college. But now. Wow. He'd blossomed into a muscled version of a modern-day Tarzan, complete with shoulder-length black hair. Was the shaggy style rebellion against the requisite buzz cut the government had imposed on him?

She'd spent too many years fighting off the heartache of losing him. To have her hormones betray her when his hands slid up her back really pissed her off. Let the Navy get excited over him. She wasn't giving into those emotions. Never again.

"You ready to go inside?" Tomas's voice broke through her mental wandering.

"Sorry." She unbuckled and got out of the car. "I appreciate you hauling me around."

"No problem. Give me a shout when you're ready to go home."

Once inside the police station, she parked her butt outside Chief

Compton's office. He was her mentor, biggest supporter and had been helpful when she'd applied for the transfer to CPS. She chatted with his assistant and waited.

"Kay." The chief's booming baritone blasted her off the chair.

"Coming, sir." Kay hurried to follow him into his office. Winning the election hadn't slowed him down.

"Sit." He waved at a chair while he rounded his desk.

His tone didn't have his usual friendly ring. He sat, leaned back, and folded his arms across his chest. Dark eyes studied her.

"I need to be part of the investigation." Pretending he didn't know who or what they were talking about would have been a waste of time. "She was killed to shut her up."

"Tomas tells me you think your attempted abductions and this murder are connected."

"Yes." She squirmed under his hard gaze. "Don't you think the circumstances are odd?"

"I do. And if you're right, you should be in protective custody." He leaned forward his eyebrows raised in question.

Shit. She'd walked right into a trap.

"You couldn't just come out and say no?"

"Kay." His chest rose and fell with a sigh. "Homicide will handle the Vaughn murder."

"But—"

He stuck his hand out indicating she should stop talking.

"Tomas and Wayne have their hands full. Two teenage girls went missing from North Park Mall Friday night. I've already asked the FBI to help out. They'll decide whether or not to open a combined investigation into Leann's death and human trafficking."

A touch of relief combined with resentment settled squarely on her shoulders. "If my boss approves the temporary assignment, I can work with the FBI."

"I spoke with her. She said you were on vacation. I suggest you take it."

Evelyn Colvin, the matriarch of child protection and the chief had conspired to keep Kay off the case.

The ray of hope she'd carried into the police station withered like an orchid under a hot Texas sun when he strolled over, opened

his office door, and then dismissed her.
 Nice try. She didn't dismiss easily.

Chapter Seven

Johnny had been behind in his responsibilities all day. He'd searched Kay Taylor's apartment at the boss's personal request. If she had that damn ring, she'd stashed it somewhere else. If he could've ransacked the place and dumped everything on the floor, he'd be on schedule, but Mr. A had given instructions to be discreet.

His nerves had him ready to choke somebody. Anybody. He had a sale tonight. Which always made him edgy. One slip and everything could go to hell.

He unlocked the door to the first holding room, recoiling at the sound of sniffling and the disgusting odors of sweat, piss, and fear. The smell jogged a memory of something bad. Something that set off a series of explosions inside his head. Something best forgotten.

Damn it, he tried to be patient, but the two new girls for tonight's auction were more trouble than the money they'd bring. Both had freaked when he'd explained how the process worked. Hard to turn a deaf ear to that much anguish.

Johnny used to struggle with the right and wrong of these sales, but he couldn't turn off his loyalty. He owed his life to Mr. A., who'd provided a safe haven when Johnny had no food, no money, and nowhere to turn. At least the boss specialized in older product, selling nothing under seventeen years old.

"Please. I want to go home," girl number one begged between sobs. She sat on the cot with her knees tucked under her chin. Long, sandy blond hair hung over one shoulder. Mascara and snot were spread across her face.

"We've been through this. You're going to a new home. How you'll be treated will depend solely on how you behave." He pointed at the sink. "Clean up. Put this on." He tossed a washrag, a nylon robe, and a hairbrush her direction. "Do something with your hair."

"No." Defiance flared in her hazel eyes while she unfurled her legs and came to a standing position. "I won't. You can't make me."

"You will. And I can." He tapped his chest, making sure she noticed the syringe.

Fuck. All he'd accomplished was more waterworks.

He didn't have an ax to grind with the young woman. Fact was, he cared nothing one way or the other. This was business, and Mr. A gave specific orders. He liked his merchandise well groomed on sale day. Johnny made sure the boss got what he wanted.

He crossed the room in three strides, grabbing a fistful of her hair. Without stopping, he dragged her naked ass down the hall to her friend's room. "Look through the peephole."

His patience dwindled when she shook her head like a dog coming out of the rain. His grip tightened as he shoved her face against the door.

"Goddamn it. I'm trying to keep you from getting the same treatment as your girlfriend here." He explained the auction process to her again. "Check it out."

She reluctantly held her eye to the peephole and looked at her friend. The girl lying across the cot, face and arms swollen, barely resembled the one Johnny picked up Friday night at the mall.

Johnny hadn't expected this girl to scream, but she blasted one out and then sagged in his arms. Done. Blank. All her fight gone. Crap. Probably should've medicated this one. He preferred not to drug them before a sale. A touch of ketamine made them more malleable, but many of the boss's customers preferred the package without pharmaceuticals in their system.

"You got lucky. She fought when Hank stopped by. He hasn't had time to get to you. Yet." Johnny shoved her back inside her holding room. She stumbled, falling to the cement floor. Pain lanced above his right ear, and he grabbed the side of his head. The headaches were coming more frequently. And damn, they were a lot more intense.

"Wherever you send me, I'll run away."

"Really?" He removed two snapshots from his inside pocket and held them in front of the crying teenager. "She ran. Talked. She can't do either anymore." He turned his back and ambled away. Then he stopped at the door and without looking at her, commented, "For your own good, wash up, brush your hair, and have that robe on when I come for you."

Jesus, it wasn't like the girls were being sold for sex. Mr. A had no reason to lie about that. They'd have a roof over their heads and three squares. All they'd have to do in return was clean or watch some bastard's kids. He pinched the bridge of his nose, trying to stem the flood of pain.

His cell buzzed. Shit. He didn't have time to talk with his so-called girlfriend. It required four shots of whiskey before he could fuck her. She meant nothing to him. But he followed the boss's orders. There were times when he feared if she grunted one more time, he might cut her throat.

As long as she provided information about Leann Vaughn's case and Kay Taylor's activities, his girlfriend was prime time.

****

Nate picked the lock on Kaycie's apartment and eased inside. The minute he stepped through the door, the hair on the back of his neck rose. She wasn't home, so why the sizzle of nerves? He shook it off.

It wasn't difficult to convince himself that looking around was purely tactical. Necessary to ensure he could protect her.

Tyrell and Marcus would arrive in an hour. The three of them were having an intervention with Kaycie when she got home. She'd protest him getting involved, but until he stopped the threat against her, she'd travel with an armed bodyguard.

The open floor plan of her small apartment lumped the kitchen, dining, and living area into one big room and made for easy defending. The solid wall of windows troubled him, but he could close the blinds, effectively eliminating the possibility of someone getting a clear shot. He double-checked the locks on the windows. He shoved his fingers through his hair, tying it off his face.

The room at the end of the hall had to be her bedroom. He moved silently, stopped just inside the doorway, and breathed in the air where she slept. Sensible Kaycie, the room wasn't elaborate or fancy. She slept on a queen-sized bed. He'd figured her for a king.

He could make do with a queen. If she was stretched out naked in it. He applied a mental head slap. No complications needed.

Every open space had been filled with books, souvenirs, and pictures. Had she kept the Saint Jude medallion? Maybe tucked it away in the back of the jewelry box or wrapped in tissue secured in one of those drawers on the dresser? More likely, she'd dropped it in the nearest trash can the day he left for boot camp.

She deserved a better man, somebody without all his baggage. Somebody who didn't reach for a weapon at every sound. Somebody who'd always be there for her.

The front door opened and closed, snapping him to the present. Nate froze. His pulse quickened. Not good. He'd let his thoughts wander and missed hearing the lock turn.

Did Kaycie have an unwelcome visitor?

Other than him?

Keys jangled, and Nate released the breath he'd held. Kaycie was home. He stifled a chuckle. Finding him in her apartment would seriously piss her off.

He silently moved down the hall. He found her in the kitchen with her back to him. Reaching up, she removed a glass from the shelf, giving him the opportunity he needed. He moved fast, trapped her between the counter with his body, and pinned her arms to her side.

She screamed and tried to whirl. Wasn't happening. She stomped where his feet should've been. Nice move, but he'd spread his legs out of reach. He leaned in tighter. He wouldn't hurt her, just keep her still. Damn, she'd mastered a few self-defense techniques over the years. He tightened his grip to immobilize her.

Inches from the nape of her neck, he fought the urge to lean down and test that spot right behind her ear. The sensitive place he used to kiss again and again until she purred.

She tried to butt him with the back of her head. Maybe, he should make her aware of who had her pinned.

"Nate, you bastard. Get off me."

Apparently, she already knew.

"That Glock on your hip is no help if it's holstered." He'd intended to rest his hand on her gun, but instead, he rested his palm on her taut belly.

He stepped back before his erection pressing against her drew her attention. She whirled to face him, her fingers wrapped around the butt of the gun.

"Don't try it," he warned.

"Get over yourself." Her tone matched the hate in her eyes. "You really think I care enough about you to shoot you?"

She unbuckled her belt, removed the holster, and placed her weapon on the counter. She opened the fridge, grabbed a beer, popped the top, and then sipped while watching him over the can.

"We still need to talk." He tried to ignore her tongue as it darted across her lips. His dick, always with a mind of its own, twitched painfully inside his jeans.

"Your memory seems to be limited and your hearing impaired. I'll speak slowly this time. No. We. Don't." Her venom-laced tone cut right through him. "I'm changing clothes. When I come back, be gone."

He waited until she disappeared down the hall before opening a beer for himself. His stomach growled as he strolled across the room to get comfortable on her couch.

She'd listen if he had to throw her down and sit on her.

"You hungry?" he yelled at her closed bedroom door. Considering her state of mind, he didn't expect her to answer. He assumed her silence meant yes.

He called Tyrell. "Where are you?"

"Almost to Kay's. You already there?"

"Yeah. Looks like we'll be here a while. Stop and pick up a bucket of fried chicken. Is Marcus with you?"

"Yeah. Our ETA is fifteen."

Nate set his cell on her coffee table and settled back. A few swallows of beer later, he sensed Kaycie standing behind him. No doubt, her dark-brown gaze shot daggers at his back. He didn't speak. The military had taught him that, on occasion, patience was a necessary maneuver.

She moved into his line of vision, twisting his insides into a knot. The jeans and faded DPD T-shirt she wore fit her like a glove. Jesus, her long black hair hung past her shoulders. She reclined in the monster-size chair directly in front of him, curling her mile-long legs and tucking her bare feet under her bottom. She rubbed her arms as if she were cold. Interesting, because he sensed she was nervous. Not entirely a bad sign.

God. She'd matured into a beautiful woman. Tall, lean and mean.

Ten years vanished.

"Why are you following me?"

"You're in danger." Would she take a swing at him if he moved closer?

"I'm aware of that. Exactly how do you know?"

The knock on her front door ended their conversation. He sank back deeper on the couch.

"I met with Tyrell and Marcus earlier today. You should let them in."

"Marcus Ricci is here with Tyrell?"

Her face lit up as she dashed past Nate. She opened the door and threw her arms around Marcus, hugging him tight. Damn, the squeal she let out sounded like she'd found a leprechaun's pot of gold. Getting together with the group might be good for him.

Nate stood and quickly found himself wrapped in Marcus's embrace. Nate had a good two inches on Marcus, but if he decided you needed a hug, it was over before you had a chance to protest.

"I heard you made it home in one piece," Marcus said with what for him was a smile.

Marcus's gaze darkened when his hands clasped Nate's shoulders. No doubt, both of their minds slipped to the missing man from their group. Donavan's chopper went down in flames while he was trying to rescue a couple of wounded soldiers. All aboard had died.

"You too, Marcus. I heard you earned a couple medals."

"They can't keep you warm at night." Marcus wrapped an arm around Kaycie's waist.

Tyrell, never one to be left out, sidled up to Kaycie's vacant side and threw his arm around her shoulder.

She ran her hands over Marcus's and Tyrell's bald heads. "What's up? You two lose all your hair while in the service?"

"Chicks like it." Tyrell preened, flashing white teeth at Kaycie.

Marcus coughed. "It's easier to keep."

Nate clenched his jaw. She wasn't through taking shots at him. Wait for it...

She turned her gaze toward him. "What's with the shaggy-dog look?"

"I'm glad you've got work for me." Marcus, always the peacemaker, weighed in, no doubt ending a possible argument. "It'll be fun helping our girl out."

Nate gave him a shut-up look. Nate could afford to part with some of his savings. Wasn't as if he'd had anything to spend it on for the past ten years.

"Helping me?" Kaycie leaned toward Marcus. "Of course, I'm happy to have my boys back together. But what's going on here?"

Time to change the subject.

"If you guys are finished mauling Kaycie, I'd like to make plans." Nate seized the bucket of chicken from Tyrell, plopping it on the coffee table.

"Somebody needs to explain the helping-me statement." Kaycie's arms folded across her chest.

"Can we eat and talk?" Marcus eyed the food. "Then we'll divvy up watch duty."

Kaycie closed her mouth, drawing her lips into a thin line, and stormed to the kitchen area. Marcus hurried to help carry plates, napkins, and the rest of a six-pack of beer. She slammed the silverware down and then resumed her position across from Nate. Wasn't him she glared at. Her gaze lobbed fireballs at Tyrell.

"This is your doing." She pointed the tines of her fork directly at Tyrell. "You asked Nate to keep me under surveillance without discussing it with me?"

"After the episode at the morgue, it was warranted." Tyrell nodded and then shrugged his shoulders unapologetically. "Couldn't do it by myself."

"Definitely warranted," Marcus said around a bite of food.

Nate let them ramble on, arguing back and forth, exactly like when they were students at UT. Kaycie had adopted Tyrell Castillo, Marcus Ricci, and Jake Donovan. The exception was Nate. She'd never mothered him. Hell, they'd been too busy screwing like monkeys.

He paid attention when she described her visit with the chief of police. The FBI had been called on the missing girls. They wouldn't react well if they learned somebody was nosing around. Nate would get the scoop on their plans and make sure he didn't piss anybody off.

"Did Chief Compton mention who at the bureau he spoke with?" Nate asked.

Kaycie turned and faced him. Her icy gaze said she hadn't forgotten he was in the room.

"He didn't mention any names."

She turned her back and resumed the argument over her protection.

"Enough." Nate grew tired of the loud debate. "You were followed by a black Mercedes today. It picked you up here, tailed you to the church and then to the cemetery. I have the license number and will check it out tomorrow." Kaycie opened her mouth, but he continued, "Until we determine if your kidnappers and the girl's death are related, one of us will either be at your side or close by."

"I'll agree to this if we dig into the human-trafficking angle." Kaycie's jaw was set. Nate remembered that look.

Nate didn't hesitate. "You got it." He smiled at her surprise.

"I can put out some feelers." Tyrell took a long draw from the beer can. "Don't know that we'll hear anything. These rings are hard to pin down. I read an article in the newspaper right before the Super Bowl. Some of these bastards are transient. They pick up and move to the next big venue at the first sign of trouble. But in this case, I'm leaning toward thinking this is a hometown syndicate."

"It's one of the fastest-growing, most lucrative crimes around. I need help, and Lord knows I appreciate you believing my theory."

"Marcus says he has time to spare, and so do I," Nate addressed her. "Tyrell will help when he's not on bodyguard assignment, which he has tonight. I'll take the first watch. Marcus, can relieve me in the morn—"

"Excuse me." Kaycie's forehead wrinkled with a full-blown frown. "I understand I'm in danger. Somebody wants to get their hands on me, and I can use your help. I'm moved and grateful you guys are willing to step up after all these years, but..."

Nate waited for a protest. She proved his premonition when she pointed a long slender finger at him.

"You are not staying inside my apartment."

Chapter Eight

Kay rolled onto her back and lay there in the dark on her cool sheets. She turned on the bedside light for the fourth time and cursed that she couldn't get Nate out of her head.

The medallion hung around her neck as a reminder to protect her heart at all costs. Tonight it weighed heavily on her chest, bringing back memories best left in the past.

Marcus had free time? She'd heard he refused the money from his wife's life insurance, sending it instead to her family. What had he been doing with his life before Nate put him on the payroll?

The thought of being indebted to Nate pushed her blood pressure through the roof. He wasn't the prince on a white stallion, riding in to save her. He was a heartbreak waiting to happen. He'd blow through like a whirlwind and be gone just as fast. She'd read that romance book. It had a happy ending. She didn't.

Tyrell, Marcus, and Nate had stayed for hours, laughing at her when she'd called them Wolfe's Pack for the first time in ten years. The four of them had discussed different schedules and ways to keep her safe. Surprise of all surprises, when she said who she suspected was behind the kidnapping attempt, they'd believed her.

She'd almost asked if any of them still had their Saint Jude medal. The protector of lost causes. She'd given each of them one at graduation, hoping it would help keep them safe. Oh, they'd made fun of her, but each left for their tour of duty wearing one around their necks. Her heart clutched. Nothing had protected sweet Jake.

She'd dated Nate exclusively, and the other three men made sure nobody else looked at her. Of course, her tutoring skills kept them eligible for football and helped hone their protective instincts. Good men, all of them.

No. The one who kept her awake was far from good. He slept

outside her apartment in his pickup, sweating out the night during the hottest summer Texas had experienced in more than twenty years. The old Nate, the one full of confidence and bravado would have wormed his way inside under the air conditioner. The new Nate had shrugged his shoulders, accepted her edict, and then strolled out the door.

Crap. People died in this kind of heat. That's why she couldn't sleep. Not because her heart did back flips every time his gaze locked on hers. And certainly not because her skin heated when those deep-blue eyes drank her in as if he were dying.

Double crap. Sighing at her weakness, she slid on a pair of jeans under her sleep shirt. Pistol in hand, she rested the grip against her thigh and plodded through the dark hall to the front door.

"Going somewhere?"

She whirled and aimed her Glock in the direction of the voice. Her end-table lamp came on, chasing away the shadows.

Stretched out on her couch, Nate awarded her with that sexy Cheshire cat smile.

"Damn it, Nate. I could've shot you."

"After being on the receiving end of that punch you threw at the cemetery, I'm not surprised you're a quick draw." He rubbed his jaw and swung his bare feet to the floor. "Mind pointing that thing somewhere else?"

Kay lowered her gun. Damn him and his blasé attitude.

"Stop breaking into my apartment." She glanced at the security chain. He should've had to break it to get inside, but there it was, securely in place. How'd he do that? Anger licked through her blood. "I double-checked to make sure the apartment was secured."

"I'm sure you did. Obviously, me on your couch is proof positive you need a bodyguard. Sleeping with your gun is a good tactic. You a good shot?"

"Don't tempt me to show you."

Nate got to his feet, stretching muscled arms over his head. His T-shirt rode up, revealing ripped abs and one thin line of hair trailing down past the button on his jeans. She dragged her gaze up to the partially exposed tattoo on the inside of his left bicep. She couldn't interpret the letters. According to Tyrell, Nate had been in a number of different countries. No telling what the darn thing meant in English.

"What's the tattoo mean?" Why she'd asked was a mystery, and when she saw the glint in Nate's eyes, she regretted posing the question.

"This one?" He slid a finger under his shirtsleeve. "It's nothing."

"Fine. Don't tell me." If he wanted to play guessing games, she was out. Kay stomped to the kitchen for a bottle of water, anything to put an end to her wandering thoughts. "I don't really care."

"Since you're up." He sauntered down the hall.

Seconds later, the bathroom door closed and the shower was running. Well, damn. She wasn't budging until he returned. Getting her financial questions answered served as a good reason to wait. She'd go to bed after she laid out the ground rules. To be sure he didn't sneak up on her again, she curled up in her favorite chair and faced the hallway.

He prowled down the hall as if he belonged in her apartment and in her life. Nate moved with a combination of grace and power. Strong movements, bold and sure, sex and swagger.

He scrubbed a towel over his thick, damp hair. Thank God, he'd dressed and covered his incredible body. Still, the tight T-shirt did nothing to hide his firm abs.

He returned to his previous spot on the couch, stretched out, and made himself comfortable. Irritation sizzled on her skin's surface. His gaze caught hers and held for a moment.

"Kaycie, I could hear you tossing and turning. I'm here, you can rest now."

"It's Kay and did something happen to your brain while you were gone?"

"A lot." He turned on his side, propped his head on his hand, and looked her in the eyes. "I get that I'm not on your Christmas list, but aren't you a little too mad at me?"

"A lot? That's all you have to say?" She blocked out the rising anger and inhaled a calming breath. "And I'll be as mad at you as I want."

He slid off the couch and knelt in front of her chair. Her alert system went off. Warm tension slid low in her stomach. She steeled herself against his charm.

"I'm sorry." He rested his hand on her knee. "What do you want me to say? That I was young and stupid? Okay. I was young and stupid. It wasn't like I surprised you with the fact I wanted to be a SEAL."

Kay stared at his hand, burning her flesh, branding her as he used to. No doubt, removing her jeans would reveal blisters. She lifted his wrist with two fingers, moving his entire arm to the side of the chair.

"I never believed you'd really go." Keeping her voice from shaking required every ounce of determination she could muster.

"You gonna hold that against me forever?"

"I get that you wanted to serve your country. In fact, I respect and admire you for it. But there's nothing here for you."

"You're still single." The corners of his mouth lifted. "I'm still single."

"That ship sailed. You're a day late and a dollar short. Opportunity doesn't knock twice. I'm sure one of those applies."

"You done with the clichés?" He tilted his head to the side. His expression reminded her of why she'd smacked him at the cemetery. He was just too damn cute.

"I have more." Her insides seized at his casual manner. "If you didn't get my meaning, you really did suffer brain damage."

She'd lost enough. The night she graduated from high school, her twin brother, Kevin, had died in a car wreck. Her father had slowly wasted away from anger, effectively shutting Kay out of his life.

Meeting Nate her first year in college had changed Kay's life. She'd let him inside, fallen in love with him, and then he'd walked away.

No more losses. No more being left behind. No more dreaming. Life was all about realism.

Yet, looking into Nate's eyes, the spark of interest, the desire flooding his gaze, sent her heart into free fall.

The difference in him was incredible. The carefree, laughing young man she'd loved with all her heart was gone.

Her hand betrayed her by inching across her lap and toward his face. She wouldn't touch him. Couldn't touch him. Another heartbreak like the last one would be more than she could take.

"You were going outside to get me. Weren't you?"

"Only because I need to clear up something."

"What's that?" The corners of his mouth lifted.

"Your protection services. What's the going rate?"

"For you? Nothing."

"Stop it, Nate. How much will this cost me? I won't be indebted to you." Her resolve strengthened when his gaze narrowed and one cheek twitched.

"It's not like I'm asking you to have sex with me. You're in trouble and I can help."

She couldn't listen anymore. She went to the bedroom and retrieved her checkbook from the drawer. Flipping it open, she returned to her chair. She poised her pen, ready to write.

"How much?"

His chin jutted out, giving him an air of arrogance. He glared at her. One eyebrow rose. "Standard retainer is five grand."

Kay could be arrogant, too. The money her grandmother had left her meant Kay had enough in the bank to never worry about money. Not a fortune, but enough.

"That sounds reasonable." She scribbled out the check and then handed it over. "This is strictly business."

His eyebrows went up at her statement as his large hand engulfed her fingers. Funny how she'd always been fascinated by them. Loved the way ... stop.

"If that's what you want." He folded the check and slid it in his back pocket. "Does this mean I shouldn't interpret being invited inside as proof you're not mad at me anymore?"

"I didn't want to be responsible if you died in your truck."

His hand moved back to her knee, warming the skin where he caressed. His scent was clean and woodsy. And male. And Nate.

A look of desire clouded his eyes. The pulse in his neck thrummed to the tune of the one between her legs. Her breath caught in her chest.

Run.

"Why was it so important to be a SEAL?"

"My grandfather was a Vietnam SEAL. One of the first, since before then they didn't exist. He was my mentor and biggest supporter. I guess I wanted to make him proud."

"You could've told me."

"I was too busy being young," he stated matter-of-factly.

"Maybe so." His reason wouldn't have changed her feeling of abandonment.

She edged away from temptation, walking with determination toward her bedroom. The room behind her went dark.

****

"Last one." Johnny lifted the limp teenager up to the truck driver, waiting until the man secured her in the sleeper compartment to hand him a bottle of water. "If she wakes, give her a swallow of this. It'll keep her calm until delivery."

"Will do," the driver said.

"Just a swallow." Johnny stood outside the warehouse, supervising the shipment of girls to their new owners. This was the last trailer to dispatch. "You let her sip along the way. She drinks the whole bottle in one sitting, and you'll pay for her."

When the trailer full of ceiling fans plus one teenage girl passed through the front gate, Johnny started inside only to find Mr. A standing aside, observing.

"Good idea keeping them tranquil until delivery." He clapped Johnny on the back and then led the way through the warehouse. "Can't have another one escape."

"No, sir. The Vaughn girl taught us all a lesson." Johnny's mood was light after such a successful sale. Time to restock. The mall was too risky with its cameras and guards. Raves were much safer. The girls were already on Ecstasy, drinking and looking for a quick fuck. The next supply would come from a huge crowd where nobody would notice his movements.

Hank, carrying his overnight bag, met them in front of the boss's office. His primary function was collections. While most sales were wire transfers, made and validated prior to shipment, every now and then, some stupid bastard tried to outsmart them. Hank made sure the customer paid his bill in full.

"Have a good trip," the boss commented to Hank as he brushed past them, pausing at the exit.

"Find my ring," Hank said over his shoulder.

Mr. A rolled his eyes and exhaled a sigh. It looked like the boss had forgiven Hank. Why was the question. The bruised face on the girl had reduced her value at auction.

"Anything for me before I leave?" The boss brushed a piece of lint off Johnny's jacket.

"Yes, sir. My girl ran the motorcycle's tags for me. Name's Nathan Wolfe. He's a private detective." Johnny's ears started buzzing and a sharp pain set off his headache. He paused to block out the pain. "I'll get more information on him tonight. When I hear, I'll let you know."

"Getting to the Taylor woman will be more difficult."

"She paid a visit to the chief. Apparently, nothing was said about a ring." Johnny continued, "The rest isn't good news. The FBI has been asked to look into the disappearance of these last two girls."

"Damn. None of this bodes well for the business." The boss poured two fingers of whiskey, offering the drink to Johnny. He quickly withdrew the glass. "I forgot you don't drink on the job."

"Never know when I'll need a clear head. The boys noticed a female friend hanging out with the Taylor woman. We might find a use for her."

Mr. A sipped his whiskey, and Johnny savored the pungent aroma.

"Maybe she would trade the ring for her buddy. Either way, when we get it back, that Taylor bitch has to die."

"Yes, sir." The KA-BAR warmed inside Johnny's boot.

Chapter Nine

The slow rhythmic beat of country music roused Kay from what had been a fitful sleep at best. Nate's shift should've ended by now, giving Kay an inexcusable pang of regret.

Marcus must've tuned in the local radio station. Catching up with him would be good. By the time she'd learned of his wife's death, the funeral had been over. Kay had planned to offer her sympathies, but Tyrell had strongly warned against it. He'd suffered guilt and pain when his sister had been murdered. His recommendation to let Marcus grieve in his own way was sound advice.

A light tap on her bedroom door sent her grabbing for the sheet. Seconds later, Nate invaded her privacy. Tall and shirtless, he filled the doorway. His broad shoulders and carved-from-granite chest tapered down to a trim waist and narrow hips.

Her mouth went dry. She couldn't force one word past the lump jammed in the back of her throat. Her gaze was drawn to a tattoo on his left pectoral muscle right above his nipple. The eagle with a trident and ship's anchor in its talons was obviously a SEAL emblem.

Something shiny caught her eye, and her gaze shifted to the middle of his chest. The earth stumbled. A vice tightened around her heart.

The Saint Jude medal hung on a chain around his neck.

He moved across the room. A predator ready to strike. "You still take cream?" He set a steaming mug of coffee on her nightstand.

His gaze swept across her face. Always perceptive, his brows knitted, his dark-blue eyes studied her.

"What's wrong?" He leaned closer. The chain swung forward, dangling her broken heart in front of her.

His warm breath stroked her cheek. His lips were close enough to kiss. His face close enough to smack again.

"Nothing," was all she managed to say.

"You're white as a sheet."

Why was he still wearing the medallion? What did it mean? Why did the one she wore under her sleep shirt burn against her skin? *Stop.* None of those question needed asking. The answers didn't matter.

Kay scrambled further up on the headboard away from him. "Get out of my bedroom."

He sighed and backed away. "Just trying to be helpful."

She stuffed her hands under the covers and refused to look at the medallion. He straightened his shoulders and strolled out of the room. Funny, as soon as he was out of sight an empty feeling rushed over her.

Kay grabbed a set of warm-ups and hit the bathroom. Anywhere she could screw her head back on straight before facing Nate again. But the shower only gave her more time to wonder why he'd kept the medallion and, more important, why she gave a damn. She couldn't resurrect a love that had died ten years ago.

The sound of Holly's laughter greeted Kay when she stepped into the hall. She rounded the corner to find her best friend entertaining Marcus and Nate.

Enthralled by Holly's bouncy personality, pixie face, and charming smile, neither man turned his head when Kay entered the room. She might as well have been invisible.

"Holly, what are you doing here?" Kay's words came out snarky, but she was getting tired of people wandering in and out of her apartment.

"Enjoying the company." Holly wore shorts and a lace cami, and her blue-streaked blond ponytail swished as her gaze shifted from Nate to Marcus. "You've been holding out on me."

"Her having a key was the only thing that kept us from putting a bullet in her." Nate shared a wink at Holly. "And I wanted to thank her for being there for you yesterday."

"If I'd known who you were, I might've shot you."

Holly sent a knowing smile at Kay, who choked down a chuckle as she refilled her mug.

"That's quite a friend you've got." Nate got up from the table and moved to lean on the kitchen counter.

He was too close. Smelled too good. Radiated far too much heat. Was this kindness part of his services?

"Yeah. She's a real Annie Oakley." Kay slid into the chair Nate had vacated. Holly's huge blue eyes sparkled.

"I do look good in my boots."

Holly could turn any situation into something funny. She was lovely, a tad ditzy, and the best friend ever. Snapping at her put a bitter taste in Kay's mouth.

"Yes, you do." Time to get down to business. "So Marcus, you're hanging out with me today?" He nodded and she continued, "Good, because we need to run by Child Protective Services. Holly works with me, and she can dig around in the system. We need to know if any of the other investigators are working cases of missing young girls."

"Be a good thing to know." Nate rinsed his cup and set it on the counter. "You said the dead girl escaped a trucker. Marcus has friends in that industry and can put out feelers. Long-haul drivers are a tight group, but most want no part of transporting kidnapped females. I'll try to find out who the FBI is sending."

"You can do that?" Kay's attention spiked. If Nate had a friend in the bureau, getting information just got a lot easier.

"I've done contract work for them since moving back to Dallas. We also need an insider to run the plates on the Mercedes. If we get lucky, the car will be registered to Hank Walsh."

Just how long had he been back? The answer might hurt worse than not knowing so she refused to ask. Being in close quarters with Nate was a mistake, of that she was positive, but she might learn more by sticking with him today. Tomas would run the plate number for her while Nate got a name from his contact.

"I'll take care of the plates," Kay said. "Nate, I'm going with you. Holly doesn't need my help."

"Neither do I." Nate's firm jaw lifted higher, and he folded his arms across his chest.

Kay opened her mouth to argue.

Nate's hands formed the universal timeout sign.

"Don't you dare shush me. Leann's death is on my shoulders. Get it?" Every muscle in her body contracted. "I will be involved in every step of this investigation."

"Kaycie" Nate's jaw muscle twitched. "You—"

"What you need is sleep." Marcus spoke directly to Nate. Kay was positive he'd interrupted on purpose. "It's you and me until Tyrell finishes his gig."

"He's not tired. He slept on my couch last night," Kay huffed, still stinging from Nate's rebuff.

"No, he didn't," Marcus said. "No shut-eye while on watch."

"I'll sleep when I need to."

Kay moved between Nate and the door. "I'm going with you, or Marcus and I will follow along behind."

Nate made what sounded like a low growl while he slipped a holster with a Glock on his belt before covering it with a shirt. He tugged a set of keys from his pocket and then glanced over his shoulder. Kay recognized his look of surrender. She'd won this round.

"Go put on a pair of jeans and some boots."

****

Nate handed Kaycie the extra helmet, fired up the motorcycle and waited for her to slide on behind him. Her thighs lay against his, breasts pressed into his back, and her arms wrapped around his waist. All reasonable thought went straight to hell.

Stupid to agree to take her along. Insane to have her body plastered against his. Ignorant to think having her so close wouldn't have an effect on him.

She cleared her throat. "We can go now."

"Sure thing, boss." He hit the gas and headed for the freeway, figuring the drive would give him time to clear his head. Not likely. Not while her skin burned his through their clothes.

Truthfully, he hadn't moved back to Dallas with hopes of starting up with her again. She'd made a life for herself. She damn sure didn't need him complicating matters. Not unless she was into shattered nerves, nightmares, and knees that sounded like cracking knuckles.

Admittedly, he was an adrenaline junkie. Away from danger too long, and he missed the rush. Forming close ties with anyone would be downright stupid.

She tightened her grip, sending him back in time to his small apartment in Austin. She'd been young and innocent, with lush lips you could lose yourself in. And breasts? They were so sweet, his taste buds tingled just thinking about them.

The problem was she'd wanted what he couldn't give. A house with a two-car garage and white picket fence. Two kids and an SUV. Christ on a crutch, at twenty-two years old, she'd scared the hell out of him. The SEALs had been his lifelong dream. A goal Kaycie hadn't understood.

She squeezed his ribs, leaned into him harder and yelled over the roar of the engine. "Where are we going?"

"No need to shout, the helmets are miked. My office is right off the freeway."

Her body stiffened. Wait for it. The next question would be how long had he been home. She'd surprised him by not asking sooner.

When he parked and she still hadn't asked, he remembered that she didn't give a damn when or where he moved.

He unlocked the front door, stepped back, and let her go ahead. "Other than me, you're the first person who's been inside. There's not much in the way of furniture. I'll drag a box from the back for you to sit on."

"Who do you know in the FBI?"

"A fellow named Dalton Murphy. I've done a few undercover jobs for them, and he's my contact. Now that I've set up an office and formed a legal company, I'm hoping for more business. Dalton's the special agent in charge of the Atlanta office. He's a good friend to have."

Nate fished out his cell. "There's a coffeepot." He pointed and started scrolling. She caught his hand with hers.

He turned and faced her. The cinnamon flecks in her sexy brown eyes flared, and her pupils dilated. Even though it lasted only a second, he recognized and remembered the warmth. Her kissable lips were too close for comfort. He edged back a step.

"Why are you doing this?"

His mind pedaled fast for an answer they both would believe.

"You're in danger."

"No. Why are *you* doing this?"

It was a loaded question. One he wouldn't answer because he wasn't sure himself. It still burned his gut that she believed his loyalty could be bought. Handing him the check had made him face one reality. Their relationship was probably better this way. Just the idea of giving up his lifestyle for a nine-to-five job, made his nuts hurt. Keeping his country safe was all he knew how to do. Government contracts would allow him to continue to help.

"You have somebody else in mind you'd rather hire?" Nate pressured. "He might be cheaper but not as good."

"Forget it." She spun on her heel toward the coffee pot. Stopped in midstride. "Hey, there's a black Mercedes parked—"

"I know. We picked up a tail right after we left your place. Ignore them."

"Why? I'll bet it's the same car. In fact, those windows aren't legal. They're too dark."

"So they are. Not your job to go remind them."

"I was a cop before transferring to CPS. Trained not to be passive when threatened. We should confront them."

"I intend to. First, I need to call Dalton. Let the boys outside get comfortable while they watch us."

Kaycie let out an old familiar huff before heading in the direction of the coffeepot.

At least she was out of the way. He didn't care if she were ex-CIA, he wouldn't risk getting her hurt. Nate quietly exited through the back door, jogged down the service alley and up beside the idling Mercedes. A confrontation in the open was the safest bet. He eased his gun out of the holster and tapped the driver's-side window.

"Lower it or I'll break the fucker."

The window slowly slid down. The passenger's door opened, and a gorilla exited the car. Tall, wide forehead, slack jaw, and familiar. His size made Nate think this was one of the bastards who'd attacked Kaycie at the morgue.

He smiled at the big ape. His fingers itched.

"You got a problem?" the gorilla asked.

"I have questions, and you have answers."

"I got your answer right here." The gorilla slid a HK MP10 out from behind his wide body. Somebody had armed this bastard well.

The car lurched forward. Nate lunged back, barely avoiding his foot being run over.

"You son of a bitch." Nate reached to jerk the door open, froze when he caught movement in his peripheral vision.

Kaycie moved into his line of sight. Feet spread, her Glock pointed at the gorilla.

Shit.

The driver's-side door swung open, knocking Nate off balance. He staggered backward never taking his gaze off her. The gorilla was half in, half out when the car sped off with both doors still open.

Nate had made a novice's mistake. He'd taken his eye off the target.

"Damn it, Kaycie. Why didn't you stay inside?" His heartbeat thundered in his ears. "You're the fucking target. If they'd wanted you dead..."

Nate couldn't speak the words. Something tripped inside, exploding in his chest. Not in hand-to-hand combat or in the middle of a firestorm of bullets, not when his men died in an ambush, had he experienced this kind of fear. Cold sweat seeped from his pores.

Kaycie's face turned redder by the second. With each step she made in his direction, her scowl deepened. By the time they stood toe-to-toe, all he wanted to do was pull her into his arms and thank God she was safe.

"Are you crazy?" She poked a finger into his chest. "You condescending bastard. Don't you ever leave me behind when there's trouble."

She stormed inside, leaving Nate to wonder why he was in trouble. Christ, all he'd done was try to protect her. He followed, locked the door, and caught up with her at the coffeepot. Adrenaline still powered through his system, sizzling his nerves when she turned her back to him.

A hint of vanilla caught his senses. His chest tightened. There. Right behind her ear. The freckle he loved to kiss. He placed his hands on her shoulders and turned her around. Her pupils flared slightly, a clear indication she'd felt the spark between them.

"I will go crazy if I don't do this." He lowered his lips to hers, bracing himself for the worst. Expecting her to shove him away. Expecting her to remind him he was in her employ. Expecting her to stand rigid as a post.

His spirit soared when soft, lush lips opened slightly. Welcomed him. He angled his mouth for better coverage and swept his tongue inside heaven. This was supposed to be just a quick kiss, a taste of her sweetness. A honey-forgive-me touch of the tongues. Desire exploded, rocketing through every inch of his body.

Nate turned ravenous. His hands roamed and smoothed, needing to experience every inch of her body. The gentle slope of her back, the slant of her waist as it nipped in at the hip. Not one inch of her had escaped his memory.

She moaned, sending shock waves of need through him. She swayed in his arms, slid her hands around his neck, and pulled him closer until her breasts pressed against his chest.

Somewhere deep within the darkness of his soul a light shone.

Chapter Ten

Kay could barely stand. Her legs had forgotten their primary function. Nate's muscular body pressed against hers, his kiss devoured her. The world shifted on its axis. Her hands tunneled deep in his hair, holding him close. Need flooded her body and concentrated low in her belly. Warmth pooled. Skin. She wanted to touch bare skin.

Oh. Hell. No. He's not to be trusted.

She'd lost her mind to let him kiss her. Logic and lust were at war inside her head. Kay placed her hands on his chest and applied pressure until his lips separated from hers. She shoved harder a second time, and he backed up a single step.

His gaze caressed her face. Navy-blue eyes had darkened to the color of midnight. Hooded with lust. His desire obvious.

Her gaze drifted to the enormous swell pressing against the zipper on his jeans. She quickly raised her eyes to meet his.

"That won't happen again." Her heart hurt, and her body protested from wanting him as she put more distance between them. At least she'd managed to speak with a small amount of conviction.

"You sure?" His gaze bore deep into hers, weakening her resolve.

Her throat closed, which was fine since her brain refused to offer up a snappy comeback. Damn, she hoped the trembling inside didn't show. She forced calm into her words.

"We merely experienced an overflow of adrenaline. It's time to get back to the employer/employee relationship."

With one menacing step toward her, he stood close enough for his body heat to weaken her resolve. The corners of his lips lifted. And that was a mistake because his arrogance pissed her off.

"I think we have unfinished business," he stated, giving her more smile.

"We don't. And give the Cheshire cat grin a rest. It doesn't work on me anymore," she lied. Refusing to blink, she held his gaze and added, "And, yes, I'm sure."

The top two buttons of her blouse had mysteriously come undone. One more and he'd have found the Saint Jude medallion. Not something she wanted to discuss with him. "Weren't you about to call your FBI friend?"

"Right. I'll do that while you call your contact at the police department. Tell them you've picked up a tail."

She'd disturbed the leather string he used instead of a rubber band when she'd burrowed her hands in his hair, and he bent to retrieve it from the floor. One black eyebrow rose while he raked fingers through his disheveled mane and secured it off his face.

Damned if her palms didn't ache to do it again.

"What was with the noble offer to take on my case for free?" Kay hoped for an honest answer. "Don't you have bills to pay?"

"You're hardly a case, and I've got enough to get by until my business gets established."

"Why this and not police work?"

"Too many rules. If I want to help somebody, I'll make that decision." Nate glanced at the front door and back at her. "You always loved kids, so I'm not surprised to find you working at CPS. But why a cop first?"

"Ambition. And I wanted to make a difference. There are different levels of investigators in the agency. I needed practical experience if I wanted to work in the field. Sitting behind a desk didn't appeal to me."

"I can identify with that." Nate filled two cups, passed one to her, and then returned to his laptop.

Kay rolled her shoulders in an effort to relax and then placed a call to Tomas Mendes. He warned her not to interfere with the case when he learned she was still on the hunt for evidence against Hank Walsh. He seemed slightly relieved she'd hired protection. In the end, he agreed to run the license plate number for her. She put Tomas on hold and walked over to Nate to ask for the number.

Waiting patiently, she listened to his conversation. He reached behind himself as if he knew she was standing there, caught her by the hand and tugged her to his side.

"Thanks, Dalton. Text me anything you can share." Nate disconnected and then slipped his hand around her waist. "I have good and bad news. My friend will keep me in the loop if we do the same."

She disengaged him from her body before her skin melted. "Is that the good news?"

"Yeah. I hoped we'd link up with the FBI agent who's been assigned to investigate. Dalton said the guy is out of the Dallas office and is a loner."

"You two should get along just fine." Kay's cell warmed in her hand. "Damn, I forgot Tomas on hold. I need the license number of the black car."

Nate passed her a business card with the digits scribbled on back. After she'd given Tomas the information, she hung up and turned the card over. Under Wolfe Private Investigation was his Texas license number.

"You're licensed but have no furniture?"

"I make do without a desk and chair. I had to have a license before the government would award me contract work. If I can establish myself, build a good reputation, the business will come."

"Am I your first customer?"

"No."

"Then how can you afford to babysit me?"

"Kaycie. I'm not in this for the money and neither are Tyrell and Marcus. This is about your safety, and we're with you because we care."

He brushed his hand over his jaw, and she remembered how his stubble abraded her chin minutes ago. "How can you care about me? You and I are total strangers. We're not those dumbass kids from college anymore."

"Right." The expression in his deep-blue eyes had gone cold. "Whatever you say, boss."

Typical Nate. She'd tried to talk, and he'd slammed the door in her face. If he was unhappy because she'd insisted on paying for his services, too damn bad.

"While your contact is checking the license plate, we can go talk to Hank's family." Nate logged off his laptop. She watched his fingers punching keys with a vengeance.

"Okay." She'd faced facts, and he'd have to eventually. The years had molded them into different people. Poles apart from the twenty-two-year-olds they used to be. Surely, he got that. Never mind that their bodies fought the idea. Common sense said otherwise.

Didn't mean her heart wouldn't shoot over the moon with him around, just meant she had to control her emotions.

"I don't leave the bike outside. I'll pull around back and come in through the back door. We'll take my truck. First we change into something more official looking."

****

Nate stopped at the bottom of the stairs, waiting while Kaycie scanned the area. They'd stopped by her place where she'd changed clothes. As soon as he'd redressed, they'd go to downtown Dallas.

"I didn't spot a tail. Did you?" Apparently satisfied, Kaycie joined him.

"I made sure we didn't have one. This place needs to stay off the grid. If things get sticky you can move in with me."

She paused and then moved on without comment. Nate held the door open to his loft and decided to lighten what had turned into a somber drive.

"I'll be right back. Unless you'd like to help me, then it will take a lot longer."

She snorted her disgust and perched on the arm of his couch, leaving him to head down the hall to his bedroom alone.

She'd been distant since they'd had their confrontation in his office. If she believed he would deposit her check and be her hired man, she was dead wrong.

Damn, the slacks and shirt he slipped on were as uncomfortable as if he'd put on a suit. Wranglers and a T-shirt were more his style. He emerged to find her in the exact same place he'd left her.

"Ready?" She sprang to her feet when he returned.

She'd rushed through their stop at her place and managed to transform herself into a sophisticated, badge-wearing, gun-toting Child Protective Services investigator. She was beautiful, but he preferred her long hair flowing down her back, her tight butt in jeans, and her soft breasts under a T-shirt.

Or wearing nothing at all.

Still pissed, Kaycie stood like a new military recruit. Back straight, eyes forward.

"Kaycie, the girl I remember used to be impulsive, a little undisciplined and a lot passionate. Where did she go?"

Seconds turned into an eternity while she stared at him.

"You remember the night I gave you the Saint Jude medallion?"

"Of course I do." He unbuttoned his shirt and displayed his. "I never take it off."

She reached inside her blouse, pulled out a chain and dropped the Saint Jude medallion on her chest.

"You still wear yours." His mouth went dry.

"Every single day." She rubbed the charm with her fingers. "It reminds me not to waste my time on lost causes."

"Meaning?" Shit, the more she talked, the less he understood.

"Meaning I loved you. Trusted you. And you broke my heart. Eventually, I grew up, got over you and moved on." She blew out a sigh. "I never made the same mistake with anyone again."

Somewhere, in the back of his mind her comments sprouted roots of confusion. She hadn't fallen in love with anybody—since him. Hadn't given her heart away—since him. Hadn't removed the medallion—since him.

Kaycie was out the door and down the stairs. He caught up with her, turning her to face him.

"I've said I'm sorry. If that's not enough, tell me what my penance is." He captured her medal in his fingers, searching her eyes for a clue. Finding none, he carefully dropped the medallion inside her blouse. "I want you. More than I want to breathe. Just know I won't stop trying."

He leaned down and grazed her lips with his. It was brief, and she didn't kiss him back, but then, she didn't bite him. All in all, he figured that was a good sign. He slid his thumb across her bottom lip with a sigh. "Now that we're all dressed up, you ready to rub elbows with the rich?"

"Yep." She moved out of his reach. "Where do we start?"

"At the top. Let's pay a visit to Hank's father."
"You think we can get him to talk to us?"
"If he cares about his son, he will."

Chapter Eleven

Kay did her best to ignore Nate. She concentrated on identifying the elevator music playing in the background while they rode to the eighteenth floor. Who could forget the theme song from *Titanic*?

"By the way, you look very professional." His breath brushed against her bare neck.

"Thanks."

"And beautiful."

Her skin warmed with the added compliment.

The doors swished open to reveal the Walsh Enterprise lobby. "Why'd we start with Hank's father?"

"Best I could learn he's Hank's only family. We'll need to ask how much he knows about his son's extracurricular activities." Nate winked and wrapped strong fingers around her elbow, guiding her across the plush carpet.

Kay moved away from him as they approached a receptionist's desk. The woman turned her perfect-toothed smile toward Nate as if Kay hadn't arrived at the desk first.

"How may I assist you?" Ms. Teeth asked Nate.

He flashed his ID and passed her one of his cards. Kay couldn't help but notice the strong set of his jaw. He was definitely in the don't-mess-with-me zone. He used to wear the same expression before a big football game, only now, he spoke with a lot more confidence.

"CPS investigator Kaycie Taylor and Nathan Wolfe to speak with Mr. Walsh."

"We have two Mr.—"

"The elder Walsh." Nate corrected his error never breaking eye contact her.

"Do you have—"

"No. Tell him it's in reference to his son."

"If you'd like to make an—"

"We'll wait."

Judging from the pink rushing up the receptionist's cheeks, if Nate interrupted one more time, the top of Ms. Teeth's head would explode. Nate leaned over the desk, his huge shoulders blocking Kay's view.

"Tell him we can speak with him or we can chat with the press. His call."

Nate stepped back and smiled, showing off his own perfect set of pearly whites. Kay bit the inside of her cheek to suppress a laugh.

The receptionist pressed a number on her desk phone, turned her back, and spoke softly into the mouthpiece. Seconds later, a door opened and a middle-aged woman dressed in a dark suit strode toward them. She snatched Nate's card off the desk.

"Tony—Mr. Walsh— will give you ten minutes. If you'll follow me."

Kay fell in step with Nate as the woman stomped across the thick carpet.

Tony Walsh rose when they entered his office. Tall, thin, and frowning, he shook hands as Nate made introductions. His office, decorated in rich, polished wood, and complemented by Southwestern furniture, screamed money to Kay. A wall of windows overlooked the busy Dallas streets. The cool reception they'd received wasn't mirrored by Mr. Walsh who waved them to a small conference table and dismissed their escort.

"You're here concerning my son?"

"We are," Nate answered.

The old man's shoulders dropped, his mouth drooping at the corners.

She hoped a female touch might lessen the blow of accusing his son. "And we'll get right to the point. I was kidnapped and after I escaped, a second attempt was made."

"I'm sorry for your misfortune, but what has that got to do with my son?" Mr. Walsh asked as he leaned toward her. Watching his expression, she read nothing but curiosity.

"We're trying to find the reason for these sudden attacks."

"I still don't understand. Why do you think I can help?"

"The first incident happened right after I visited a young woman in the hospital who'd accused your son of abducting and raping her."

"Hank is innocent of those charges." His back straightened. "I see no correlation between her false accusation and your unfortunate attack. What are you insinuating?"

Nate's expression hardened. "Surely you'll admit it's more than a coincidence connecting the death of the only witness to your son's crime and the abduction of the girl's caseworker."

"Look, my son may be spoiled, but he's incapable of hurting anyone. If I believed those charges, I'd have insisted he seek psychological help and own up to his responsibility."

"If he's responsible, as you put it, now would be a good time to tell him to back off. I'd be very upset if something happened to Ms. Taylor."

Nate's tone sent chills straight to Kay's spine. His message was a mix of threat, hate, and vengeance. Mr. Walsh's eyes flashed wide.

"Threats should be directed to my attorney." Tony Walsh glanced at his watch. She sensed he was through talking. He rose, hurried to the door and opened it.

Kay paused on her way out, placing her hand on his arm. The older man trembled under her grasp.

"We didn't come to upset you. We came to gain insight."

"I've told you my son is innocent. Direct any additional questions to the offices of Hammond and Hammond."

Mr. Walsh opened the door and motioned to his assistant. Before Kay could ask anymore questions, she and Nate were whisked out of the building like yesterday's dirt. As soon as they hit the sidewalk, Kay spun to face him. "What the hell was that macho act you pulled?" She stabbed a finger in his chest. "We went to talk not piss off an old man."

"We went to send a message. You can bet Hank will get an earful."

Nate's hand closed around her hers, pulling it to his mouth. Kay watched mesmerized as his tongue slipped out to lick the tip of her finger. Moisture zinged straight to the juncture between her legs.

"That's twice you've poked me in the chest. Do it again and

there will be consequences."

"You think you can scare me?" Kay straightened her five-eight frame and cocked her head to the right, delivering her version of a don't-mess-with-me glare.

"Yeah. I do." He shrugged. "Call Holly, see what she and Marcus dug up."

Tugging her cell from its holder, Kay slid into Nate's pickup, muttering to herself. He'd grown into the most frustrating, confusing, arrogant, sexy man she'd ever met.

She wouldn't give into his charms. "No way."

"No way what?" Holly's voice boomed over the line. "Are you talking to me?"

"Holly?" Kay didn't remember hitting speed dial. Apparently, she had. And if the expression on Nate's face was any indication, she'd been talking out loud. That damn grin, the one she'd told him didn't work anymore, was plastered across his face.

"What's up?" Holly asked.

"Nate and I are headed to my apartment." Kay struggled to keep her voice steady. "Where are you and Marcus?"

"Walking to the car. Meet you there in twenty."

Kay ended the call and gazed out the window while Nate drove onto the freeway, heading south. She froze when his hand gave her shoulder a shake. The look she gave him was a warning to never mention what he'd overheard.

"Sweetheart, old man Walsh wasn't going to tell us anything. Parents protect their kids."

"I know that. I deal with them all the time. But his son is a monster."

God. He'd stopped calling her Kaycie and switched to sweetheart. She'd relaxed her guard and allowed him to move in.

"Hank needed to know you're not alone. If we tracked him down and told him, it would mean nothing. Dad telling him with fear in his voice might carry more weight."

"You could've mentioned your plan to me. That's twice you've treated me like I'm less capable than you. Do it again and there will be consequences."

She'd turned his words on him but with a different connotation.

This time his gaze carried no humor. She was glad he'd taken her statement seriously.

"I'm trying to help," he growled.

"And I don't doubt that. Not for a second." Her heart softened a tad at his declaration. "I'm a hell of a lot more capable than you think."

"Are you a good shot?"

"Trust me. In a duel, put your money on me."

"Beautiful and deadly. That's an image I'll take to bed with me tonight."

****

Nate choked back the urge to pull Kaycie behind him. To demonstrate his confidence, he let her enter her apartment first to ensure no surprises waited for them.

He'd made her angry enough for one day. Now wasn't the time to test her patience.

She was working too hard to push him away. None of her tactics would stop him from protecting her or from trying to win her forgiveness. Like the old cliché said, he'd rather be sorry for something he did than something he didn't do.

"Place is clear." Kaycie waved him into the room.

Nate went back down to his truck and brought in the snacks and beer they'd picked up. They moved around each other in her kitchen as if they'd done this a thousand times before. She removed two beers, handing him one. His hand covered hers. Lightning strikes shot up his arm when she didn't move.

She dodged his grasp, moving to a CD player and a collection of hundreds of discs.

"Place is too quiet. You still like country music?"

Nate followed her, reaching around to help choose. Her body went stiff. She grabbed his hands, backing the two of them to the middle of the room. When she faced him, her expression telegraphed fear.

"I have a question, and I need a truthful answer."

"I'll never lie to you." He tensed.

"When you broke in, did you touch anything?"

"No. Why?"

"My CDs are kept in alphabetical order. It may mean nothing, but a couple are out of place."

"I didn't get near your music." He remembered the eerie feeling he'd had after he'd picked the lock and entered her apartment. He'd blown it off, thinking the chill had come from being close to her things. "Show me."

Sure enough, the first few were clearly out of order.

"The radio was on this morning. Did anybody play a CD before I got up?"

"No. Look through the apartment. You'll be able to spot anything missing or moved."

Nate followed her from room to room. A massive hand clamped around his chest and squeezed. Could her apartment have been bugged? It was a long shot but not one he could overlook. If a camera or microphone had been hidden, he'd find the damn thing.

He methodically searched and probed in every spot he could think of. The knot in his shoulders eased when he was satisfied the place was secure.

He walked back to Kaycie's bedroom. "Anything else out of place?"

"Nothing."

He opened a drawer on her dresser. "Underwear not disturbed?"

"No." She crossed to him, reaching to close the drawer.

He caught her hand in his. Her gaze lifted, met his and held. Longing darkened her smoldering brown eyes. He moved closer.

"Hello," Holly yelled from the living room, and Nate silently cursed.

"Let's see if they found anything useful." She turned and left him standing there.

He rubbed at his temples, forced his libido to the back burner, and followed her into the living room.

Holly's eyes flashed wide, and she threw her arm around Kaycie's shoulder.

"Did we interrupt something?"

"No."

Kaycie snapped her answer a hair too fast, which pleased Nate immensely. It also pleased him to find Marcus and Tyrell were with

Holly.

"Somebody's been in Kaycie's apartment," Nate said.

"Any thoughts as to what they were looking for?" Tyrell asked, following Kaycie into the kitchen.

He opened a cabinet door and removed mugs. Nate bit back the haunting question of why Tyrell seemed to know exactly where things were stored.

"None," Kaycie said. "A few CDs were out of order. Nothing else was disturbed."

"That she could tell," Nate interjected.

She pulled her bottom lip in between her teeth. Damn, she pretended this situation didn't scare her, but he knew better. The urge to wrap her in his arms and tell her not to worry nagged him.

Right now, he needed to concentrate. He rolled his shoulders and stretched his arms overhead, trying to get his blood moving.

"You look like shit," Marcus commented. A smile spread across his face.

"Thanks." Nate returned the grin. "I'm glad you're here to point that out."

"You're dead on your feet," Marcus continued. "Let's wrap this up. Let you get an hour or two of shut-eye. I'll take watch tonight."

"No. I'll stay," Tyrell piped up. "I'm between gigs. Time for me to pitch in."

"Fine," Nate agreed. "Let's hear what Holly found."

The small team gathered at the table. He inwardly hoped Kaycie hadn't stumbled onto a human-trafficking ring. They were the scum of the earth. People who operated without remorse or conscience. Her situation moved up the critical ladder if she was right.

"The number of missing teenagers spiked around the time of the Super Bowl." Holly slid an Excel spreadsheet to the center of the table. "Law enforcement expected these bastards to show up. Human trafficking and prostitution increases in every town before and during a large sporting event. Here in Dallas, the number of operations didn't diminish as it did in other major venues. Three other investigators reported a rise in missing girls after the game was over."

Marcus's eyebrows pinched. Nate remembered the quiet man liked to collect his thoughts before speaking. Marcus glanced up from the documents. "The numbers are high, and so are the girls' ages. These pedophiles prefer seventeen-or-eighteen-year-olds."

"What?" Tyrell turned his gaze toward Kaycie. "That not usual. Is it?"

"No," she said. Sadness filled her tone. "They've found a niche in the market."

"So how do we stop it?" Marcus asked. "Should we expect pushback from the cops?"

"Count on it. From the FBI too, just as soon as they learn we're digging around," Kaycie answered. "First thing in the morning we need to see if we can link the missing girls. Where'd they hang out? Where were they last seen?"

She impressed Nate with her take-charge attitude. The young girl had become a woman who'd truly come into her own. He liked this stronger, more independent version. Her self-assurance made her even more beautiful. If that were possible. He folded his arms over his chest and let her run with the ball.

Kaycie removed a picture of Hank Walsh from a file she'd set on the table. "And were any of them seen with this man?"

Chapter Twelve

Kay kicked off the covers and stretched to the soulful sounds of Tracy Chapman. Tyrell must've taken charge of the radio and found a station that better fit his music preference.

She showered, put on a pair of jeans, a lightweight blue blouse, and her Western boots. If Nate had ridden his Harley, she'd be ready.

She walked down the hall to a surprisingly quiet apartment. Considering Holly's monster crush on Tyrell, her morning chatter should be filling the kitchen with charm and cheer.

"Morning." Nate leaned against the counter, looking entirely too comfortable. Tyrell lowered the newspaper and smiled.

"Back at you," he said behind a flash of teeth.

"I'm shocked Holly's not here yet." Kay reached for the cabinet door, pulling down her favorite mug.

"Haven't seen her." Nate took the cup, filled it with coffee and handed it to Kay as if this were his apartment. "Marcus is late too."

Kay breathed in the aroma of caffeine before she moved to the living room. Marcus and Holly had only met a few days earlier, but her spirited friend had been known to act impulsively. Kay shook off the thought. Marcus, although handsome enough to turn heads, might be too quiet for Holly. His somber mood and gray eyes painted a mysterious picture. Unfortunately, after his wife's fatal car wreck, he'd taken himself permanently off the market.

"I'll bet they're here in a few minutes." Kay sat on the couch, propping her feet on the coffee table.

Tyrell strolled over, eased down beside her, and then dropped his arm over her shoulders. His soul patch was expanding to his chin line. She rubbed his whiskers. "You trying to look like that guy on *Criminal Minds*?"

He narrowed his gaze. "He'd be lucky to look like me."

Choosing to ignore his vanity, she suggested, "Let's talk about who's doing what today."

Tyrell nodded. "Nate and I are going to try to find a connection between the missing girls. We'll talk to their families and friends. You call those DPD buddies of yours and tell'em not to freak out if they hear we're digging around." He patted the back of her head. "Marcus will hang with you here."

Heat rose until her cheeks burned. Who'd he think he was? Bad enough Nate thought he could boss her around. Tyrell's voice droned in the background. It was time to stop him before she popped a blood vessel.

"You've gone completely out of your mind. Hell, I'm better qualified to investigate this case than both of you. Neither of you know crap about being a cop."

"Kaycie, you're right," Nate commented, seemingly unfazed by her outburst. "But if you go anywhere, you're safer with Marcus watching your back."

Nate stretched his long legs out in front of him, the denim barely containing his muscular thighs. His gaze followed the line of Tyrell's arm. She considered his expression for a second before realizing what was wrong with him. Nate was jealous. A piece of her heart twisted.

"Don't think I'm not aware of that, but don't treat me like I'm a child. You two may know military warfare, but that doesn't automatically equate to analytical." Their raised eyebrows stoked her anger. "Look in the dictionary. You won't find the word 'smart' used in the definition of brawn."

"Did she just call us stupid?" With a grin and feigning hurt feelings, Tyrell scooted to the end of the couch.

"She's the boss. Doubt her ability and you could face consequences." Nate chuckled. His black hair spilled around his face. He raked it back and tied it off.

"What the hell does that mean?" Tyrell asked, glancing at Kay.

She gave him an I-don't-know shrug.

"It means Kaycie's picking up the tab. She'll work with me today. You and Marcus team up."

Kay shook her head. "Nobody's going to talk to those two

brutes. They'll just scare people. One of you go and take Holly. She's never met a stranger."

Marcus arrived with a box of bear claws, ending the argument. Kay decided Holly should be in on the jobs assignments, so she retrieved her phone from her bedside table and punched the speed-dial number. The call went to voice mail. Sleeping in wasn't like Holly. Her missing the chance to spend one minute with Tyrell was downright unbelievable.

"I'm waking up Sleeping Beauty," Kay said as she rejoined the meeting.

Three gorgeous men rose to their feet at the same time. Nate with his long black hair, strong jaw, and navy-blue eyes. Tyrell with his caramel skin, a mixture of his African-American and Latino heritage, and black flashing eyes. Marcus, the gentle giant with gray eyes and cupid's-bow mouth. That they'd rally to her defense after all these years moved her. How had she not fallen in love with them all? Actually, she had, just in different ways.

Had Tyrell or Marcus kept the medallions she'd given them? That Nate still wore his stirred emotions she kept packed away in the recesses of her mind.

Nate's broad shoulders moved into her line of vision, blocking her view and snapping her to the present.

"I'll go with you."

"Her apartment is across the hall and down two. You can stand in the door and watch me." Kay stepped around him and made a show of clipping on her holster. She marched down to Holly's door and knocked.

Warmth sizzled up Kay's neck. She turned to check, and sure enough, Nate had stepped into the hall.

Waiting. Watching. Protecting.

"Hey, you. Wake up." Kay tried the door. Panic sizzled up her spine as she turned the knob. "I'm coming in."

Their floor plans were identical, and Kay easily spotted Holly's purse on her blue faux-suede couch. Her car keys were on the oak coffee table. Kay listened for the sound of the shower running or anything to indicate her friend was awake. Her scalp tingled when she was met with silence. This couldn't be good.

Kay hurried straight to the bedroom. A chill rushed up her spine and slammed into the base of her skull. The bed was empty. Covers were strewn across the floor. She opened the bathroom door a crack.

Empty. "Something's not right," Kay muttered. Scanning the bedroom, she noticed a throw pillow on the bed that was normally on the couch. A small cell phone lay on top.

Not Holly's iPhone.

"Oh, God." Bitter coffee rose in her throat. She looked closer, hoping for anything that might help. She slipped her gun from its holster.

She wanted to run. To scream. Procedure demanded Kay call in the crime and leave the scene undisturbed.

Instead, she stopped and considered the cell. Who but her was supposed to find it? She approached the bed nervously.

Holly's life could depend on Kay making the right decision. She blew out a breath, wrapped her trembling fingers around the cool plastic and slipped it inside her jeans pocket.

She whirled to leave and ran face first into rock hard chest. She screamed and struggled to get free of the hands gripping her arms. A mixture of fear, anger, and embarrassment burned her cheeks.

"Easy, sweetheart. I've got you."

Nate's strong hands held her in place, calming her jagged nerves while his gaze swept the room. The muscles in his jaw twitched.

Had she pocketed the phone before he saw? Could she convince him that she was supposed to find it? For Holly's sake, Kay wanted to determine the purpose of the phone before confiding in anyone. Her gut said she had to surrender the cell to the police, but her heart insisted she keep it. She, Nate, Marcus, and Tyrell could devote their undivided attention to finding Holly. Nate had said it best. They didn't have rules and restrictions like the cops did.

"Holly wouldn't leave without saying something to me." Guilt triggered a torrential downpour coming from her eyes. "Somebody forced her out of her bed and made her leave with them."

"I know." He tilted her head up with his fingers. "We'll find her." The conviction in his eyes brought no comfort to Kay.

"We have to." She leaned against him as he led her toward the door. She prayed silently that God would let Holly return unharmed.

"Let's get out of here," he said. "We'll call the cops from your place."

Tyrell and Marcus had followed and were waiting in the hall. She had no way of telling how much they'd heard, but they listened intently while she called for help. Then, without hesitating, she dialed Tomas. Her call went straight to voice mail. The message she left pleaded that he and Wayne come right away.

Marcus opened his arms, gathered her close and she broke down again.

"This is my fault," Kay sobbed into his chest. "Who would take Holly?"

"Stop blaming yourself," Nate scolded, pulling her away from Marcus. He gripped her shoulders, his intense gaze locked on hers. "Pull yourself together. If you don't, you'll be more of a hindrance than a help."

He was right, and she knew it. His strength telegraphed assurance to her. Together as a team, they'd find Holly.

"I'm fine." Kay stumbled to the kitchen sink and splashed cold water on her face. "It just caught me off guard."

Tyrell's expression turned cold and hard. "I'll kill the son of a bitch who harms a hair on that woman's head. Cut his nuts off and feed them to him."

"You can do what you want as soon as we find her." Kay refused to expect anything other than a safe rescue for her friend.

"I will. She's family. Like you."

Within minutes, someone pounded on Kay's door. She opened it to find two uniformed officers waiting. A patrol car must've been nearby for the officers to arrive so quickly. She let them in, identified herself to the uniformed officers, and introduced everyone. Kay let the police in Holly's apartment then returned to her place to wait.

She paced, unable to relax until they finished looking around. They returned unconvinced and reluctant to call in a CSU team. Instead, they theorized since there was no evidence of foul play, Holly could've gone off on her own .

Kay's anger bubbled over. The cops would listen and believe.

"The place has to be dusted for prints. Questions have to be asked of the neighbors." The doubtful expression on the cops' faces made her consider turning over the cell in her pocket.

"Ms. Taylor, wait forty-eight hours. See if she turns up."

"No way. Here's proof." Kay ran out on the small balcony where she had the perfect view of the parking lot and pointed. "See. Her car's right next to mine."

"There was no sign of forced entry." The young cop edged toward the door, eyeing Nate, Tyrell, and Marcus as if maybe Kay had partied too hard with them last night.

"Doesn't mean a thing." Kay didn't try to hide the bitterness in her tone. "My apartment was broken into twice without showing signs of a breakin."

"Did you file reports on those incidences, ma'am?"

"No. Nothing was taken." The more she talked, the deeper the hole she dug. "This isn't about me. My friend has been kidnapped."

A knock on the door interrupted the argument. Kay breathed a sigh of relief to find Tomas and Wayne standing in the hall. "Thank God. Maybe now somebody will take action."

Wayne and Tomas relieved the first responders, sending them back out on patrol. Kay made introductions again and waved everybody to the living room. With Tyrell on one side, Marcus on the other, and Nate standing as if about to be inspected by the admiral of the fleet, either unable or unwilling to bend his knees and sit, Kay repeated the facts.

Tomas and Wayne took turns quizzing her, filling in the blanks. Their gazes were solemn and attentive.

"We've worked a lot of cases together," Kay insisted. "I need you to believe I'm right about this."

Wayne nodded. "There are still protocols to follow. Questions have to be asked and answered."

"This has to tie back to Hank Walsh," Kay insisted, knowing the most important clue was in her pocket. Something unexplainable made her keep it. She just knew it was left for her.

She needed Tomas and Wayne to leave so she could check out the phone. She'd find out if there was a message and then decide who to involve.

Guilt shredded her insides.

"Kay," Wayne said in his official tone. "We're waiting for the

Crime Scene Unit to finish. CSU don't need us tromping around in the way."

"They're here?" Relief washed over her. They'd believed her. A surge of hope rushed over her.

"I called them after I listened to your message." Tomas stood, casting a steely glance at Nate, Tyrell and Marcus. "We appreciate that you have private protection, but all of you need to listen up. Stay out of this investigation. Let the professionals work the case. If your friend's in trouble, we'll find her. And if Walsh is connected, we'll take him down."

Her apartment fell silent as a tomb. Kay nodded and escorted Tomas and Wayne to the door. The cell was an important key, and she couldn't wait any longer.

"I have a headache. Think I'll rest for a while." She spoke in her firmest, leave-me-alone voice. She swallowed hard. Lying to Nate and the guys was hard. They were on her side. If her hunch was right, Holly had been kidnapped, and the people who had her wanted to talk to Kay, not three angry men.

Nate moved from where he'd stood for the past hour and blocked the path to her bedroom. She'd never seen his expression this hard and unyielding.

"If you're desperate for quiet time, why not leave the phone with us? Or were you keeping that all to yourself?"

"What's he talking about?" Tyrell snapped out the words like a bullwhip.

Her shoulders sagged. That Nate hadn't betrayed her to the law meant more than he could imagine or she could say. She pulled the throwaway from her pocket, trudged to the couch, and then sank down. "He's referring to this. I found it in her apartment. It's not hers."

"Damn it, Kay. Why didn't you give that to the cops?" Sweet Marcus didn't sound sweet anymore. "You've handled it, wiping out any fingerprints that might have been usable."

"Because she's guessing whoever snatched Holly wants to be able to contact Kaycie." Nate came to her defense, giving her a measure of confidence that she'd done the right thing. "It may be a stretch, but what else do we have? The cops would've confiscated the damn thing, and we'd never learn what these assholes want." He rested his hands on her shoulders, leaned over the couch and studied the cheap cell.

"It's time to turn it on," Nate said.

She found herself leaning back, breathing in his warm, musky scent.

Marcus moved closer, his expression full of concern. "Nate's right. Won't do us any good if they call and the phone is turned off."

A blast of adrenaline hit her as she pressed the button and the small screen lit up. The cell vibrated almost immediately. "There's a message."

Nate's breath brushed her cheek as he stilled her hand and studied the screen.

"We listen on speaker. One of us might pick up a background noise, any sound to help us figure out where the message was recorded. I don't think you can trace calls from these throwaways, but new technology comes out every day. I'll check with a friend."

"Good. 'Cause the company I work for won't help. Too afraid of losing their license." Tyrell squatted and rocked back on his heels. He was calm and all business. "To get Holly back, we're gonna break a few laws."

Marcus cleared his throat, and all eyes turned toward him.

Kay had no idea what was running through his mind. "You okay with this?"

A slow smile crept across his face, giving him a much younger appearance than thirty-three. He moved to the chair, his pen and notepad ready.

"For you? Hell, yeah."

"Then let's listen." Kay placed the cell on her coffee table, pressed Menu, and then scrolled to messages. Nate eased down next to her. His presence gave her strength.

"Go ahead, sweetheart. We need to hear."

Chapter Thirteen

Nate gripped Kaycie's knee reassuringly. She seemed to have pulled herself together. He was damn proud of her resilience.

He moved closer when she leaned forward and pushed the button.

An automated voice informed them of one message, recorded this morning at two o'clock. "If you're Kay Taylor, and you're listening to this message alone, you have a chance to get your friend back alive. You have something valuable that I want." The man's voice was a whisper, and everyone leaned closer. "And I have someone you love. You'll trade or she'll die."

Kaycie reached for his hand. Nate wound his fingers through hers for support.

"Keep this phone with you," the male voice instructed.

The automated voice returned with instructions. Nate hit five to save. He hadn't picked up on any outside noise on the call other than what might have been Holly struggling. Kaycie wrapped her arms around her middle. She'd pull away if he hugged her, so he tucked her under his arm.

Something other than lust stirred deep inside him. A protective instinct to keep her safe gripped his lungs and squeezed out precious oxygen. He'd opened his agency to work special operations, expecting to run into danger and violence. He hadn't expected to find it in his backyard. If anyone harmed Kaycie or her friend, that person would meet his maker. This, Nate promised.

"What does he think I have?" Her words came out in a strangled cry. "Why didn't Walsh come out and say what he wants?"

Marcus scrubbed his eyes with his hand. "We don't know who 'he' is. Not for sure."

"We don't have ironclad proof," she agreed. "But the only

controversial case I've had this year was Leann's. She identified Hank Walsh from a photo array and now she's dead."

"You recognized his voice?" Marcus asked.

"No. I've never spoken with him. DPD interviewed him." She shook her head, and her lips curved downward. "He probably searched my apartment. Makes me sick to my stomach to think he might've touched my things."

Tyrell paced, running his hand over his bald head. Nate tried to measure the tension in the room. Judging from the snarls on Tyrell's and Marcus's faces, they were ready to go to war. Nate dug deep and forced his rage to the back of his mind. Losing their tempers would help no one.

"She's right. We'll operate on the assumption Walsh is behind Holly's disappearance." Nate turned Kaycie around to face him. "Think back. Did Leann give you something? Ask you to hold on to anything?"

"No."

"The search wasn't random. He was looking for something in particular," Nate said.

"Apparently, he didn't find it." She wound her fingers through his and squeezed. "Why not trash the place? If I hadn't noticed the CDs, we'd never have known."

"The answer to that question might be important." Tyrell stopped pacing. "We damn well need to figure out what he was looking for and soon."

"I agree," Kaycie said. "And I'm betting CSU won't find any fingerprints in Holly's apartment. Nobody's that stupid." Her voice gathered strength as she talked. "They'll go door to door, but after they leave we should double back. In the meantime, let's see if we can beat them to the site manager. I want to take a look at the parking lot cameras."

Nate said nothing, recognizing she needed to feel in charge. A sense of controlling something, while everything around her crumbled, would help her stabilize her emotions. She fastened her long brown hair in a ponytail and rose to her feet.

"Marcus, go with her. If they give you access to the security disks, call. We'll come down." He gave Tyrell a slight nod, holding him in his chair. Nate had a second thought, "Marcus. You armed?"

He scoffed and lifted his long-tail shirt. "Am I a Texan?"

"Nice." Tyrell acknowledged the Sig Sauer. "That a P226?"

"Yep. Nine mil."

Nate pointed at the door. "Go. Don't let her out of your sight."

Nate waited until she closed the door. He turned to Tyrell and asked, "Does the company you work for do surveillance?"

"No. We stand around, glare at people, and keep our weapon in its shoulder holster. We keep fans away from hotshot sports figures or visiting movie stars. Why?"

"We need to monitor Kaycie's movements. I'll pick up the equipment and get a tracer on her. Regardless of which one of us she's with, we'll know where she's located. If I'd thought Holly was in danger, I'd have monitored them both."

"You think Kay will go for it?"

"I do." Nate wasn't worried she'd refuse. She was street savvy and too smart to try some stupid-ass heroic stunt. "Tracking devices are nothing anymore. I can download it on a laptop and have it activated within minutes. I'll download an app to our phones, and we'll monitor her movements."

The door opened, and both Nate and Tyrell reached for their guns. Kaycie's expression said she didn't have good news.

"The camera on the west side had been disabled. Nobody noticed until we asked." Her face flushed red, and her lips faded into a thin line.

"Intentionally?" Tyrell ran his fingers over his bald head.

"Oh, yeah. Wire was cut." Marcus's jaw appeared to be locked.

"What else?" Nate asked

"We had..." Marcus shifted his gaze toward Kaycie. "She had a run-in with the CSU team. They showed up while we were in the manager's office. Before I could get Kay out of there, they'd issued a stern warning. Threatened to report her to Chief Compton." Marcus finally allowed a smile. "She told the guy to go fuck him—"

"Okay. I lost my temper." Kaycie's cheeks got redder. "The jerk couldn't have been twenty-five and had the balls to try to intimidate me."

"I'll give you that," Marcus conceded. "He was a smart ass."

Nate choked on a laugh, dodged her fiery glare, and decided against reminding her that she was only thirty-two. Her cell vibrated, probably keeping him out of trouble.

"My mother's calling." Head down, Kaycie moved to the far corner of the kitchen.

Tyrell launched into a conversation about tracking devices with Marcus, but Nate kept his gaze on Kaycie's mouth. He couldn't read her lips verbatim, but he got the gist of the argument. If he read her body language and compared it against her conversation, Kaycie would rather run naked down Interstate 635 during rush hour than attend a Sunday family get-together.

Her relationship with her dad had been a sore topic back in their college days. She'd steadfastly refused to discuss the subject, always referring to it as a family rift. Apparently, it was now an abyss. Her gaze came up from the tops of her boots and caught him staring. Those hot-fudge eyes turned icy cold. Damn, she did pissed better than anyone he knew. She turned her back, lowered her voice, and quickly ended the call.

"Did you get all that?" she muttered to him, brushing past him to join Tyrell and Marcus.

"Enough to offer my services." Nate moved as close as he deemed to be safe.

"Services?"

"I'll be your date. You can introduce me to your folks." His wisecrack was flippant, but he'd try anything to relax her tense shoulders.

"Why would I want to do that?" She spoke as if asking the village idiot. "It's not open for discussion. I'm not going."

"I don't think I can download a tracer app," Tyrell said, ending the confrontation. "Marcus probably can. He has a smartphone."

"You don't have to buy a new phone, keep up with her on your laptop," Nate answered as Kaycie peered over Tyrell's shoulder at the computer screen.

"Tracer app?" Kaycie's eyebrows pinched.

"Yeah. You and I are going shopping. I want you to wear one until this is over."

She angled her head slightly. "Good idea. What else do you have planned?"

"Marcus and Tyrell will locate Hank Walsh and take turns following his every move. If he's involved, we'll know soon enough."

****

Johnny cursed the storm brewing in his head. Drugging and bringing much younger girls in to be sold didn't bother him. Sure, Hank's treatment of them ticked off Johnny. Bruises reduced their value, and Mr. A wanted his merchandise to sell for large sums of money. After all, only the super rich were among his elite clientele and they could afford to pay top dollar.

Johnny swiped his card-key across the reader. His cheek twitched. A new reaction. He slammed the door open.

A startled Hank glanced over his shoulder. The bastard was ripping off the hostages clothes.

"What the fuck?" the weasel snarled. "Get out. I'm not done with her."

For a moment, Johnny lost contact with his surroundings. His hands squeezed his temples to hold back excruciating, burning pain.

When his vision cleared, Hank had zipped his pants.

"Yeah. You are. You get out," Johnny ground out the words, advancing into the room.

Hank puffed out his chest, spread his legs, and brought his hands up in fists. Johnny chuckled and planted his eel-skin boot solidly into Hank's unprotected nuts, folding him like a piece of paper. Johnny shoved the moaning Hank into the hall and closed the door behind him.

The woman Johnny had taken from her nice warm bed this morning was curled into a ball, sobbing the words "no more" over and over again.

"Stop that." Johnny scrubbed his hand across his chin. His violent response to her mistreatment confused him. "I'm not going to hurt you," he lied.

She lifted her head. Her lips curled into a snarl as tears streamed from her eyes.

He'd thought her pretty this morning when he'd picked her lock and taken her against her will. Now his stomach roiled at her swollen eye, split lip, and soon-to-be-purple cheek.

"Well, that bastard did." Sobbing, she wrapped her arms around her body and rocked back and forth. "He was going to rape me."

She tugged at her torn sleep shirt. Her face was a study in fear, yet her gaze never strayed from Johnny, making his nerves jump around inside. He didn't like the feeling. He steeled himself against any emotion.

"Why did you stop him?"

"Hank's a scumbag," Johnny said, unsure he knew the answer. "You're barter. When we get what we want, you can go home."

"You can't let me leave. I've seen your face, and the worm's who hurt me."

"We agree on one thing." Johnny studied her pale hair with the pink streak down one side.

"That you're going to kill me?" The pitch of her voice rose, echoing off the thick walls.

"No. That Hank's a worm." He stuffed his hands in his pockets to keep from touching her spun-gold hair. "Why do you do that?"

"What?" Her eyebrows pinched together, her face filled with confusion.

"Forget it." He turned toward the door.

"Please don't leave." She dragged her fingers through the tangled strands of hair.

"The pink. Why the color?"

"I don't know." She struggled to cover herself as she pushed to a sitting position. "Maybe I like being different."

He nodded. Not that he understood. Being noticed outside his little world meant trouble.

"What am I barter for?"

"Your friend has something I want. If she values you, she'll trade."

"Are you talking about Kay? She couldn't possibly have anything you'd need."

Johnny leaned against the door, unable to pull his gaze from her slim body. "Yes, she does. If she wants to see you again, she'll bring it when and where I tell her to."

She spoke as he swung the door closed behind him.

"If she does, you'll kill us both."

Chapter Fourteen

Kay slid her laptop down the table next to Nate's. His gaze came up, catching hers for a long, lusty moment. He'd tied his long hair back, showing off his handsome face. He winked and went back to installing the tracking software. Their phones had been set up and soon the guys would be able to monitor her every move.

Before the trip to the spy store, she'd considered herself knowledgeable where technology was concerned. The sales clerk had proved her to be severely challenged.

A loud knock on her door sent her jumping to her feet. "Sheesh. No more caffeine for me."

"Take your gun." Nate's caution was unnecessary because she'd already reached for it. She opened her mouth to say "yes, sir" but his gaze had already shifted back to the computer screen.

"This waiting is killing me. Why haven't we heard something?"

"I'd say his tactics are working," Nate mumbled without raising his head. "He's letting you think about his threat."

She held her pistol against her thigh, leaned down, and peered through the peephole. "It's Tyrell." Kay opened the door and stepped back.

Nate glanced their direction. "Is Marcus on Walsh's tail?"

"We haven't found him. None of his neighbors saw him come home last night or leave this morning. His apartment's a pigsty."

"Did anyone spot you breaking in?" Kay made no effort to keep the alarm out of her tone.

"Excuse me?" His voice and expression were the definition of a man who'd been insulted. "I was finessing my way around and into people's houses when you were still holding your mama's hand to cross the street. I'm invisible."

"Six-two, black and bald." She rolled her eyes. "I'm sure nobody noticed you."

"But Marcus is still camped outside Walsh's apartment?" Nate studied the screen on his cell. Apparently satisfied, he slid it into the clip on his hip.

"Yeah. I stopped by to let you set up my new cell. I can't be the only one without a smartphone."

Nate grabbed the iPhone and settled back at the computer. He shoved a small box toward Tyrell without looking up. "We bought a tracer for Hank's car. When he comes home, plant this under the fender of his car."

The corners of Tyrell's mouth lifted into a truly evil smile. "I like it. Gives us the leeway to hang back and not take a chance on him seeing us."

Nate handed Tyrell his phone. "You're all set. Use this icon to find Kaycie's location and follow the bouncing ball. I'll activate the second one after you alert me the tracer's been planted on Walsh's car."

Kay's heart did a funny tumble listening to Nate talk. The mark of a leader was evident when he spoke. What job did he have as a SEAL? They hadn't talked about the past. He'd deliberately steered their conversations away from his personal life. They might be strangers, but she liked this new Nate.

"Hey." He leaned down close to her face and snapped his fingers. "Were you daydreaming about me?"

"Not hardly."

"Let's go, sweetheart." Nate opened the door, swinging it back. "We're paying old man Walsh another visit."

Tyrell went down the stairs with them. "After I drop off the tracer, I'm catching some shut-eye. I'm taking the late shift."

"We might be arrested and put in lockup for this visit," Kay said. "You may have to get up and come bail us out."

"I can do that." He gathered her in for a hug and then disappeared into his car with a wave.

Nate's gaze caught hers and held. No escaping the flicker of desire when his navy eyes turned to mysterious cobalt.

Her hormones surged, sending blood coursing through her veins. Once inside his pickup, she composed herself and prayed he hadn't noticed her reaction to just a look.

They rode in silence until Nate parked across from Anthony Walsh's office. Nate turned in the seat to face her.

"When you were taken, you woke up in a warehouse district. After we shake up Hank's dad, we have to identify every facility he owns. I can do it, but if you know somebody who can get that information for us faster, it would help."

"I know the right person." Her grandfather had friends in every department of Dallas government. Papa's request for a favor would be acted on immediately. "Thank you for not trying to make me stay home."

His perfect mouth lifted at the corners. There was the grin that warmed places she shouldn't let heat up for him. Unbuckling his seat belt, he reached and cupped her face. His thumb stroked her cheek.

The world moved in slow motion as he leaned over and pressed his lips to hers. Not an all-consuming flamethrower to curl her toes. Instead, his touch was soft and gentle. An I'm-here-for-you kiss that tied her heart into a knot. She pulled away seconds before she lost her soul.

"I didn't want to face the consequences." He winked and pressed the release on her seat belt.

Unable to form words, she turned her back to him and got out of his truck. She couldn't allow him to witness her tongue slide over her lips, savoring his flavor. Coffee, toothpaste, and Nate's distinctive taste flooded her senses. Her breasts were heavy and ached for his touch.

Odd how an old heartbreak and many nights of pain could fade from memory.

"You coming?" He stood waiting on the sidewalk, his hand extended.

"Yeah." Unable to resist touching him, she wound her fingers through his. "What's the purpose of shaking up Mr. Walsh again? I was joking with Tyrell about needing bail earlier, but Walsh might actually call the cops on us."

"It's not a coincidence that Holly was taken right after our last chat with him. He knows his son is evil, and it's time he faced facts."

"You think he's involved?" The idea sent Kay's mind spinning.

"Maybe not criminally, but he knows something. If he's covering for his son, he's as guilty as Hank."

The throwaway vibrated and sent shock waves through her body. She quickly removed it from her pocket. Nate caught her arm, moving them closer to the building and away from foot traffic.

"Deep breath." His gaze held hers, never wavering as she took the call.

"Kay Taylor." No way would she use a casual greeting with this bastard. She held the phone between her and Nate, straining to hear over the street noise.

"Your friend is in pain. Do you want to be responsible for what happens next?"

"Please don't hurt her." A queasy feeling rushed Kay. Her stomach cramped, so she leaned on Nate for support. "I'll do whatever you say."

A dark shadow passed over Nate's gaze. He motioned for her to keep talking.

"Tell me what you want."

"Be ready to hand it over the next time I call." The muffled voice sounded hard and uncaring.

"Wait," Kay cried. "I don't know what you think I have." The silence made her wonder if he'd cut her off, but the screen showed the call was still connected. "Please," she begged. Fear and anger boiled through her system.

"The ring. Next time I call, you be ready to trade."

"Don't hang up," she screamed. Two passersby stopped and stared. Kay slammed her mouth shut.

"He's gone, sweetheart."

Nate closed his hand over hers, pushing down until she slipped the throwaway into her pocket. A weight pressed on her shoulders. What had they done? Sweet, friendly Holly was hurting, and Kay couldn't help.

"I don't have this ring." Her body shook as her imagination flooded her mind with images of Holly being hurt and alone. "How do we stop him?"

"You're sure the girl didn't pass anything to you? Could she have dropped something in your purse when you visited that last day?"

"Who knows? I woke up in the hospital wearing a standard-issue gown. My purse was never found."

"What happened to your clothes?" Nate dried her cheeks with gentle strokes of his thumbs.

"I'm sure they're in the evidence room." Kay massaged small circles on her temples. "Holly brought things from my apartment for me to wear home."

Kay called Tomas and asked for his help. She lied to him about why she wanted access to her clothes.

"I'll call down and have the clerk go through your stuff. From the tone in his voice, he doubted her watch was in one of the pockets.

"No," she snapped too quickly. "Really, I'd rather handle my own underwear."

She heard his groan. "Fine. Have the front desk call me when you get here."

Kay ended the call hoping Tomas didn't plan on standing over her. "If the ring's not there, we're screwed."

"Kaycie." Nate's tone was soothing. "We'll never give up."

****

The elevator door closed with a swish. Nate's chest expanded, swelling with pride. Kaycie handled pressure better than anyone could expect of her. She rolled her head and shoulders as if preparing for a confrontation.

They stepped into the corridor and found Ms. Teeth and Walsh's assistant speaking with the elder Walsh. Kaycie ran past the desk straight to him.

"Have these people escorted out." He barked orders at the receptionist.

"No." Kaycie's cry echoed off the walls. "Please, it's a matter of life or death."

Mr. Walsh glared down at her. He was tall and thin, gaunt looking, as if his health might not be good. He held up his hand, and the call to security ended abruptly.

"Make it quick."

"My friend's been kidnapped." Kaycie's tone was soft and pleading. "I believe your son's behind her abduction."

The old man's shoulders drooped. His chin sagged, aging him right in front of Nate's eyes. The expression of defeat was all over his face.

"Why would you possibly think such a thing?"

"Sir." Nate spoke, keeping his tone calm. "We can't locate Hank."

"He's been out of town visiting customers. He only returned today." Mr. Walsh sighed something that sounded like relief.

"Are you sure?" Kaycie reached out, clutching his arm.

Nate followed the elder Walsh's gaze down to her hand.

"We will end this nonsense. I can prove my son was nowhere near your friend."

Walsh whirled and stormed into his office. Nate caught Kaycie's elbow and guided her inside. The old man's bony finger stabbed a number on the desk phone.

"Yes, Mr. Walsh?" A male voice spoke briskly. "You need the car brought around?"

"No. Did you pick up Hank today?"

"Yes, sir. His plane landed around one-thirty."

"Where is he?"

"I dropped him off at his apartment. He said he had errands to run. I offered to drive, but he loves showing off that new sports car you bought him."

"Thank you." Walsh disconnected and tapped a second button on the phone. "There's a man and woman on their way down. Make sure they don't come back to the eighteenth floor."

The color had drained from Kaycie's face, and Nate held her arm tighter. "Let's go. He's never going to believe us."

"Keep this pursuit up and you will find yourself in civil court."

Nate led her from the building. The trembling of her body worried him. The pressure was getting to her.

"He's lying." She spoke through clamped teeth. "Or he's blind to what a monster he raised."

"Kaycie." Nate was at a loss for words. If Hank was really out of town, the chances of Holly being rescued dwindled.

Kaycie rushed into traffic and crossed the street. Nate followed, relieved to find she was seething mad, not breaking down.

"Maybe the chauffeur lied. He could be working with Hank."

"True. There's nothing we can do here. Let's talk to that person you said will help locate the Walsh properties."

The cinnamon flecks in her brown eyes sparkled in the sunlight as she rose to her tiptoes and initiated a kiss.

"Get a room," somebody in a passing car shouted, jarring them out of the clench.

"Thank you for believing me," she whispered into his lips.

Nate waited until she got in and closed the car door to comment. He ignored the temptation to check his stomach. Somehow, she'd reached into his guts and tied them into a knot.

"Thank you for forgiving me."

Chapter Fifteen

Kay chatted with the front-desk clerk at the morgue as she signed in. She asked the woman to let Doctor Taylor know they were headed to his office. Nate caught her in three strides. His gaze was hooded as they headed down the hall.

"Take a right." Kay brushed too close and caught a whiff of his scent. Heat spikes shot across her skin. *Business relationship*, she mentally chanted.

"Who's the Taylor at the morgue?" He tapped a finger on the sign next to Papa's office. "Is this the dad you refuse to talk about?"

"My grandfather." She'd never told Nate why she and her dad weren't close. The truth was too painful to discuss. Standing outside Papa's office, she prayed he'd leave the subject alone. She took Nate's hand and proceeded through the door.

"Kaycie." Papa's voice boomed across the small office. Shelves along the wall were stacked high with reports and medical magazines. She'd bet money he knew exactly where everything was located.

Nate's grip tightened for a fraction of a second. Had he noticed Papa used her full name too? Kay pulled her hand free, sailed into a bear hug from her grandfather, and then made introductions. Papa ushered them to a small couch. After she and Nate sat, he dragged over a chair directly across from her. Something about his demeanor set off her warning bells. Papa wasn't happy.

"Are you the hired gun protecting my granddaughter?"

Oh, shit. Family might be a safer topic.

Nate leaned forward, his expression the picture of calm. "Yes, sir. You could call me that."

"Papa ... " Her brain spun, came up blank. No believable excuse for not telling her grandfather she'd almost been kidnapped from the morgue's parking lot came to mind. "You're busy and I—"

Papa cast an Alaskan glance at Kay, stopping her midsentence. She shivered from the chill.

"Kaycie, I do leave the morgue from time to time. And I often have breakfast with the chief. Why did I hear about your attacks in the middle of my bacon and eggs?"

"I'm sorry." God, he could make her feel three inches tall when he was right.

"I refrained from calling and chewing your butt out because Chief Compton assured me you were okay."

"Dr. Taylor, we need your help." Nate put the visit back on point and kept her from stumbling over another apology.

Papa shoved his glasses to the top of his head, ruining his Einstein look, and pursed his lips. Clearly, he was scrutinizing Nate.

"Mr. Wolfe, how can I help?"

Her punishment for keeping Papa in the dark was to be totally ignored while Nate laid out the events of the past few days. Thank God, he kept the threat she'd received via the cell phone to himself.

A couple of times Papa adjusted his glasses, raking his fingers through his hair. He glanced at her when he heard Holly was missing, and his gaze softened. Another time Kay would've been upset that they talked around her. Today she rested the weight of the moment on Nate's shoulders.

"I'm due a few favors, and the information you're seeking isn't private. But it's late." Papa moved to his desk and opened a screen on his computer. "It might be morning before I can gather this much information." He turned to Kay, his gaze warm and forgiving. "How will knowing the locations of Walsh's facilities help? You can't search the buildings."

"I'm hoping I recognize the area." She refused the doubts creeping into her thoughts. "We'll find a way."

"I don't suppose telling you to—"

"No, Papa. I can't leave this to someone else. Holly was snatched because they couldn't get to me." His eyes widened, and Kay realized she'd said too much.

"Kaycie..." Papa rubbed the bridge of his nose and faced Nate. "You keep her safe." Not a request. Instructions.

"Come hell or high water." Nate rose and offered Papa his hand.

"Good man." Papa slapped his palm firmly in Nate's grasp. "I'll e-mail the information to Kaycie."

"Papa—"

"I understand the urgency." He cupped her cheek, leaning down to kiss her forehead. "When this is over, you'll owe me. And you know how I'll collect."

She all but stumbled down the hall, reeling from Nate's use of the old cliché. Damn him. Trust was a commodity she didn't issue without reason. He'd protect her all right, but at what cost to her heart?

****

"Tyrell placed the tracking device on Hank's car." Nate breathed easier as he watched the ball bounce in place. Hank was home.

Sitting across from him at her kitchen table, Kaycie smiled over the top of her computer screen.

"Did you call off the in-person surveillance and send Tyrell home?"

"No. We'll keep the tail on Hank. The tracer allows us to stay further back. Undetected. Close enough to move if something breaks."

Her long slender fingers rubbed her temples. Dark circles under her normally feisty eyes worried Nate. Her sluggish movements confirmed his suspicions. Kaycie was exhausted.

He should've insisted she wait until morning to meet Tomas at the jail. After she'd dug through the evidence bag and didn't find the missing ring, her nerves had crashed faster than a blowout at Daytona. She needed rest, but here she sat, refusing to quit.

"Let's get you to bed."

"Holly's probably not sleeping." Kaycie's gaze dropped to her laptop screen. "I'm reviewing the case files she downloaded. According to three CPS investigators, the missing girls Leann's age are all from one geographical area."

"Show me." Nate finished linking his cell with Hank's tracer then moved next to her.

"This area." She drew a circle around Handle Park. "They all lived within twenty miles of each other. Different schools. Probably different friends."

Nate reached for her cell. His arm passed close to her breasts, and her breath hitched setting off blood spikes to his system. She'd showered and changed into a pair of gray warm-up pants and a yellow T-shirt. Her hair hung in loose waves down her back. He imagined burying his face in those mahogany tresses.

Nate finished setting up her phone and then leaned in to study the map on her screen.

"These girls hung out somewhere. Click nearby venues and then shopping. You might've found the kidnapper's hunting ground." She turned and met his gaze with hers.

The dark circles under her eyes tore him apart. Tomorrow morning was soon enough for her to continue researching. "You are going to bed. I'll try to narrow down the likely places."

"I'll get you a pillow." She rose and walked slowly out of the room, moving as if putting one foot in front of the other required major effort.

Nate hopped into the shower, expecting her to be sound asleep when he emerged. Not only was her light still on, but she hadn't returned with the promised pillow.

He rushed down the hall and found her on the floor in front of her closet. The room looked as if it had exploded. Drawers were ajar, and everything had been dragged out and opened.

She whispered, "I searched again."

"I see that."

He dropped behind her, leaned her back against his chest and rocked.

His heart folded. A knot formed in his throat as he scrambled for the right words to comfort her.

"Shh." He stroked her sweet-smelling hair away from her face, smoothing his fingers across the soft skin on her cheek. His body tensed at the contact of her body against his. "Did you get a phone call while I was in the shower?"

He almost missed her slight headshake. She held up a small box. No way was he letting her out of his embrace, so he flipped off the lid with one hand. Inside, he saw a charm bracelet with red parrots and white cockatiels interspaced around the circle. He understood immediately.

"Holly's birthday?"

"Next week." Her words were soft yet saturated with pain.

"We'll have her home before then."

Kaycie twisted in his arms, turning her tear-stained face toward him. Her gaze searched his, no doubt looking for the truth.

He kissed her. Her lips parted, and her tongue found his. She tunneled her fingers into his hair, pulling and tugging him closer. His body reacted immediately.

Her touch sent flames licking through his blood, blanking his mind to the outside world. Soft skin vibrated under his touch.

She scrambled to fully face him. Straddling him, she settled her crotch directly over his throbbing erection, rocking back and forth. Her gaze drifted down and then back up. The soft moan might have been his. Her eyes, now black as night, fluttered closed when he brought his lips down to hers.

Jesus. He ravaged the inside of her mouth with his tongue. Need boiled from deep inside his soul as he spread his fingers on her back and pressed her breasts to his chest.

He'd missed this. Missed her. Missed feeling alive.

Her hands coursed across his shoulders, rubbing, touching, and kneading his flesh. Her body molded against his, imprinting, bringing the past forward.

He couldn't do this to her. Couldn't have sex with her when she was in this state. Couldn't.

His erection didn't agree with his brain, and it strained against his jeans.

Shit. He grasped her shoulders and reluctantly peeled her off him. The smoldering in her eyes sparked with surprise and stirred a longing deep inside his soul. Her kiss-swollen lips leaned into him once again. Her tongue slid across his closed mouth, seeking entrance.

Desire pushed forcefully against his zipper. Painfully hard, he stopped her hand right before she covered him.

She wasn't looking for sex. Her heart was breaking, and she needed escape. She'd be full of remorse in the morning if they made love tonight. He couldn't deal with seeing regret in her soulful eyes.

"Kaycie." His voice croaked like a frog.

He got to his feet and then swung her into his arms. She moaned softly into his neck, her warm breath blistering his flesh. Oh, hell. She'd misread his intentions.

Fighting the lust consuming his body, he moved across the room. He jerked the covers back and then laid her on the bed.

"Sleep." He slid the sheet over her, leaned down and kissed her forehead.

Her fingers wrapped around his wrist, sending rockets of electricity up his arm.

"You don't want me?" The circles under her eyes contradicted the desire in her gaze.

Nate dropped to his knee next to the bed, afraid to touch her. Afraid he'd lose control, climb on top of her and bury himself deep inside her body. Afraid she'd despise him in the morning for taking advantage tonight.

"Sweetheart, I want to rip those clothes off you and kiss every inch of your body. I want your pupils to do that sexy flare when I slide inside. I want to hear you cry out my name when you come. I want that more than the very air I breathe. But you'd hate me in the morning, and I don't want that."

He stroked the back of his hand down her ivory cheek, reluctantly eased from the room and flicked off the light on his way out. His boots weighed at least a thousand pounds. Aches screamed through his body in places he didn't know could hurt.

"Nate?"

He froze, standing still in the dark. "I'm right here in the hall."

"When did you get out?"

"A couple of years ago." That she'd asked the question didn't surprise him. He hated to answer while her exhaustion had her emotions and nerves raw.

"Why didn't you come home?"

A heavy weight filled his chest. "After the military, I ran a few off-the-record ops for the government. My head wasn't in a good place. To get it back on straight, I turned down the last job they offered and kicked back for a while. Shot the rapids in Colorado. Let the universe talk me down." He waited a split second. Had his answer satisfied her? "Goodnight, Kaycie."

"Will you stay until I fall sleep?"

He closed his eyes for a moment. Crawling in bed with her would be a true test of his control. He returned to her bedside, toed off his boots, lay down, and spooned her against him. No words were necessary as he draped her body with his to give her comfort.

Soon her breathing settled into a nice steady rhythm. This was his shift and no way he'd close his eyes. Besides, he didn't need to be wrapped around her when he dreamed. Not with his nightmares.

He refused to move, torturing himself with each inhale and exhale. In and out. In and out. The citrusy scent of her hair flooded his senses. Her warmth burned his skin through the bedclothes. Her body molded against his causing fire in his groin. Need swept over him. Yet, he refused to move for fear he'd disturb her much-needed rest.

He worried they wouldn't find Holly alive. Truth was, and Kaycie knew the odds, most kidnappers didn't allow eyewitnesses to live. She'd never forgive herself or him if Holly died.

Chapter Sixteen

Kay forced her way out of the dream where she and Nate were in bed, snuggled against each other. A ringing noise disturbed her peaceful sleep.

The throwaway phone.

"Oh my God," she gasped, kicking the covers to untangle her feet.

The mattress shifted, and cold air washed across her back. Nate. She'd asked him to stay, and she'd fallen asleep inside the protection of his strong arms. His body radiated incredible heat. Her skin chilled from missing his warmth. He turned on the small lamp next to her bed as she swung her feet to the floor.

"You awake enough to talk?"

She nodded.

"Ask for proof of life."

"Okay." She pressed the button. "Yes?"

"How can you sleep when your friend needs you?" The tone sounded angry, venomous.

"Please don't hurt her."

"I will if you don't bring me the ring."

"There is no ring." Frustration poured through Kay's words.

"Find it and be ready to meet next time I call. Unless you want me to kill her."

"How do I know you haven't already?"

"You'll have to take my word for it."

"Let me talk to her."

"No."

"Don't hang up." Kay's blood ran icy. "Hello?"

"Asshole's gone," Nate growled out his words.

"God. I'd kill this bastard if I could." Kay shivered at her own declaration. She'd wanted to smack a few parents but never hated another human being. Until now.

Nate knelt in front of her. His hands caught hers. She remembered how he used to bury his feelings. Worked hard at hiding his emotions. Not now. The picture of doom on his face was easy to read. Like her, he feared Holly might already be dead. No. She had to believe her friend was alive.

He grabbed his cell and connected with the tracker, turning the screen at an angle, allowing her to see. "Walsh's car is at his apartment," Nate said to her.

"Tyrell would've called if Hank had gone out. Wouldn't he?"

"If Walsh budged, we'd have heard. The fact he's not babysitting Holly makes me think he's high up in the organization. Got somebody doing his dirty work for him."

Kay ran her fingers through her tangled hair, pulling up and clipping the whole mess to the back of her head. "Damn it. I should've asked what the ring looked like."

"Let me see the throwaway."

She passed it over and waited while he pushed keys with a frown. "What?"

"His number is blocked. I checked the calls received the other day, but since we were doubling back I wanted to try again."

"So he's tech smart."

"Yeah. He's made sure you can't track him down. He'll call back. You can ask for a description then."

Nate rocked back on his heels, staring at the wall. The tendon in his jaw jerked.

"What are you thinking?" Kay asked.

He shook his head as if trying to break out of a fog. "Something about the voice on the phone."

His gaze met hers. The dark expression scared her. "You recognized him?"

"Not him. His intonation. He's a killer. Cold. Calculating. Deliberate."

"You knew people like him?"

"I was him." His words, void of emotions, came cold and harsh.

Kay crawled across the bed to sit next to him. Cupping his cheek in her palm, she forced his distant gaze to meet hers. Nate had gone somewhere else in his mind. The icy stare sliced right through her. She had to bring him back.

She ignored the warning her heart sent, accepting she'd face one hell of a heartbreak when he left. But right now, tonight, he needed her, and her body ached for his touch.

"No. You did what you had to do. What you were trained to do. That's not who you are."

"You don't get it. Most of my kills were by rifle, but a few with my bare hands or a knife. Whichever way, a lot of people died." His expression was solemn. "Don't misunderstand. I don't regret my actions."

"And you shouldn't." She wanted him to unburden and share his pain.

"I was proud of what I did for my country. My team went places where most men would've died. We were selected because we'd get the job done, regardless of the cost. Some of us didn't come home. Part of me wonders, why was I spared?"

"Maybe there's something you have to do before you die." Her heart ached for all he'd been through. She rested her hand on his back, the muscles tightening at her touch. Arguing that he wasn't to blame for lives lost during war would be futile.

His scoff said he didn't agree. "Right."

"Is that when you got out of the military?"

"No. I went back to Afghanistan after a few weeks R&R. Things got ugly after that." A cruel smile lifted one corner of his mouth. "Hate can take control, snake up from down deep and squeeze the compassion right out of your soul. Trust me, I recognized the guy on the phone."

He'd spoken the words with such hate and thick emotion Kay realized she'd stopped breathing. Her mind searched for words of comfort and found none appropriate.

"I don't know how you survived, but I'm glad you did. You're home now. I promise the world offers plenty of reasons to be alive, but the only way you'll find them is to move on."

"The way you moved on?" His cool gaze pinned her. "This rift between you and your dad, is it your brother? What about his death weighs so heavily you can't take your own advice?"

She squirmed at the shift in conversation. "We were talking about how you survived Afghanistan."

He pushed off the bed. "Bullets, blood, and memories kept me alive." In two long strides, he'd left the room.

She went back to her search, wondering if the ring had been passed to her before her last visit to the hospital. She dug through her briefcase, while trying to remember what she'd worn to an interview with Leann the week before she was murdered. Kay searched through pockets, found two dollars and a dry cleaner claim check but no ring.

The light in the living room was still on. Kay succumbed to the urge to walk down the hall.

Nate had unbuttoned the top snap on his jeans and stretched out on the couch with his eyes closed. Long black eyelashes cast shadows on his cheeks. A white T-shirt hugged his chest, outlining the hard ridge of the Saint Jude's medal tucked inside. Even at rest, Nate's body looked coiled and ready to spring.

She ached to run her fingers though the shoulder-length black hair, to rub her palm over the day-old scruff across his chin. Longing, desire, and need settled deep inside her, low in her belly.

She ignored the craving inside and reached to turn off the light.

"Don't. I'm not asleep."

His eyes opened, hitting her with a sultry gaze that shot through her and left her feeling naked. Years ago, that same expression had melted her resistance and rendered her unable to think straight. Tonight, she discovered it still had the same effect.

He lifted up on one elbow. "Did you come to talk about your brother?"

"I didn't. We all carry guilt tucked away somewhere private Let's leave it at that. Like I said, some of us move on." She stood over him, dumbfounded, as he reclined, closed his eyes and effectively blocked her out.

Frustration boiled through her, and she slapped the claim check on the coffee table, gritting her teeth when he didn't look at her. "I'd forgotten all about picking up my cleaning. I need to do that in the morning."

"Whatever you say, boss."

****

Johnny paced up and down the hall outside the woman named Holly's holding room. He'd fucking gone over the edge. The boss would be at the warehouse in a few hours, and Johnny still wore yesterday's clothes.

He scanned his card and slowly opened the door. The tiny bundle curled into a fetal position lifted her bruised face, eyes wide and full of horror. Her body trembled.

"Sit up." He waited until she'd righted herself before snapping a picture with his cell. The Taylor woman wanted to know her friend was alive. He'd send her something to prove his point.

"Did you come to kill me?" The blonde shoved her matted hair over her shoulder and stared wide-eyed at him.

"Not yet. Your friend wants to be sure you're alive."

"Let me talk to her."

"Not unless you know where the ring is." He advanced a step, and she cringed. Her reaction sent a blast of pain over his right ear.

"I'm freezing," she said. "Can I at least have something warm to drink?"

"This isn't the Ritz." He couldn't hold back a smile as he tossed her the blanket he'd brought, which she greedily dragged up and under her chin.

She'd kept her shit together, at least momentarily. Brave. He liked that. He lifted his phone to get another shot. Damned if she didn't do a faux quick draw with both hands and point at him just as the camera clicked. "You like to have your picture taken?"

"Not particularly. I'm betting I look like shit. My appearance will motivate my friends to find me. It won't be pretty when they do."

"You've got a smart mouth." He narrowed his eyes to make a point. "I'd advise keeping it shut when Hank or the boss is around."

Her bravado withered, and oddly enough, he preferred her defiant side. He texted both pictures, slipped the cell back in his pocket and turned to leave.

"You seem like a nice guy, not like that bastard Hank. Please let me go."

Without turning around, he huffed out a breath and said, "I'm not a nice guy. Not sure I ever was."

****

Nate blasted off the couch and was standing next to Kaycie's bed before she picked up the throwaway phone. Was the bastard trying to keep her awake? Nate could go for days without sleep. Been trained to rejuvenate on twenty minutes of shut-eye. He didn't know what to expect from her. How long would she hold up to pressure when she was running on adrenaline?

"Nothing's written in the text, but there's an attachment." She opened the first picture and gasped. "Oh God."

Nate wrapped a protective arm around her and pried the phone from her grip. He studied the proof-of-life snapshot on the small screen, memorizing every bruise. He'd seen worse than this. A hell of a lot worse, but this was Kaycie's friend who'd been beaten. He opened the next picture. Holly's eyes and face still reflected agony, yet she'd hiked one eyebrow and pointed her index fingers at the camera.

"I don't get this one," he said to Kaycie, whose head was turned into his chest. "This one is different. It looks like Holly posed for him."

"Maybe he made her," Kaycie's tone was filled with hate.

Her voice grew weaker with each word. Worried she'd cave, he gently maneuvered her to sit on the bed. He turned the phone Kaycie's direction, hating to hurt her but needing her help.

"Maybe he did."

"If we argue, and it turns out I'm right, Holly pulls her finger weapons and fires. It's her way of joking around."

Kaycie stood and paced around the room.

She spun to look at him. Inhaled sharply. "I think she's telling me I was right about Hank Walsh." Her words, dripping hate, chilled the air. "That bastard hurt her."

Chapter Seventeen

Nate opened the door quietly. He shushed Tyrell before allowing him to enter Kaycie's apartment. "She had a rough night. I'm letting her sleep a few more minutes."

"That's cool. I have an idea to run past you."

"Coffee's hot." Nate waved toward the kitchen and returned to his chair. He'd brought his and Kaycie's phones plus the throwaway out of the bedroom and placed them next to her laptop, ready to intercept any incoming intel. She'd left her e-mail logged on, and he watched for the information from her grandfather. "Talk to me."

"We should pick up a change of clothes or two and crash here. Be together if something breaks. Neither you, me, nor Marcus need a lot of sleep. We'll rest when this is over."

"Agreed." Nate had no doubt Tyrell's training as a Ranger had taught him how to stay awake for days. "Kaycie needs as much support as we can give."

"Holly's been missing for twenty-four hours." Tyrell scrubbed a hand over his chin. "Somebody needs to brace Kay for the worst."

Nate didn't disagree. "She knows."

Tyrell collapsed in a chair across from Nate. "So you back for good?"

"Wouldn't have opened an office otherwise. You looking for a job?"

"Maybe, but I wasn't talking about work. I meant Kay. She's nursed a grudge and a broken heart because of you for years. I'd hate for you to fuck up her head again."

"That subject's not open for discussion." Nate leaned back in his chair and folded his arms across his chest.

"Kay and I have been friends for a long time. Love her like a sister, and I take exception to anybody messing with my family."

A frisson of resentment rushed Nate. "Don't preach—"

Tyrell held both hands up in the surrender position. "I'm just saying."

"Duly noted." Somewhere in the recesses of his mind, Nate appreciated Tyrell's concern, but needed him to concentrate on Holly's rescue. "You talk with Marcus this morning?"

"Yeah. I'll let him know he's bunking here for the duration. You hear anything?"

"She had two calls early this morning."

"And?"

Nate pulled up Holly's picture on the throwaway and passed them over. "The asshole left no doubt what would happen to her if Kaycie didn't come up with the ring."

"I'm gonna kill the motherfucker who did this." Tyrell's jaw worked from side to side as he gritted his teeth.

"I'm in." Nate explained their visit with Kaycie's grandfather. "He's gathering addresses on all of Walsh's properties. It's thin, but what else have we got? Our best bet is for Walsh to lead us to Holly."

"Maybe we should encourage him. Nothing's keeping me from showing up at his door with a buttload of questions."

"Go for it. Take Marcus and do that scary shit Kaycie was talking about." Nate paused at the sound of the bathroom door closing. "I'd hoped she'd sleep longer."

"How's she holding up?"

"Not good." Nate refilled his coffee and set it on the table. "The call and then the pictures wound her up. She took her bedroom apart looking for that fucking ring."

"Didn't you already search?"

"Exactly." The ping from her computer grabbed Nate's attention. "Hang on." He opened the attached file and silently cursed the affluent senior Walsh. "Seven properties." Nate's gaze swept the room. "We need a Dallas city map."

"Do it online."

"I could and then print it. I'd rather have paper first."

"Think I have a map in the console," Tyrell said, heading for the door.

Within minutes, he was back, leaning against the kitchen counter and marking spots on the map while Nate read locations from the information Kaycie's grandfather had sent.

Kaycie wandered in after her shower, dressed in jeans and a faded George Strait T-shirt. She accepted the coffee Tyrell poured. She lifted the steaming cup to her nose and breathed in deeply. Steam rose and drifted across the dark circles under her eyes.

Tyrell opened his arms, and she stepped into a bear hug. A ping of jealousy sizzled up Nate's spine at the sight of another man holding her closely. The sizzle flashed to a burn when she wrapped her arms around his waist and squeezed.

Kaycie moved to sit next to him. She studied the computer screen. "I knew Papa would come through." She leaned closer, shaking her head. "That's a lot of places to figure out how to get inside."

Her scent, clean and fresh, washed over Nate. He forced himself to concentrate on the business at hand.

"Tyrell's going after clothes. He and Marcus will bunk here. We'll take turns on the couch. When it's time to take action, we need to be together."

"Goin' now. Little Mama, you got an extra key?"

"I don't. Holly's the only one who does. I'm not sure I should go in her apartment until I check with Tomas. I'll call the complex office and ask them to let you in."

"Tell'em I'm your cousin." Tyrell winked. His wisecrack about the difference in ethnicity didn't draw a response from Kaycie.

"We'll get extra keys made today," Nate said, walking his old friend to the door.

Kaycie hadn't eaten worth a damn since this whole thing started. Breakfast was about the only meal he could cook, but he scrambled a mean egg. He opened the refrigerator and removed items.

"The city has changed since I lived here. While I cook, familiarize yourself with each of Walsh's addresses. Eliminate Hank's apartment and the old man's home. We can search them if we need to. First, we'll drive by the warehouses and through the area where you escaped. If we're lucky, something will trigger a memory."

Nate cracked four eggs into a bowl before rummaging around for a fork. Suddenly, the scene was so domestic his feet itched. It was his custom to run from the idea of having an apron hanging from his neck, yet here he was, like a lovesick clown, making fucking breakfast. While the eggs cooked, he toasted and buttered four slices of bread. He fixed their plates, draped a kitchen towel across one arm, and served her with a bow.

"Eat up." He sat next to her and dug in to his breakfast.

"Thanks. This looks great." Her words belied her actions as she pushed her food around on her plate with her fork.

She shifted in her chair and glanced in his direction every few minutes. The silence while they ate prompted Nate to inhale his food and finish dressing.

He'd pulled on his boots when she stood and walked over to him. "What's on your mind?" He studied her face and body language, unable to read her emotions.

"You did the right thing last night." She drew in a breath. "Sex would've just complicated matters."

"Sweetheart, sometimes sex is just sex and doesn't have to complicate anything."

"I'm sure you could explain it away as nothing. Still, I appreciate you not taking advantage of my emotional state."

"That's me, chivalrous to a fault. I wouldn't want the word to get out I'd slept with the boss." He waited for a blink or reaction.

She didn't flinch. "Right. I'm ready to hit the cleaners if you are."

She slipped on a long-sleeve shirt, covering the pistol on her hip, and strolled down the hall as if she thought the subject was closed. It wasn't. Last night he'd voiced, in explicit detail, exactly what he wanted to do to her body. Maybe neither of them wanted permanent, but both were fighting a fire only sex would extinguish.

****

Johnny broke the news to Mr. A that as of the last conversation with the Taylor woman, she was still insisting she didn't have Hank's ring. "We've had the hostage over twenty-four hours. Seems kind of odd she's not willing to give it up."

Mr. A's eyes turned steely hard, causing Johnny's heart to jackhammer against his ribs.

"If Hank is wrong ..." The boss stopped outside the holding room. "The friend is in here?"

"Yes, sir. You sure you want to go in?" Johnny's hand hovered over the lock.

"Because she'll get a look at me?" The boss's eyebrow rose. "Dead witnesses don't testify."

Johnny blew out the breath he'd been holding and swiped his key card. His caution was an act. He wanted nothing more than to show the boss Hank's handiwork because the woman called Holly looked even worse this morning. With one eye purple and swollen almost shut, her lip and face the color of grapes, she looked pathetic. Surely, this time the boss would sanction action on Hank.

"Johnny. Was this necessary?" Mr. A moved closer to the small bundle of bruises.

Johnny's brain hiccupped. He opened his mouth to defend himself but couldn't. His code of honor kept him from throwing Hank under the bus.

"That man Hank beat me." Holly ground out the words over a busted lip.

"I should've known," Mr. A said, returning to stand over her. "My apologies. He gets rambunctious sometimes."

"Rambunctious?" She threw the blanket back and slid her torn shirt to the side, revealing teeth marks on her breast. "He almost raped me." Her gaze burned with hate. "He's disgusting."

Johnny could taste the need to gut Hank. The woman and the boss glared at each other for a long minute. Jesus, she had balls of steel. And Mr. A's tolerance level for insubordination was low.

"Be done with this." The boss exhaled a long sigh. "Kill this creature, the Taylor woman, and Hank."

Chapter Eighteen

While Nate drove, Kay lined up their stops on the GPS. She turned her head away from him and tried to figure out how she'd managed to screw up thanking him. He'd exercised kindness and good judgment last night. Somehow she'd come across rigid and uptight.

Deep inside, part of her wanted to believe she'd given him a taste of being rejected, although that wasn't the truth. Her body craved his, flushed when he brushed past, her breasts ached for his touch.

She trusted him in all things except with her heart. He'd proved his thrill-seeker adventures and need to fight the good fight meant more to him than she ever had.

Could she have a "sex is just sex" relationship? Why not? She was an adult with needs. People had sex without emotional ties all the time. Right?

One thought nagged at her confidence. Last night, she'd all but climbed over him, and he'd said no thanks. Regardless of all the sexy things he'd claimed he wanted to do, if he'd truly wanted to make love to her last night, they'd have been naked, in bed and smiling by now.

The car stopped. She glanced up to find them parked in front of her dry cleaners. Nate's hand was thrust out with a claim check.

"We didn't have to do this now," she said, remembering his non-reaction to her appearance in the living room.

"You're the one who tried to knock down the coffee table with the receipt. I'm following the boss's orders." His tone carried a razor-sharp edge.

His blue eyes reflected nothing. He'd put a mental wall between them. On the other hand, maybe she'd built an insurmountable one by refusing to talk about her relationship with her dad.

Stewing like a boiling pot, she slammed the door a little too hard and then stormed into the store.

The owner's wife rushed to the counter.

"Ms. Taylor, I almost called but knew you'd be in soon."

"You lost my favorite slacks?"

"No." The woman chuckled as she opened the cash register. "We found your ring."

She dumped the contents of a small envelope into Kay's hand. In that surreal moment, Kay's hearing failed. The only sound was the swish of blood pumping to her brain. The world spun, forcing her to lean against the counter for support.

"Was in your jacket pocket."

Kay realized the clerk was speaking. "Thanks." She forced the word out.

"I'll get your cleaning."

She glanced over her shoulder at Nate, who had his cell to his ear. Their gazes locked for a split second. He dropped the phone, erupted out of the car, and raced to her. He burst through the door and gathered her in his arms. Her heart twisted, swelling painfully inside her chest.

God, it felt good to be forgiven. It felt good to lean into his chest and listen to his heart pound. It felt good to know she held the key to Holly's freedom in her hand.

"I'm here." Strong arms wrapped around her and guided her to the lone chair. He knelt before her. "What happened?"

She unfurled her fingers. His gaze dropped to her hand.

"You have got to be kidding." He tapped the ring, rolling it around on her palm.

Lost in a haze of confusion, she said, "Leann had to have dropped it in my pocket during one of my visits with her."

"Why pass it off to you?"

"She must have been afraid Hank knew she had it. Look at the initial." She turned the W up where he could see.

"This changes everything. Can you walk?"

"I'm fine. My legs got rubbery for a second."

"No doubt. We've got work to do."

Kay paid the bill, thanking the owner for returning the ring. The woman's wide eyes indicated her curiosity as to what had just happened, but Kay didn't try to explain.

He loaded her along with her cleaning into the car and then drove toward her apartment.

"I'm hitting redial. I have to tell him I have the damn ring."

"Not until we have a plan." He was using his don't-fuck-with-me voice. "I won't risk losing you both."

"We're running out of time. Maybe I can stall him by telling him I'll swap the ring for Holly. It will give us a chance to figure out a plan."

"First I need to talk to Tyrell. He and Marcus were about to knock on Hank's door when you almost collapsed. They need to know about the ring. Will you at least call him first? Let him know what's happened. Tell him we'll meet back at your place later."

Kay's heart did a flip. Hope filled her chest for the first time since they discovered Holly missing. "You're right. We'll want to be together to plan the swap. If the kidnapper picks a drop location, I need to deliver the ring."

Nate held a hand up, supposedly to stop her arguing, which she ignored.

"No. It's me he's been talking with. He won't allow it. Besides, you and the boys will protect me."

"You do understand Hank's people aren't planning on trading. Two more dead females mean nothing to them."

"I know. And we won't let that happen." Coffee backed up into her throat.

Her call with Tyrell lasted only a few minutes. He passed the phone to Marcus who wanted assurance he wouldn't be left out when it came time to go after Holly.

Kay dug the throwaway from her pocket. She couldn't wait any longer.

Nate's hand gripped her knee. "Try it. With the number being blocked, it may not go through. If it does, tease the bastard, let him know you have it, but don't promise anything. You want to talk to Holly."

****

Johnny pressed his palms against his head and squeezed. Surely, the searing hot pain would boil his brain. The intensity jumbled his thoughts, blurring his vision.

The sudden vibration in his pocket startled the shit out of him.

Should he care the Taylor woman was calling? Hell, yes. If she really had it, Mr. A would want the damn thing returned. Wouldn't change the outcome, just delay it.

The memory of the bite marks on Holly's breast flicked through Johnny's memory. How many more had she not shown?

Clenching his teeth against the headache, he brought the phone to his mouth. "I'm glad you called. You can listen while I kill your friend."

"I found it."

Johnny raked a hand through his hair, closed his eyes, and took a moment before speaking. Hank had been right all along. Christ, this meant the boss would forgive that fucking slime-ball again.

"Too late."

"Hurt her and kiss your chances of getting this ring back goodbye."

Johnny laughed at the woman's bravado. "You're as mouthy as Holly."

"Thanks. We're a lot alike."

A male voice drifted through the receiver. Johnny barely heard the man tell the Taylor woman to hang up. She shushed whoever was with her. Trouble in the ranks benefited Johnny's purpose because he had to separate her from her bodyguards.

"You won't be alike when she's dead."

Johnny decided to let the two women speak to each other. He strode into the hall and opened the door to the holding room.

Holly was bent over the small sink, splashing her face. She'd draped the blanket he'd given her around her shoulders. She yelped and scrambled backward, slinging a trail of water across the floor.

Christ, how had he not noticed her size? She couldn't be more than five-four.

She stopped when her legs bumped into the cot. Tears welled. "What now?"

"Your friend's ready to trade." He brushed her hair over her shoulder, instantly regretting the feel of gold silk against his fingers.

He thrust the cell in front of her, leaving it tilted so he could hear what was said. "Say hello."

"Kay?"

"Holly?" The Taylor woman's voice shot up two octaves. "Thank God."

"Don't-give-him-shit-he's-going-to-kill—"

In the middle of her run-on sentence, Johnny ended the call and glared down at Holly. "Do you ever do what you're told?"

"Why should I?" She tilted her head back, never flinching. Her defiance made him crazy.

"Because Hank will be here later today. You'll need a friend then."

The low cry that burst from her sounded like a lost kitten. She climbed further back on the bed and scrunched into a ball.

"Please don't let him ..." Her bottom lip quivered.

"He won't hurt you again. I'll kill him first."

Big blue eyes, full of doubt and confusion, lifted and studied him. "Why? What do you care?"

"I don't."

She blanched as if he'd struck her. Her fiery eyes and pale skin fascinated him. The deep bow in her upper lip tempted him. He bit back the urge to reach out and touch her mouth. Disgust at himself balled in his belly. Hank wasn't the only degenerate.

"You do. Or you wouldn't protect me."

"Has nothing to do with you," he lied. "I hate that son of a bitch."

"So do I," she muttered.

"Do you need something for the bite?"

"You afraid I'll die from infection before you get a chance to kill me?"

He couldn't hold back the laugh that rolled up and out from somewhere deep. "Your wiseass remarks should probably piss me off, but Christ, you've got guts."

"Why do you kill people?"

"It's my job."

"Johnny. Killing isn't a job."

His name rolled off her lips for the first time. He wanted to hear her say it again.

"I think it's what I was trained to do."

"What does that mean—you *think*?" She sat up. Her gaze locked on him.

"And I'm good at it." He'd said too much and gone way past the boundaries he kept between himself and the girls brought in for sale. But she wasn't going on the auction block. He opened the door.

"How did you know my name?"

"Your boss called you Johnny. What's your last name?"

"Darling, but don't think knowing that will help you. Your friend is the only one who can."

"Don't go. I'm not gutsy. I'm scared."

He couldn't glance back at her. Couldn't take those blue eyes searching his face, looking for a human being with real emotions. Couldn't bear that she'd see nothing but a void.

He returned to his office and called Mr. A, who was already furious because the ring had taken priority over gathering merchandise and having a sale. Johnny listened patiently while he was reminded cash-paying customers expected quality young women to be available on demand, and they'd go elsewhere if their needs weren't met.

The boss's instructions were as expected. Forget killing Hank. When the ring was in his possession, he would eliminate both women.

A plan began formulating. He had orders to follow. And he'd do his job.

How many people knew about the ring? How many had to die because of Hank? How many times would he escape facing consequences for his behavior?

Chapter Nineteen

"Got a problem." Marcus's tone came through edgy and nervous over the cell, standing the hair on the back of Nate's neck on end.

"What's up?" Nate put the call on speaker. He wouldn't keep anything from Kaycie.

"The monitor on Hank's car is useless if he doesn't drive it. He just rode off in a limo. An older dude went in the building. A few minutes later the two of them came out together."

"Tall, thin, salt and pepper hair?"

Kaycie's gaze heated Nate's neck even before he glanced at her. "Yeah. About the same height as Hank."

Nate snapped his attention back to the moment. "That's probably Hank's dad. Stick with them."

"Yeah. I'm laying back. Wouldn't do to be noticed."

"How'd the visit with Hank go?"

"The bastard wouldn't talk to us. Coward kept the safety chain on."

"Tyrell demanded to be let in. Threatened to kick the fucking door open and interrogate him our way."

"You stirred his shit. That was good enough." Nate chuckled. Any normal person would panic if they opened the door and found Marcus and Tyrell standing there. "We're headed to the first Walsh property on our list."

"Is this the industrial park where Kay was found?"

"No." Kaycie spoke up for the first time in the conversation. Nate hoped talking would help her relax. "That's our third stop."

"Nate treating you okay?" Marcus asked.

The corners of her mouth lifted slightly, and a stupid zing of jealousy flashed in Nate's blood. She used to smile at the sound of his voice.

"He doesn't feed me as often as you do," she said, leaning across the car closer to the phone, bringing with her the scent of lemons and spring mornings. "Other than that, he's doing okay."

"I don't like being stuck out here," Marcus said, huffing out a breath loud enough to be heard over the speaker. "You stay in touch."

"Will do." Nate dropped the cell on the seat and parked a block away from a huge rambling warehouse. Eighteen-wheelers were backed up to unloading docks by the dozens. Kaycie rubbed her eyes. A frown darkened her face.

"What's going on inside that pretty head?" He dropped his hand on her knee.

She blinked. "Memories of running for my life flood my brain every time I get close to a warehouse."

"I'm not convinced finding the place you were held will do any good. The place has probably been scrubbed of all clues by now."

"You're probably right. At least we accomplished one thing. The voice on the phone will get in touch with Hank. He'll get the message we've got the ring and we're not backing off until Holly's home safe."

****

After they drove past a second warehouse, Nate had stopped at a burger joint. She'd ordered but demonstrated no interest in her food. "You told Marcus I didn't feed you. Don't make me tell him you refused to eat." Nate picked an onion ring off her plate, held it up, and waited until she took a bite.

"You ready to go?" Without waiting for him to answer, she stuffed her food into the trash bin, kept the cup of coffee, and headed for the car.

"You're the boss." He said it jokingly, hoping to get a rise out of her, a spark of defiance. Got nothing.

The next stop, less than a mile away, was in the same industrial park where she'd escaped and run to freedom. To him all the buildings looked alike. The only difference was their size. Judging from her body language, she was on full alert and determined to find the warehouse. Her hands were rolled into fists, and her gaze scanned the area.

Nate's respect for her grew because going back had to be

traumatic as hell, yet she never complained. If returning meant sparking a forgotten memory that would give them an edge, she was all for it.

They'd paid particular attention to the vehicles at each location, looking for the white van and the black Mercedes. If they found either, chances were good they'd uncovered an important location.

A hand gripped his arm. "Why hasn't that lunatic called?"

"I wish I knew. He's probably planning how to pull off a swap with no witnesses. He can't afford to allow anyone to walk away."

Kaycie's shoulders dropped down further each time they stopped at an unfamiliar place.

It was as if she carried the weight of the world on her back. Her only concern was her friend's safe return. He wanted to lift that load, to lighten her burden.

He turned the corner, slowed the car, and waited for her to react.

"I recognize that building." She pointed at the big-box spread out over probably half an acre. The sheer size made the first two they'd visited seem small.

"This is where you were rescued." He'd started to begin here first, but the other two had been on the way.

"Yeah. I ran toward the loading docks." With her hands folded in her lap, she closed her eyes.

Nate parked next to the curb and let her slip into deep thought. Her body shivered as if a chill assaulted her. He wanted to drag her into his arms and hold her until she warmed. Instead, he moved across the car and held her hands between his, slowly rubbing her cold skin.

"Turn right," she whispered, looking over her shoulder.

She leaned forward and scanned the area. He followed her directions, keeping one eye on her and one on the street signs.

"This road takes us to the third property," Nate said as he swung into an empty parking lot. "City records indicate it's vacant. Sure looks deserted."

She was out of the car before the engine died. Moving fast, she tried the front door. Locked. Her eyebrows drew together. The strain on her face worried Nate.

Her eyes widened. "I ran out the back into the trailer lot. There's another entrance."

Shit. She tore off in a run, her long black hair billowing out behind her. Nate hustled to catch up. Her reaction confirmed his suspicions when he'd read the report this warehouse was unoccupied.

When he caught her, she'd reached a side door. "We have to get inside."

Nate stepped around her. Peered through the glass, ensuring the place was empty. Expecting an alarm would scream bloody murder, he gave the handle a tug. The metal screeched and scraped the floor as it opened.

She didn't hesitate or give him time to issue a caution, she just blew right past him.

"Damn, you could've let me make sure nobody else was here."

"This is the place." Ignoring his frustration, she pointed overhead at an exit sign.

"We got in too easy. I don't like it." His voice echoed off the open space. He moved closer, wrapping an arm around her shoulder. A surge of anger rushed him when her body trembled.

Her fingers grazed the wall as they traversed the hall, further into the cavernous building. This had to dredge up the horror of that night.

She led him to a small empty room. "In here."

His palms itched. His skin crawled as the need for vengeance roared through his blood. What he'd give to wrap his fingers around the neck of the bastard who'd hurt her.

"My hands were taped." Her shaky fingers hovered above her right ear. "And I had a gash right here."

She shocked him by stretching out on the floor. "I don't think that's a good idea." He offered her his hand, but she ignored him.

"I woke up in this very spot. What's that smell? Bleach? Bastards cleaned up my blood." Her hands covered the side of her head where she'd been injured. "I've never been so scared."

"But you kept it together. Hell, you rescued yourself! Be proud of that. I am."

"Tomas and Wayne will send a forensic team out here. I'll bet my blood seeped into the cement. No scrubbing gets all traces. It will put more pressure on them to look closer at Walsh."

Nate reached down, and she grabbed a hold of his wrist. Her clammy, trembling hands worried him. Maybe reliving her time in this room wasn't a good idea.

The sound of car doors slamming stopped them both.

Nate whispered, "If it's security guards, I'll try to bluff our way out. Be better if you give your information directly to your DPD friends."

"What if it's not security?"

"They didn't try to sneak up on us." Nate rested his hand on his gun when the side door opened just to be safe. "Wait here."

"You're not leaving me behind," she whispered, but the power in her tone was clear.

"What if I'm wrong?" He stroked the backs of his fingers across her cheek. "I can't take that chance."

"Police," a male voice called out. "Step outside into the open with your hands where we can see them.".

She opened her mouth, but he rested his finger on her lips. "Shh."

The cinnamon in her eyes flared, but before Nate answered, he bent his head and kissed her.

"Coming out," he yelled. He leaned close to Kaycie's ear and said, "You stay close behind me."

"And if it's not the police?"

He patted the gun on her hip. "You know how to use that thing. Don't you?"

Nate breathed a sigh of relief when two uniformed officers waited just outside. The youngest of the two stepped forward.

"You folks keep coming."

"We're just looking around," Kaycie protested.

"Do you have permission to be here?" the cop asked.

She opened her mouth and Nate tried to cut her off.

"Show them your PIs license."

Judging by the look on both cop's faces, this was going to be a long afternoon.

****

Kay sidestepped Tyrell when, half-asleep, he stumbled down her hall and swept past her with a surly grunt. Based on the frown and way his jaw twitched, his frustration level was as high as hers, and catching a few hours sleep on her couch hadn't helped his mood.

"Good morning," Kay said, lifting her voice an octave and flashing a smile to his snarl.

He lifted the coffeepot to his nose, sniffed the black liquid and poured a cup.

God. He was going to drink it cold. "Give me that."

She stuck the mug in the microwave. He might've gone for days without sleep while in the military, but today signs of exhaustion painted his ebony skin with a gray sheen.

"Tyrell, you need to eat. I'll make sandwiches."

"Don't worry 'bout me. How you holding up, Little Mama?" He stopped her by dropping an arm over her shoulder. Together they watched the cup circle as the coffee heated.

"I'm tired of waiting for the phone to ring."

The microwave pinged, and Tyrell retrieved his cup. Soon they all sat at the table, staring at the small throwaway cell.

"How'd the site visits go?" Tyrell asked, finally sounding awake. "See any place they might be holding Holly?"

"No. But we almost got arrested for trespassing. And Nate shushed me as if I were a trained Labrador retriever." A scoff came from Nate. She continued, "Somebody noticed Nate's car in the parking lot and called the cops."

"And?"

"Let's say they weren't impressed with my private investigator license," Nate muttered. "Stuck us in the back of a squad car while they contacted Kaycie's pals downtown. Took them an hour to decide not to haul us away in cuffs."

Tyrell sipped his coffee. He grimaced, letting her know she'd overheated his caffeine fix. "So you have the ring, but we're no closer to finding Holly," Tyrell ground out the words. "I don't do cat-and-mouse very well."

Nate shoved hair off his face. His eyes were clear and steady. She searched for signs of fatigue, instead found determination, confidence and a whole lot of dangerous.

"The bastard on the other end of the throwaway has to lead us to her. Hank must be allowing him to call the shots." Nate leaned back, folding his arms across his chest.

"I agree. I don't think the caller is Hank." Kay moved the cell around in a circle with a finger, willing it to ring.

Nate nodded. "For now, we're at his mercy. We wait to be given instructions."

Tyrell ran a hand over his shiny head and nodded his agreement. "If you don't mind, I'll use your shower before I head out."

"Go." Kaycie removed the stale coffee from Tyrell's hand and set it in the sink.

A few minutes later he reappeared, dressed in jeans and his customary black shirt. "I'm heading out. Phone's on." He patted his pocket.

"You want a sandwich or something before you go?"

"No, thanks. I'll pick something up for me and Marcus. He'll probably run by his place for a change of clothes. Don't expect him for a few hours."

She accompanied him to the door. "If this runs into tomorrow, you sleep on my bed. That couch is a killer." She fisted her hands on her hips to indicate her word was final. Because in this case, it was.

Nate moved close to her, apparently showing solidarity. "We'll call if something breaks."

Tyrell clipped his holster on his belt, sliding his Sig home as he closed the door.

Her apartment could've been a tomb. Neither she nor Nate spoke as they moved back to the kitchen. He opened the fridge and stood staring inside. Sunlight drifted through the bank of windows, shimmering across his face. She closed her eyes, and for a few seconds, the tension and stress slid away while she remembered the young man he was long ago.

The soft touch of lips against hers sent her floating on a cloud. Had she fallen asleep on her feet? The kiss shifted to demanding and strong hands splayed across her hips, crushing her into a hard-as-steel body.

Her eyes popped open. Knees weakened. Nate's mouth covered hers. He leaned his head back a few inches, his blue eyes now the shade of midnight.

This wasn't the boy she daydreamed about.

This was a man.

Chapter Twenty

Kaycie had closed her eyes, and she swayed slightly. She drew Nate to her like a magnet. Drove him to cover her inviting lips with his. Her gaze met his and answered his unasked question. Her brown eyes had darkened to obsidian.

He hauled her against his body and kissed her again, teasing her lips open with his tongue. Somebody moaned, probably him. The honest sweetness that was pure Kaycie flooded his senses. She tunneled her fingers through his hair and leaned into him.

He'd dreamed of holding her like this for years. Nurtured the pictures his mind had taken and filed them away for ready retrieval. The image of her lying beneath him, her beautiful body trembling with passion, had never faded.

His hands traveled, molded, pressed, and refreshed his memory of every inch. The clothes separating their bare flesh drove him crazy. The need to touch her soft skin was too much. His attempt at being suave failed when his fingers shook and turned clumsy. A deep breath failed to calm him, so he gathered a handful of material on either side of the buttons on her blouse and ripped. They popped, flying across the room.

His gaze feasted as her chest expanded, rising and falling rapidly in surprise. He one-handed the bra clasps and then slid the beige, satin straps from her shoulders.

His heart stumbled, hurt. She was magnificent.

"Beautiful."

He cupped her breasts, lifted them, supporting their weight in his hands. Her low moan powered blood to his groin. Rosy nipples begged to be touched, and he circled them with his thumbs. His insides coiled tighter as they pebbled under his touch.

Her head tilted back, and he kissed the pulsing vein in her neck, her collarbone and the creamy flesh above her breasts. Her fists closed around the hem of his shirt and lifted. Nate stepped back far enough for her to jerk it off in one fluid motion. Small hands imprinted streaks of fire as she trailed her fingers up his rib cage to cup his face.

He lowered his head and pulled her rigid nipple into his mouth, laved the tip with his tongue. A shiver pulsed through her as she pressed harder against him. Her encouraging soft mewl only made him tug harder.

Nate wanted more. Needed more. His name. He wanted to hear her cry it out at the moment of release.

"I love the way your body responds." He moved to the other breast, tasting, savoring, and nipping with his teeth. His hands traveled, exploring, and enjoying.

God, her scent. Woman, citrus and sexual arousal, raced through his system like a shot of exotic aphrodisiac. Her skin, soft and creamy, begged to be loved.

She unbuckled his jeans, forced her hand deep, wrapped her fingers around him and squeezed. He stopped breathing. Jesus, he'd explode if he let her continue for long.

"Enough," he managed to force out.

He grabbed her thighs and hoisted her up to straddle his hips. She squealed and followed with a laugh. She locked her legs around him and spread bites and licks across his bare shoulder. With her in his arms, he couldn't get down that hall to her bedroom fast enough.

He placed her on the bed, shaking his head no when she reached for him. He wanted to pounce on her, devour her, and then bury himself deep inside her body but wouldn't. This would not be a quickie. He'd make love to her body and mind.

"Raise up, sweetheart." He stripped her jeans and panties off in one pull. Stood over her, staring down at her naked body, waiting for him. Only for him. "My God. You're incredible."

He shucked his own jeans, and his throat closed when her gaze traversed his form. Up and down. Sultry, hooded eyes stopped on his swollen erection.

A sexy grin lit her face. "So you do want me?"

"Damn right, I do." He crawled over her, nudging her thighs

apart, wedging himself against her heated flesh. How long had he wanted to do this? How many nights had he closed his eyes and prayed to dream about her? "I told you I wanted to kiss every inch of your body."

"Oh, I remember, but I questioned your truthfulness."

"Never doubt me. I have a particular spot picked out and know exactly where to start."

He kissed her, drinking in her essence. Allowed himself the time to wallow in the lushness of her breasts, touching and tonguing each one until they were pebbled peaks. Then he worked his way down. Past her sleek hips to her legs and started back up. By the time he licked her inner thigh, her body was quivering. He switched to the other side. Closer and closer to heaven.

"Nate, please." Her voice, throaty and breathless, was barely a whisper.

He parted her with his thumbs and blew softly.

"Nate!" This time her tone was more commanding, and hearing her cry out his name sent a rush straight to his heart.

That she was louder and full of frustration, prompted him to lick her damp skin in one long sweep. She dug her heels into the mattress and raised her hips. Then he feasted.

Her hands wound through his hair tightly, holding him taut against her silky smooth core. Over and over he brought her to the brink. His thumb and finger found her clit and gently squeezed, and she detonated under his tongue. Her hips rose higher from the bed, thrusting her center deeper into his mouth. She cried out his name. Again and again. The sound filled the room. Filled his soul. Filled his mind with promises of forever.

Jesus, he loved the sound of her coming.

Memories of the past, of what they'd had, of what they'd shared, of what he'd missed flooded him. Memories he'd clung to all those long nights. Memories that were now a reality.

His throat swelled. Heart hurt. And the word *mine* circulated through his mind while he kissed his way to her lips.

"I need inside you." He dug a condom from his billfold, held it to his teeth, and tried to rip it open. Damn his shaking hands.

****

Nate's body loomed above hers. Beautiful. Strong. Virile. All male. His muscles tensed, tendons stretched tight, his face the picture of determination as he fought with the condom package. Kay's pounding heart raced even harder.

"Stop. Let me." She wrapped her fingers around him and felt the power of steel underneath the velvet soft skin. She stroked her hand up and down, marveling that he grew still larger and harder under her touch. He hissed out a warning breath and groaned.

His gaze caught hers. The hunger blazing almost incinerated her. If he stared at her with such longing much longer, she'd be nothing more than a pile of ashes.

Overwhelming need had settled at the juncture of her thighs. She couldn't remember wanting anything as badly as she did Nate.

"You're headed toward disaster if you don't stop. And we're nowhere near finished." One jet-black eyebrow rose, which she figured was a warning, so she leaned over, kissed the tip of his erection and then rolled on the latex protection.

He'd uncovered something buried deep inside her. Something that relaxed the twisting and squeezing and tightening that had kept her from trusting him.

"I'll hold you to that." She needed more from him. Wanted more for him.

"At last," he whispered as he slid inside her. His words almost sounded reverent.

Kay sighed as the feeling of coming home filled her lungs, squeezing her heart. His size required some adjusting, but her body quickly molded around him. The sensation of him stretching and filling her heightened her already sensitive nerve endings.

He stayed very still, rested his weight on his elbows, his gaze locked with hers. She tilted her hips and wrapped her legs around his waist, taking him deeper.

"Yes. At last." Her eyes fluttered closed as he moved inside her. She met him thrust for thrust, move for move, until she couldn't tell where she ended and he began.

He rose up on his knees and lifted her legs over his shoulders, exposing her in the most vulnerable of ways. His hand slid between their bodies. His magic fingers found her clit.

"Look at me. Say my name again." He almost withdrew until she locked her gaze on his.

"Nate," she whispered. "Don't stop." She lifted her hips to encourage him.

Sounds wrapped around her. Sounds of pleasure. Sounds of two bodies moving together. Sounds of two lovers about to shatter into a million pieces of light.

Every nerve ending fired, directing all pleasure sensation to her core. She wanted the feeling to last forever even while an orgasm roared from deep down in her soul. Climbing to the top of the roller coaster and then racing down the tracks only to rise to the pinnacle again and again. She abandoned all reason. Soared through the clouds.

"Nate!"

His back bowed and ecstasy etched his beautiful face. He pulsed inside her and then collapsed on top of her.

Kay brushed his long hair off his face. Wove the silky threads through her fingers. Covered with a layer of sweat and gasping for breath, she held tightly when he rolled to the side, taking her with him.

He pushed up on his elbow, leaned over, and claimed her mouth. Just as he'd claimed her body. Just as he'd claimed her heart.

"My God." His smile chipped away another piece of the protective wall. "I can't get enough of you."

Nate's gaze glided almost casually down her naked body. Kay considered herself a modest woman, but with Nate, she had no such inhibitions. He whispered she was beautiful again and again. She had to strain to hear his words.

She refused to question if they'd been wrong to make love. She wouldn't think about the answer. There was only today. Right here. Right now. Right this minute.

Even though she willed the outside world away, reality was never far from her mind. Marcus would arrive soon, and while she certainly wasn't ashamed of making love with Nate, it was an intimacy she didn't care to share.

"We should shower and dress."

"Naw." He protested by circling her nipple with his finger.

"Marcus will be here—"

"Oh shit." Nate all but sprang off the bed. "That fine-looking body ..." he swept an open palm through the air in her direction, "is for my eyes only. You shower first."

She raced past him with her arms full of clothing and the always present throwaway phone in her hand. She yelped when he swatted her bare bottom.

Standing under the warm water, while her body still tingled from their lovemaking, reality crept in. Her chest ached as if a strong north wind swirled around her heart, tightening and chilling. Reminding her this situation with Nate was temporary.

When Holly was home and Hank behind bars, Nate's job would be finished. And he'd move onto something more dangerous. She couldn't compete with the excitement of some threat in a foreign country.

The pain in her chest hit with such a force, she braced her hands against the shower wall for support. Deep breaths and determination helped her pull her thoughts together.

She wouldn't cling when the time came for him to go, and she'd tell him that. She was okay with his mysterious missions and danger. She expected it. Hell, welcomed it. With her resolve in place, she dried off, dressed, and went to tell him.

Nate's voice drifted to her ears. "If the Colombian op can wait, I'm interested. I can't take the job right now. I'm committed to this case I'm working on."

She paused in the hall, eavesdropping on a phone call and not feeling one bit guilty. She'd missed the first part of the conversation, but she'd heard enough to figure out Nate's FBI contact needed him for a mission. Good Lord. Colombia? Had she heard yearning in Nate's tone? If not for his commitment to saving Holly, Kay had no doubt he'd be gone tomorrow. A little piece of her heart broke off.

She rolled her shoulders to loosen the tension and joined him in the kitchen, just as he ended the call. Kay breathed out a sigh. He'd tell her about his next mission, and she'd let him know she understood. The time was right to clear the air.

He looked up and hit her with a smile. "Marcus isn't coming here. He's headed home."

Too stunned to speak, she nodded. Was he really keeping his phone conversation, or the fact he'd be leaving as soon as Holly was home, a secret? How had she been so stupid as to think he'd actually discuss his plans with her? She reminded herself he hadn't contacted her when he first got back.

He had an awkwardness in his tone as he rambled on about Marcus.

"We need to talk." She backed away when he started toward her. Her skin sizzled from embarrassment. "Seriously."

That stopped him. "Shoot."

"About what just happened between us." She tried to swallow, but the knot in her throat prevented her from continuing. His gaze swept across her, lust painting his incredible face.

"I believe it's called sex, not 'what happened.' And since Marcus won't be here anytime soon, I'm thinking we should go back to bed."

Flames licked through her blood, sending a coil of need straight to her lower stomach and putting her breasts on full alert.

"First, we need ground rules."

Both his eyebrows went up. "I followed orders while I was in the military. I'm not good at it anymore." He advanced a couple of steps.

"Well, we need to be clear. The sex was great. Wonderful. But that's all it was. Sex. When this is over and Holly's safe, we go back to our old lives. Parting as friends."

His eyes were unreadable. Void of all emotion. He hadn't loved her enough to stay ten years ago, and she didn't believe he did today.

His chest rose and fell with an audible breath. "That's the way you want it? No strings?"

"No strings."

He nodded once before turning and heading to the fridge. "No problem. Want a beer?"

His blasé attitude and cold words told her he was fine with no emotional attachment.

Chapter Twenty One

Determined not to forget Mr. A's directions, Johnny held the phone to his ear with his shoulder and wrote down every word. Later, he'd commit them to memory and then shed the document. That the cabin was a couple hours outside Dallas and not on the map was good news, but transporting Holly across the state line was dangerous. The feds were already in Texas looking into the missing girls and, if he got caught, his trial would be in federal court. It was no secret their prison sentences were much harsher.

"You sure nobody will be around?" Johnny rarely questioned the boss, but this was too important to leave to chance.

"The place hasn't been used in years." He snorted a sound of disgust. "Maybe I'll take you hunting someday ..."

His voice trailed off, and Johnny waited a second, knowing not to pry. As far as he knew, the boss wasn't close to anyone and had probably thought better at being too friendly.

"And the front-end loader?"

"In a small barn. And in perfect working condition." The boss blew out a breath. "I'll call Hank with instructions."

"Keep him away from me. I've got enough problems."

"I understand. However, I'm sending him to the cabin first thing in the morning. He'll come in handy if you're right and the Taylor woman brings her entourage."

"Don't need him. I like working alone."

"Out of the question," Mr. A snapped. "This is his mess, and he can help clean it up."

"Yes, sir," Johnny fired back, wishing he'd reined in his temper before speaking. His tone of voice had pushed him over the boundary of acceptable behavior. "Sorry."

"How long since you slept?"

"Awhile. I don't need much."

"When this is over, there's a considerable bonus waiting for you. Take that girlfriend off somewhere, lie on the beach for a few days. That's an order."

Johnny shuddered. She was a clerk in the Dallas police chief's office, and he had no intentions of spending time with that bitch. This afternoon, she'd shared how the FBI investigation on human trafficking had uncovered one of the boss's competitors. Other than that, she'd provided nothing of value.

"Yes, sir." Johnny dropped the phone's receiver in its cradle, rubbed his throbbing temple, and thought over the directions to the hunting cabin.

He didn't trust Hank. Would rather he had been kept in the dark. If this plan leaked, the feds would hit Oklahoma like a swarm of killer bees. Nobody in their right mind fucked with them.

Not knowing the lay of the land spelled disaster. Johnny needed a couple of exits in case something went wrong. Reconnaissance wasn't a luxury. It was a prerequisite. No way was he waiting until morning. He knew how to map the spread in the dark.

Wondering how he knew to do that started his head hurting.

After the sun went down, he moved his car behind the building and parked close to the door. He opened the trunk before he went inside after Holly. Steeling his emotions, he refused to consider the trauma he was about to cause her.

He unlocked the door and stepped inside. "Get up." He threw her a set of scrubs he'd picked up earlier at a secondhand store. "Put those on."

Her small hands shook as she reached across the cot and snatched both pieces into her arms like a hungry beggar grabbing at food. She hugged the closest thing she'd had to clothes in days to her chest. Her mouth worked, but no sound came.

"You want me to dress you?"

Through trembling lips came, "No. I want you to turn your back."

He amazed himself when he did as she asked. He had nothing to lose by giving her a moment of control. No way could she overpower him.

The rustle of cotton sent images of her naked, diminutive frame.

"I'm ready," she said on a whisper.

"Walk left down the hall and then out the door." He grabbed her elbow when she wobbled. It didn't surprise him that she was weak-kneed. She'd picked at the food he'd brought her, refusing to eat. She stepped outside, paused, and shook her head.

"No. I won't. You can't make me get in the trunk." She grabbed a fistful of his shirt. "Kill me here."

She seemed to grow two inches as she straightened her shoulders. Her gaze was full of hate, and he felt it clear to his soles. Her words dripped with venom. Her face was beaten and bruised, but determination filled her eyes.

Damn, he liked her bravado. But it wasn't enough to dissuade him. He didn't have to like his job, but he did have to follow orders.

"I removed the emergency release, so don't think you can pull it and save yourself."

She struggled when he tied her hands behind her back. Stiffened her entire body as if she were an ice cube, forcing him to pick her up and make her bend her legs. Shit, putting her in the trunk was a precaution he had to take. She pushed against him so he held her close. Holding her against him flooded him with warmth. Sent all the wrong messages to his brain.

"Let me ride up front with you," she pleaded. "I'll cooperate."

"No," he said. She kicked her feet out at him, making him jump back. He grasped her by the ankles, shoved her legs down, and closed the trunk lid. Good job, hero. You stuffed a hundred-pound woman in the back of your car. While he'd tried not to hurt her, he'd scared the shit out of her.

When he crossed the border, he fished the cell from his pocket. The Taylor woman answered on the first ring.

"Be in Madill, Oklahoma, at nine tomorrow morning. Park outside the Dairy Dream and wait for my call."

He disconnected. Had no desire to argue with her. Nor did he intend to waste his breath by telling her to come alone. He had no doubt she would bring help. He could only hope she'd kept their secret from the law.

Holly hadn't once stopped kicking or screaming since he'd

closed the trunk lid. Enough. He drove onto a dark side road and parked.

The smell of sweat slammed into him the second he popped the trunk. He shined a flashlight across her face. Wild blue eyes full of anger met his. Something inside him broke.

"Now what? You going to kill me or did you grow a heart?"

****

"Kaycie." Nate spoke sternly to talk her down. She'd erupted in a string of curse words, fury exploding from her after the phone call with instructions on where to wait in Oklahoma. "If you want, I'll call my FBI contact and fill him in on what's going down. Dalton will see to it we have backup."

"No. We have to do this." She leveled her gaze on him. "Between you, Tyrell and Marcus, I'll be protected. What you three do to those rat bastards after Holly's safe ... well, I don't care and don't want to know."

Nate's antennae went up. Did she realize she'd given him the go-ahead to kill Hank and the scumbag working for him? The law frowned on outright murder. Of course, if a person acted in self defense ...

"The shit will get deep when the law learns we've withheld important information. We have to accept that fact. All four of us could face charges. Your association with DPD could be damaged beyond repair."

She glanced at the door as if willing Tyrell or Marcus to arrive. "This won't get your license revoked. Will it?"

"That's a nonissue." He went to her, unable to keep his hands off her. He cupped her face in his hands. "If it does, so be it."

"Thank you." She rose up on her toes and kissed him.

"Marcus will be here first." Nate reached for her, but she moved away. "Tyrell is borrowing earbuds from his bodyguard job. We'll be in contact at all times."

He couldn't speak the words, wouldn't tell her this whole deal scared the shit out of him. The idea of her being out front on this rescue was eating him alive. Her life would be on the line, and if he couldn't get to her in time...

The heat from her body skewed his thinking. He moved to the

living room to help his focus.

"Nate?"

Her voice fell like velvet from behind, sliding across his skin. He shouldn't hold her. Knew not to. But he whirled and dragged her against him, hard. Held her tight. Breathed in her recently showered scent. Grapefruits or lemons swirled around her freshly washed hair.

"I have an idea," he said, taking one more breath. "Marcus might be able to help."

"What's that?" Her face rested on his shoulder, and her palm circled the spot over his heart.

While Nate explained his idea, he ran his hands up and down her back, across her arms, her gorgeous face. If she really meant their relationship was temporary, he'd have to honor her decision. So he memorized every crest and valley. How unmilitary was that?

"You really think Marcus can get his hands on an eighteen-wheeler?" She kissed the vein in his neck, and his pulse thumped harder under her lips.

"Be the perfect vantage point to watch that Dairy Dream and keep an eye on you." He thought a minute. "The container has to have a ramp. Loading and unloading a car or my bike would be a snap."

He tipped her chin up and stared down into her deep-brown eyes. "I don't like you being in the middle. Not one damn bit."

"Me either. But we didn't get to choose."

A knock on the door pulled her away from him.

She peered through the peephole. "Tomas and Wayne."

"What the hell do they want?" Nate scooped the laptop and throwaway cell off the kitchen table and carried them to her bedroom. A second knock came as he jogged back to Kaycie. "You have to get rid of them."

"I know. We'll let them think they interrupted a private moment."

She reached over and removed the leather thong he used to keep his hair back, the same hair he intended to have cut after this was over, and jerked his shirt over his head.

He reciprocated by unbuttoning the top two buttons on her blouse and mussing her wavy mane.

Arm in arm, they opened the door. Tomas and Wayne exchanged glances. Their gaze shifted from Kaycie to Nate.

"We need to talk," Tomas growled, pushing his way inside.

Chapter Twenty Two

Every nerve in Nate's body went on alert. Cop or not, nobody barged into Kaycie's apartment, and they damn sure didn't boss her around.

"You better have a warrant in your pocket. Else you can bully your way right back out that door." His hands flexed of their own accord, itching to pound the arrogant bastard.

"Wait." Kaycie stepped in front of Nate. "Have you learned something? Anything?"

"Nothing to help us locate your friend." The cop named Wayne spoke directly to Kaycie. "And if you keep interfering, we may never find her."

Nate dug back in his memory bank to fish out the guy's official title. "Detective Kern, isn't it?"

Nate shook the extended hand. He ignored Tomas altogether. "Exactly what brings you out this late in the day?"

"You can blame my partner's curious nature." Wayne's words came out slow and casual. He turned, facing Kaycie. "Why were you nosing around the Walsh warehouses today?"

"Since when is it illegal to look?"

"You keep poking around, you're likely to hit a sore spot and get hurt," Tomas said directly to Kaycie.

"Not on my watch," Nate countered, pulling her closer to him.

She wrapped her arm around his waist. "We were hunting for the white van or the black Mercedes. If you two remember, I told you I wanted to find the warehouse where I'd been held."

"And what did you learn?" Wayne asked.

"You first," she countered, sending a sense of pride swelling in Nate's chest.

"Working with the FBI, we've uncovered a human-trafficking ring. But we couldn't connect Hank Walsh to the organization." His hand went up to silence any possible interruptions. "That doesn't mean we're discounting your theory."

"What about Holly?" Kaycie asked.

"The crime scene team found nothing. We have zilch." Wayne's eyes narrowed. "Her parents are on alert to ransom demands. But living out of state and not having any wealth to speak of, they don't expect to be contacted. Have you heard anything?"

Kaycie looked Wayne in the eye. "Nope. That's why I still have my protection."

Tomas scoffed, his gaze scraping across Nate, no doubt noting his bare chest and messy hair. "Exactly what is he protecting?" he asked, nodding at Nate.

"You have something you want to say?" Nate moved a step closer to Tomas, and Kaycie stepped between them.

Wayne cleared his throat. "We're leaving." He locked his gaze on Kaycie once more. "You're sure there's not something you want to tell us?"

"I'm sure." Her back was straight and she held her head high as she opened the door and waited.

Nate wanted nothing more than to reach for her when they were alone again. He stopped himself. She'd spoken directly to Tomas and identified Nate as her protection. And she'd intervened damn fast. Which man was she protecting?

A question slapped him across the face. Was he an old itch she was scratching? Getting him out of her system before returning to her regular life? Maybe she really did want temporary.

He pushed their tattered relationship out of his mind and called Marcus. Nate hated to wake Marcus after only a few minutes of rest, but had to update him on the phone call and upcoming meeting in Oklahoma. Then Nate asked about access to a big rig that included a loading ramp.

"I have a friend who came off the road last night. He'll let me drive it, but he's not putting his livelihood on the line for free."

Nate moved down the hall out of Kaycie's earshot. "I'll cover the charge. We have to be able to get a car and my bike in and out with ease."

"Fuck, man, this is really going down." Marcus sounded more

enthusiastic than he had in days. He'd gone from sounding sleepy and groggy to full-on Army badass. "When do we need it?"

"Kaycie has to be outside the Dairy Dream in Madill by nine in the morning."

"Don't make it too easy on me." Marcus chuckled. "If I'm going to pull an eighteen-wheeler out of my ass, I'd better get busy."

"How does meeting right outside Tyrell's apartment sound? At oh-three-hundred. You can park on the shoulder and drop the ramp."

"That'll work."

"I'll ride with Kaycie until outside Madill. Then I'll join you and Tyrell. We'll go into town first, and the truck can break down. Shit ..." Nate closed his eyes for a second. No doubt the bastard Kaycie was meeting would be there early, too. "Won't work. Three men our size in the cab would be too obvious."

"Naw. This rig has sleeping quarters. One of you can crawl back there. I'm driving."

"Tyrell will fit just fine."

Nate walked back to the living room, parked in the monster easy chair, and made the second call. Tyrell answered on the first ring. Tyrell was about to turn rabid. Waiting had never been either one of their strong suits. The decision to end the surveillance on Hank was hard, but if the shit got nasty, having Tyrell or Marcus to help cover Kaycie was a smart thing.

Nate hit end and then dropped his cell on the table. He scrubbed his hands over his face, battling exhaustion. He and Kaycie needed sleep. Rest upped the odds on their side.

She wrapped her arms around her waist and rocked, her eyelids drooping. Worry lines bracketed her mouth. He just might kill the motherfucker who'd caused her this anguish and despair.

"Go to bed." The words "before I pull you into my arms" clung to the tip of his tongue unspoken.

"Is that an invitation?" she asked.

"No. You need rest." He finished the beer he'd opened earlier. He could tell by the determination on her face, she was building toward arguing that she couldn't sleep. "Count sheep. Do whatever relaxation techniques you can to slow down your brain. You have to be sharper than any of us tomorrow. Go."

She'd made it plain he was only passing through. If that's the way she wanted things, temporary would be over tomorrow.

"What about you? You laying down with me?"

"I don't think that's a good idea. I'll grab a shower and stretch out on the couch." He didn't wait for a response. Another round of temporary with her and he'd be screwed. He grabbed his bag from her room and hit the shower

****

"Stop staring at me." Even in the dark, Holly's eyes on Johnny's face warmed his skin. Her voice poured over him like a blanket, soft and warm.

Why he'd given into her pitiful cries was a mystery. He didn't like puzzles. He had too many of them in his life already.

"You're not a bad person, Johnny. I know that in my heart."

The pain over his right ear seemed to ease at the sound of her voice. "You know nothing. Shut up, or I'll toss you back in the trunk."

A soft whimper drifted across the open space between them. "Please don't."

"You haven't eaten since lunch. I can't trust you in a drive-thru. If you get hungry ..."

"No food," she said quickly. "Really. I'm fine. Can you tell me where we're going?"

He saw no reason to keep their destination a secret. She was never leaving the property anyway.

"The boss has an isolated cabin. Sounds like a good place to make the swap. I want to get there early enough to do reconnaissance. I need an alternate way out in case things go bad."

"That's a military term, isn't it? Recon. What branch were you in?"

Was he in the military? Hell if he knew. He ran his hand over his chin and concentrated. Nope. Nothing.

"Johnny?" She spoke so softly he almost didn't hear.

A small cold hand gripped his bicep, startling him and causing him to jerk out of her grasp. The noise she made didn't sound human. Shit, he'd scared her again.

"Sorry, you surprised me." He hoped she'd say his name again. She didn't. "Did you want something?"

"What happened to you?"

"Don't know what you're talking about." The pain over his ear heightened.

"People don't get up one morning and decide they're capable of killing on command. Do they? Why else would you be involved in this?"

"I'm good at what I do. Orders are easy for me to follow."

"So if I order you to stop the car and let me out, you'd do it?"

"It's not quite that simple." He allowed a smile to creep up his cheeks. He huffed out a breath. No reason she shouldn't know his story. It wasn't like she'd ever tell anyone.

"Help me understand," she persisted.

"When Mr. A found me, I was living under a bridge, filthy, and starving. He gave me a job. Gave me the clothes on my back. Hell, he gave me my name."

"You didn't know who you were?"

"Correction. I don't know who I am."

****

Kaycie's couch wasn't all that uncomfortable, but Nate had been up and down. His brain refused to shut down. Too bad this wasn't the military, where you rescued the hostage, killed your enemy, and never looked back.

Kaycie kept creeping into his thoughts. He moved to the oversized chair, hit the lever, stretched out, and forced his eyes to close. He ran the different options, including one where he asked her for a second chance, through his head. She didn't trust him, and he wasn't sure how to restore her faith.

The hair on his arms rose. Without moving, he opened his eyes to confirm what he already knew. Kaycie had entered the room. A full moon streamed through the bank of windows, casting an ethereal light over her. His throat closed. His chest hurt. Jesus, she was beautiful.

He wanted to feel her skin pressed against his. Needed to bury himself inside her and give her pleasure.

His heart thumped a staccato rhythm against his rib cage. Even though she was on the other side of the room, he hardened and throbbed inside his Jockeys. He remained silent, barely breathing. She passed the empty couch, headed straight toward the chair.

In one motion, her T-shirt went flying. A second had her panties sliding down her hips to the floor. Had he fallen asleep and this was a dream? He prayed not to wake.

No dream. His muscles contracted as her slim, warm, naked body climbed on top of his, enveloping him with a warm and velvety sensuality. He breathed in. Images of clean, fresh sea air crashed his senses.

She settled one knee on either side of his hips and lowered herself over his erection, swiveling until he rested in the juncture between her thighs. Nothing separated them save for his cotton skivvies.

She leaned down. Her warm breath brushed across his cheek seconds before she captured his lips. Her tongue swept inside his mouth, stroking and stoking the fire building.

His hands traced her back muscles and down to her heart-shaped bottom. Smoothing and memorizing before he reached around to cup her luscious breasts. She lifted her head and shoulders, positioning a nipple over his mouth.

Eager to taste, he pulled her in and rolled his tongue around the tip. Her back bowed, forcing herself deeper.

He slid his hand between her thighs and found her hot and wet. "You're awesome."

He slipped a finger inside her moist heat, his heart folding like a piece of paper when she mewed like a kitten. Her legs spread, giving him better access as she pressed down on his hand. Her muscles tightened, and he recognized the signs. She needed release, and he'd give it to her.

"No," she gasped, jerking her hips away from him. "Inside me. I need you to love me. Now."

Need controlled him. Shut out all worries. There was nothing in his life but the woman whose eyes begged him to make love to her. Damn underwear. Off they came, and before he could recover, she'd taken him inside her body.

"Yes," she whispered, sliding down his full length. Her satin flesh gripped him, tugged him deeper.

He'd never been inside of her body without a condom separating them. The sensation almost made him come on the spot. He clamped his hands over her hips to stop her, but she bucked out of his grip, pressed down, moving back and forth.

"Oh, God. Sweetheart. You feel incredible." He lifted his hips to meet hers, reveling in the skin-against-skin sensation, wishing he could stay buried in her forever. "Stop. Condom."

"No," she cried out. "Don't stop." She swiveled her hips, sparking wild charges through his groin. "I want to feel you. You and me."

Her delicious breast brushed against his lips. She raised her body slightly then drove herself down, grinding against him. He knew better than to continue but couldn't deny her. Couldn't deny himself. Couldn't pull out. She dropped her hands to his chest, braced herself, and rode him hard. Pushed him to the brink. Struggling to keep from losing control, he hung on with every molecule of determination he could muster.

"Let go, Kaycie. Look at me and let go."

She cried out, moving faster, driving harder. She detonated around him. Her tight inner muscles contracted. Unable to resist the vice-like grip, he erupted in a series of explosions. She collapsed on him, their bodies damp with sweat.

He shifted to his side, pulling her close to him in the big chair. He stroked her cheek, moved her disheveled hair off her face, and kissed her forehead.

"Sleep now." He held her in the quiet of the night, loving the sated expression on her face. Well, not loving. Right? He liked the sated expression on her face.

"Nate?" Her tone sounded sleepy and thick. "I'm on the pill, if that's worrying you."

He swallowed. Hard. "I'm not. Doesn't matter. If you got pregnant, I'd be there with you every step of the way. I'd be a good dad." And he would. A child with her didn't scare him like it had ten years ago, and that surprised the shit out of him.

She rose up on her elbow and opened her mouth. Oops. He'd said too much.

"Shh." He silenced her by resting his finger against her lips. Then he added, "Now's not the time."

Chapter Twenty Three

"You can't go with me, and I can't leave you here free to wander off." Johnny bit the words out, refusing to allow Holly to plead against being handcuffed to the bed.

"Johnny," she said softly. His skin burned when she gripped his arm. "Where would I go? What would I find if I ran into the woods? Acres of trees, underbrush, and God knows what."

Why did she argue? The sparsely furnished one-room cabin had a bed, a table with two chairs, and a couch. A hot plate, motel-sized coffeepot, and small apartment refrigerator lined one wall. It was handcuff her to either the rusty metal headboard or the bathroom plumbing.

"Ever heard of Stockholm syndrome?"

She jerked her hand from his bicep as if she'd been electrocuted. Stepping back, her blue eyes reflected shock. "You think I'm falling in love with you?"

"It crossed my mind."

"Well," she huffed, "you did save me from that dickhead, Hank. But rest assured, I don't love you. I do however, think you need help."

"And you can get it for me. Right? A prison cell with a top-notch shrink to make me all better? Get real." His temple throbbed, and he wanted to pound the side of his head until it stopped. Instead, he grabbed her wrist and led her to the far wall of the small cabin. "Sit," he commanded. She meekly complied, not uttering a sound while he secured her to the rail on the headboard.

"I don't believe you'll kill me."

He turned his back to her, needed to walk away. "Today."

"You can't."

Just like turning off the radio, he tuned her out.

The size of the isolated deer-hunter's cabin allowed him to get outside with a minimum of strides. He breathed the fresh air in the pitch-black darkness.

His headache progressively got worse, and disappointment filled his gut. He'd been wrong. The pain didn't lessen when he was around her. How fucking stupid he was to have ever believed such an idiotic idea.

Shitty luck. Not a star or sliver of moon was out to illuminate the area. Good thing he'd brought two flashlights.

The cabin sat at the back of the property a couple miles off the nearest dirt road. The lean-to the boss called a barn barely provided shelter for the tractor. If it didn't start, Hank could hand-dig the graves. The idea of killing Holly turned his stomach over.

Maybe he'd add Hank's body to the count. Accidents happened.

Johnny moved further away from the cabin. The heavy tree line behind the house offered good coverage. It helped him but also provided protection to whomever the Taylor woman brought with her. And she was too smart to come alone. The trick would be losing her hired gun.

An alternative exit still had to be identified, and Johnny would scout again at dawn, but daylight was still a few hours away.

Damn Holly and her offer to get him help. Was he supposed to believe she wouldn't cut his throat if given the chance? Nobody took care of him. To survive, he'd take care of himself.

He didn't need her or anyone else.

****

Wrapped around Nate's warm body, Kay rested her cheek on his bare chest. She'd never understood why she bought such a big recliner. Now she silently thanked the sales clerk who'd talked her into purchasing the space hog.

Nate's heartbeat was slow and steady, beautiful music in her ear. Could've been angels singing, and the gentle rhythm gave her great pleasure. These few precious hours could be her last with him. Her heart clutched, tempting her to wrap her arms around her rib cage. The pain of losing him a second time would be much worse than the first.

The chair creaked, and his lips brushed the top of her head.

"You think too much. Go to sleep. Even an hour will help."

"Hmm," she said on a sigh. Cuddling closer, she rested her leg across his body. "Hmm," she repeated with more enthusiasm. "Somebody's not too sleepy."

His chuckle vibrated under her cheek. "Somebody can't get enough of you. I get hard when you walk in the room. Don't expect less when your naked body is draped across mine."

"You talk prettier than you did ten years ago."

"I was a stupid, scared-shitless kid. And I behaved like one."

"Stupid? Maybe. But you've never been afraid of anything." She lowered her hand, trailed down the narrow line of soft hair that led to his silky erection.

"I was afraid of you. Of marriage, kids, responsibility. Afraid I'd be thinking about you and walk into a trap. Or worse, lead my men to their deaths. Afraid I'd let you and my country down."

Relief washed over her, warming her soul. He might be leaving soon, but once upon a time, he'd loved her.

"I didn't know." She turned her head to kiss his chest. "I was caught up in what I wanted and didn't realize you were struggling too."

His hips lifted, brushing his erection against her fingers. She understood. He was through talking about the ten-year-old subject.

So she slid all the way on top, reached to the side of the chair and pulled the lever, sitting him up. In one motion, she dropped from the recliner, knelt between his legs, and took him in her mouth.

"Oh. Jesus. I really did die and go to heaven." His hands wound through her hair.

His words inspired her. Regardless of what tomorrow brought, she'd make sure he never forgot tonight.

****

Nate preferred to stay in bed. His fingers stroked Kaycie's hair, which was currently spread across his chest. She'd given him a special gift last night. Her mouth had almost driven him out of his mind.

Afterward, he'd promptly scooped her into his arms and carried her to bed.

He wasn't a saint. He'd had his share of sex over the years. But the woman in his arms brought out a need in him that burned its way to the very core of his soul. At times, he was sure his life's breath depended on being inside her body.

She'd fallen into a deep sleep. With her at peace, he'd closed his eyes for a few minutes. An hour's rest was plenty for him, but she'd need more than caffeine to keep going.

With a quick kiss to her forehead, he reluctantly eased her head onto a pillow. His feet hit the floor, and her hand brushed across his back, stopping him. Damn. He'd disturbed her.

"Time to go?" she asked, her voice soft and drowsy.

"Soon. I'll fix coffee. Madill's over a two-hour drive, and we have to get my bike first. Then I'll follow you to Tyrell's."

"I'm up." She rose and stretched her arms over her head.

"There's time for you to rest a while longer."

"Coffee sounds good." She slipped on a T-shirt and tossed him a smile as she strolled from the room.

Pride swelled inside his chest. She had more guts and stamina than a few of the men he'd gone into battle with. He respected her strength and devotion to her friends. Loved her for the woman she'd become.

No. Not love. She'd made it clear he was supposed to go away when this was over. Falling in love with her would be as smart as intentionally stepping on a land mine.

Nate hit the shower, stepping out to meet her coming in. "Need your back washed?" he asked, knowing that's all they had time for. Her laughter started his dick thinking otherwise. He wrapped the towel around his hips, but not in time for his erection to go unnoticed.

"Hold that thought for ..." Her gaze shifted to stare at the floor.

'Nuff said and without additional words. Her unfinished sentence reminded him today was the end of the line. As soon as Holly was safe, this case was over and his employment would end.

And didn't that take care of the tented towel?

"I'll get out of your way." He didn't take her extended hand. Time to move on.

****

Damn him. Kay bit back the urge to grab his broad shoulders and shake him. Him going to Colombia wasn't her fault. She wasn't the addicted-to-adrenaline junkie. Hell, he'd already lined up another job. The more treacherous, the better.

A shower soothed her sore muscles but did nothing for the ache in her chest. Her body hummed with need. His nearness brought out a side of her she hated to lose. This feeling of being wanted, of being alive. No one had ever filled the void he'd left. No one ever would.

Enough. She toweled off, dressed, pulled her damp hair into a ponytail, and headed for the kitchen ready to fight.

What she got was a cup of coffee and an omelet, which they split, while he talked her through the plan one more time. All military, all business. She wanted to smooth away the furrow between his brows. Didn't trust herself to touch him.

The plan was based on the assumption the kidnapper would force Kay to go with him. The eggs in her stomach flooded the back of her throat at the idea of getting into the car with the bastard. Her skin dampened with sweat and then chilled. To still her hands, she wrapped them around the warm mug. She could do this. Would do this.

"Tyrell borrowed equipment because it's imperative we stay in constant communication with you. Most earbuds are small enough not to be seen. If it's noticeable, you may have to leave your hair down to cover your ear. We'll be able to hear what you say and follow using the phone app. The laptop will be in the cab of the rig. At no point will you be off the grid."

"It won't matter if he decides to shoot me or Holly. Nobody can protect us from a bullet." She tried to mask the worry in her voice.

His eyes closed, jaw twitched, and the nerves in his face tightened. "I hate this plan. Let's go back to my original idea. Let me take the ring to the bastard."

"It won't work. I was just letting my nerves do the talking." She covered his hand with hers, relaxing just a smidge when he encased her cold fingers between two warm palms.

"We can call this off with one word from you."

Kay drained her cup and stood. "Can't. Let's go meet the rest of Wolfe's Pack."

She didn't get the laugh she wanted. Instead, she settled for a grunt of acknowledgment at the use of the old nickname.

Nate rinsed their dishes, dropping them in the dishwasher. "Ready?"

Somehow, he'd separated himself from her already. In warrior mode, his posture was rigid. Eyes a blank slate, void of emotions. Lips closed in a straight line.

She followed his lead.

Now wasn't the time for self-pity.

She clipped on her holster, slid the Glock home, and then slipped into a long-tailed shirt to stay within Texas law. Her fingers slid between her jeans and the holster, checking to ensure the small tracking device was still attached. Satisfied, she stuffed the throwaway cell in her pocket and then picked up her purse. A second tracer was located in a small zipper compartment. A backup in case the first one was discovered.

A deep breath. A short prayer for Holly, and Kay was ready.

Chapter Twenty Four

Between Marcus's complete silence and Tyrell's war-zone posture, Nate was ready to kick both their asses. He got it. They were all ready to take this bastard down.

Along with the extra pistol and clips he'd brought, and with what Marcus and Tyrell were packing, they had enough firepower to take out the population of Madill.

They'd stopped the eighteen-wheeler and let Tyrell unload his pickup. Then Marcus had driven the rig into town and parked on a main thoroughfare a half-block away from the Dairy Dream. Nate popped the hood to give the appearance of a breakdown, which allowed Tyrell to arrive a few minutes later without raising suspicion.

Soon Tyrell and Nate hung over the engine, pretending to discuss the problem. Hiding his eyes behind dark sunglasses allowed Nate to visually sweep the area unnoticed.

There were no cars in the ice cream joint's parking lot when Kaycie drove down the street, pulled in and parked.

Adrenaline flooded Nate and every cell in his system went on high alert.

"So far so good," she said. The tremor in her voice sent flashes of concern through him. Were they asking too much of her?

"We're here, sweetheart. I can almost touch you." Every muscle in his body tightened while his brain screamed he was crazy to place her life in jeopardy.

Hell, he thrived on danger, but not when Kaycie's wellbeing was concerned. Nate wanted to wrap his arms around her, to form a cocoon to protect her against harm. He considered aborting the mission, taking her place, and telling the kidnapper *tough shit* if he didn't like the swap.

The blood in Nate's veins turned to ice at the sight of a black

Mercedes with tinted windows moving slowly toward the Dairy Dream.

Tyrell's muffled string of curses said he'd spotted the car too. "Showtime, Kaycie. Whatever happens, don't look at us."

He assumed her way of confirming she'd heard was the cough that tore through his eardrum.

The Mercedes slid into the spot next to her. Nate tried but couldn't get a visual on the driver behind its dark windows.

A phone rang, and he watched as she held the throwaway to her left ear.

"I'm where you said to be. Where's Holly?"

"You bring the ring?" Choppy words came through the earbuds loud and clear, sending a shiver of relief through Nate. Hearing the conversation was critical but worsened the urge to go drag the bastard out of his car and beat his head on the pavement.

"Yes." She held it up. "I need to see Holly."

"You don't give orders. You follow them. Now slowly remove your pistol, show it to me and then set it on the passenger's-side floor mat."

The clank on the glass indicated she'd smacked the Glock against her window pretty hard. Her anger comforted Nate. Let her get mad. She'd keep the asshole talking.

"Done. Now give me Holly."

"Where's the ring?"

"In my pocket."

Nate kept an eye on Kaycie. At the same time, he pointed at the engine, pretending to discuss the problem of the eighteen-wheeler.

He asked Tyrell and Marcus, "Can you guys tell if there's anyone else in the Mercedes?"

"Windows are too dark," Tyrell answered.

"Nothing from here." Marcus set a clipboard down inside the back of the trailer and then lowered the ramp.

"He's awful sure of himself." Nate's anger worsened. His hands balled into fists. His palms itched, and that always meant trouble.

"Come get in my car," the jerk ordered Kaycie.

Again, the kidnapper's voice resonated with Nate. This bastard's tone was chilling, monotone, making the hair on the back of Nate's neck stand.

Kaycie stepped out of her Camaro and swung her handbag over her shoulder. Nate was constantly impressed with her ability to keep the stress from showing on her face.

"Leave the purse," the voice on the phone instructed. "And hurry it up. I'm not waiting around for the cops."

"I didn't call the police."

"But your friends are close by. So move your ass."

Still holding the throwaway to her ear, Kaycie complied. The calm look on her face did nothing to ease the tension between Nate's eyes.

Killing this bastard would be a pleasure.

"Shit, there went one tracer," Tyrell complained.

Kaycie opened the passenger-side door of the black car and was jerked inside, sending Nate's heart plummeting. Her audible gasp hit him like a spear to the heart.

"Oh my God!" she cried out. "Jake?"

"What the fuck did she say?" Marcus ran to the front of the truck. His eyes were wild.

"Name's not Jake," the man said.

"We thought you were dead." Her voice was at least two octaves higher than normal.

"You don't know me," the man insisted.

"Why are you lying?"

"Holy fuck. This is crazy." Nate jumped from the rig to the ground. "Abort. Abort. Kaycie jump out." He had no idea what the hell she was trying to say by calling the guy their dead friend's name. Something wasn't right and now wasn't the time to analyze.

Whatever she was trying to tell them, her driving off with him was not an option anymore. Nate hit the ground running.

"Take him down," he commanded, as he bolted across the quiet street.

Seconds. That's all he needed to get to her. The distance between him and the car closed quickly. Nate's legs pumped, his heart hammered, seemed to count the steps left between him and the woman he loved.

He'd put a bullet in the driver if he could get a shot.

Nate swore when the Mercedes revved the engine and then shot forward with the passenger's-side door still open. He caught a glimpse of Kaycie grabbing for the seat belt as the heavy metal door slammed shut. The car sped straight at him, missing by inches, but only because he vaulted out of its way.

"Son of a bitch." Off balance, he tucked and rolled across the pavement. He regained his footing, spun, and ran to the back of the rig. Tyrell and Marcus were already unloading the bike.

Thank God, the second tracer was on her holster.

My fault. The two words pounded in his head to the rhythm of his heartbeat. He should've insisted she tell her DPD friends Tomas and Wayne. Jesus. Guilt swarmed Nate. If something happened to her, he'd never forgive himself.

"I know you!" she exclaimed. "Where have you been, and why did they tell us you were dead?"

"Not dead. And not Jake," the kidnapper's tone had shifted. Anger weighted his tone.

"What's she trying to say?" Tyrell's ebony skin had turned ashen. "Jake's been dead for two years."

"You see his body?" Marcus asked.

"Nothing to see when the box came home. When a helo crashes and burns, there's not much to ID," Tyrell snapped.

"We don't have answers, and it doesn't matter if the guy looks like Jake's identical twin. He's probably taking her to Hank." Nate stopped the discussion, throwing a leg over the Harley. "You two follow in the pickup. Stay far enough back ... you know the drill."

He secured his cell with a small bungee cord where he could tell at a glance which way the Mercedes was headed and started the bike. It roared to life under him. Powerful and ready to go. "This bastard won't keep her or Holly alive for long. Not after he gets that ring."

****

Kay squeezed her eyes closed hoping to force her lungs to work properly. Her eyes were playing tricks on her. He couldn't be Jake. One more cleansing breath, and she'd check him out again.

The confirmation glance set her mind spinning. His baby face had filled out, which was to be expected. Jake's rigid posture and steely eyes gave him the air of a warrior. The sweet blond-haired kid she remembered still had broad shoulders and a sharp jaw. All doubt disappeared when she saw the small mole below his right eye.

"Jake, tell me you didn't hurt Holly. She's okay, right?"

"I don't know if you're confused or stupid, but I've already told you I'm not this Jake. Yes, your friend is alive. It's you I should kill and dump on the side of the road. That way your cop friend will know what I do to liars."

"I didn't lie." Her trembling hand tightened on the door handle. Nate's command to abort had her weighing the pros and cons of jumping from a moving vehicle.

She had to stick this out or Holly would pay the ultimate price. The car whizzed by telephone poles. Kay prayed a local cop would spot the speeding Mercedes.

"I'm not an idiot," he snapped, glancing in her direction. "I didn't expect you to come alone."

She couldn't hold back the shiver. His used-to-be-full-of-fun slate-gray eyes reminded her more of a shark than the playful young man everybody had loved in college. She refused to give up trying to understand why he didn't seem to recognize her.

"He's not a cop. Didn't you recognize him when you almost ran him down? He's Nate Wolfe. Your friend."

"Never heard of him. And I have no friends."

"You must remember him. What about Tyrell Castillo or Marcus Ricci? You have to know them."

"Whatever game you're trying to run, it ain't working."

Fear surged to anger as he continued to deny her and his old friends. "Right back at you. I don't believe you don't remember us. Wolfe's Pack was legend on the UT football field. You used to tell people I was your baby sister."

His hand went to his head and massaged, digging his fingers into his wavy blond hair. He moaned the sound of an injured animal.

"Shut up," he whispered. "Leave me alone."

Kay bit back a scream when Nate spoke through the earpiece. Even over the roar of the Harley, his voice came through as if he were sitting next to her.

"You're doing great," he said. "I want you to be sure about this nutcase. If you say this guy is Jake Donovan, then that's who he is.

Maybe he has amnesia. We'll try something. See if he reacts. I'll tell you his favorite football play, and you repeat it to him. Don't explain or elaborate. Let it simmer in his mind."

"Okay," she answered Nate. Oh. My. God. She slapped a hand over her chest, turned toward Jake, and faked a cough. Could she be more careless?

"Okay what?" Jake asked. His eyebrows pulled together.

The equipment Tyrell borrowed was state-of-the-art for sure. She'd answered Nate like he was in the seat next to her. "You said shut up," she said with a frustrated grunt. "I said okay."

The Mercedes slowed and made a sharp right. She casually rested her hand on the door handle, wrapping her fingers around the cool metal. Could she break through to Jake? What had happened to him? Why did no one know he was alive?

"Nice recovery," Nate's voice helped her relax her grip on the door handle. "I want you to wait a few minutes. Let him think about what you've said, and then snap these words at him. Spread, Slot Right, 357 Seam, on 2."

"I remember that one," Marcus said, reminding her she had lots of backup.

Another turn and the potholes in the road worsened, forcing the car to a crawl. The thick underbrush and weeds on either side of the dirt path provided the perfect shield. They were hidden from the main road's view.

Jake stopped at an old metal gate.

"Open it, and then close it when I drive through."

Her eyebrows went up. "You're letting me out?"

"You'll come back if you want to see Holly alive. Be quick about it. Not that it's any of your business, but Hank Walsh hurt your friend. He may be there alone with her. Do you want that?"

Kay scrambled out and ran to the gate. They had to keep Hank away from Holly. Her mouth went dry from images flashing through her mind of her friend's bruised face.

"Is this bastard nuts?" Nate said, his voice came through clearly, assuring her they hadn't lost coverage out here in the backwoods. "Be careful with him, he's obviously unstable."

"Good to know Hank's coming. I don't like surprise visitors."

Tyrell's baritone voice rolled through her earpiece. "You're doing great, Little Mama."

"Stall if you can." Nate's voice ended the chat. "Give us a few minutes to get situated. But if Hank's already at the hideout, speak the play before you leave the car. If not, get a visual on Holly and then say it loud and clear."

Kay slapped her hand over her heart when the horn blared behind her. Jake's patience with her fumbling must've worn thin. She gave the heavy metal a shove, waited until he'd stopped, and then closed it.

Chapter Twenty Five

Johnny had never considered suicide before, but if the inferno inside his head didn't cease, a bullet to the brain was definitely an option.

The Taylor woman kept throwing names at him. Do you remember this? Do you remember him? Johnny didn't remember shit. The initials J D were all he'd had until the boss came along and gave him some ancient crooner's name.

Jake? Who the fuck was he? Name didn't set off any revelations. Johnny kinda wished it had.

He slammed his foot on the accelerator when she finally quit dickin' with the gate and re-entered the car.

"I told you I was in a hurry to get back. Now I see how much you care for your friend."

She whirled toward him just as the car hit a large pothole, bouncing her around the front seat.

"You could've waited until I buckled up."

Johnny didn't have time to wait. His gut was gnawing through its lining. If Hank wasn't at the cabin, he would be soon. And wouldn't that pervert like to find Holly handcuffed to the bed?

"I was right. You're as smart-mouthed as Holly." The clearing ahead gave him his answer. Based on the dust settling, somebody was ahead of him.

"Holly? You two are on a first-name basis?"

"Give me the ring."

She dug a tissue out of her pocket and held it up. Ah. Finally. He reached across the car, pulling his gaze off the road for a second. They hit another deep pothole, the car bounced like it had no shocks and the ring bounced off the windshield.

"I dropped the damn thing," she snapped.

"Tell me something I don't know. Find it. You see the dust up there?" He pointed a finger toward the distance. "I'm betting a red sports car is up ahead of us. Hank's about to find Holly all alone."

The Taylor woman grabbed his arm. "Jake. Hurry. Please, don't let Hank hurt her again."

"Name's Johnny Darling. And Hank had better not touch her."

"It's Jake Donovan. Don't you find it interesting the initials are the same? And I'm Kaycie Taylor. We went to college together. You joined the Marines."

"You're the second person to ask me if I was in the military." The burner inside his brain turned up the volume. He pressed three fingers against the one spot in his head he wanted to rip out with bare hands. The pain intensified with each headache, making him wonder how much longer until it drove him insane.

"What's wrong?" She moved her hand to his shoulder, which he shrugged off. "Let me help you."

"Find the ring," he yelled over the roar inside his head.

She dug around under her feet, apparently having trouble. At last, she leaned back and offered it to him.

"Here. Take the damn thing. I hope it's worth all the pain you've caused."

"I agree that too many people will die because of Hank, but it has to be done." Johnny laughed when she gasped. For some sick reason, he liked that he'd frightened her. Maybe she'd quit dogging him about who he was. He snorted. "Wonder if Hank's ready to die too?"

"You were right. He's here," the Taylor woman announced as if he was stupid. "Stop him."

The red car was empty, and Johnny didn't have time to chat. Anger had taken full control of his senses. The desire to protect Holly countermanded the boss's orders.

****

"Do it now, Kaycie." Nate's voice rang in her ear. "Call the play."

Fear cut off her oxygen. For the first time since seeing Jake, Kay had to battle back panic clawing to get out.

She erupted out of the car with Jake. "Spread, Slot Right, 357 Seam, on 2." She spoke loudly and with authority.

He stopped in his tracks. Something was happening to him. A

spark of understanding? Kay bit her tongue to keep from telling Nate. Jake rubbed the side of his head a lot, but now he appeared to be digging a hole.

His shark-like eyes cleared right in front of her. The taught nerves in his face seemed to relax. For the first time today, the boy Jake, the sweet defender of the innocent, stood in front of her, his lips curving in a shy smile.

"Jake," she pleaded. "You remember the play?" Repeating Nate, she added, "It was your favorite. You used to bug Nate to call it. Promised him a touchdown every time."

They moved a couple steps toward each other. Confusion clouded his handsome face. He closed his eyes briefly.

"I remember ..." He shook his head. "Nothing. I've accepted not having a past."

A woman's scream ended the conversation.

"Hurry," Kay begged.

Jake burst through the door with her right behind him. "Hank," he shouted.

Holly, handcuffed to the bed, kicked wildly. The bastard was unzipping his pants.

"Stop," Kay screamed and ran past Jake toward her friend.

Hank grabbed her around the middle, lifted her off the floor and threw her on the small bed next to Holly.

He leered, turned to Jake, and said, "Two chicks. Two men. Let's have some fun with them before you kill 'em."

Kay dragged the trembling Holly close and held her tight, whispering, "It's okay."

Kay wasn't sure where the huge knife came from, but Jake was wielding it like he knew what he was doing. The shark's eyes were back and locked on Hank. Her insides cramped, and a chill raced across her back. She had never witnessed such hate in a person's eyes as she saw in Jake's.

"What'd I tell you about her?" Jake advanced just as Hank pulled a gun from behind his back. "I told you to keep your hands off."

"What do you care? The bitch is as good as dead. Her and her friend."

Jake advanced a step and said through gritted teeth, "You almost lost your nuts the last time you touched her. Today you'll lose more than that."

Let them argue. This was the perfect opportunity for Kay to gather her thoughts. Perhaps she could capitalize on the distraction.

"You don't give me orders. You're a bum. Were living under a bridge when you were brought into the organization. I knew then you were trouble."

Holly clung tightly to Kay. Where were Nate and the boys? How far behind were they? "Hurry," she whispered, praying one of her rescuers heard.

She couldn't wait for someone else to save her and Holly. Kay battled back her own panic and set out to free her friend while the two men circled each other like wolves ready to attack. Their attention was on each other, and she'd use that to her advantage.

She placed her feet against the headboard, inhaled a deep breath, and wrapped her fingers around the bar holding Holly hostage. Pushing with her legs and pulling with her hands, she summoned every ounce of strength and said a short prayer.

The headboard cracked. The loud noise reverberated through the room. Hank whirled and aimed the pistol at Holly.

Without thinking, Kay shoved her friend flat on the bed and used her body as a shield.

Kay didn't see the knife leave Jake's hand, but Hank's eyes went wide, and his gaze lowered. His hand clutched his belly where only the handle protruded. The blade was buried deep in his stomach. His knees buckled, and he fell to the floor.

The door burst open, and windows on either side of the house exploded. Three men rushed inside, with Nate in the lead. A gunshot reverberated through the small cabin.

Nate stumbled, gathered himself and kept coming toward her and Holly. Kay had never been so happy to see him.

Tyrell and Marcus stared as if Jake had dropped in from Mars. Both shook their heads as if to clear away the shock. Then they went after the man who called himself Johnny Darling. The man who couldn't be anyone but Jake Donovan raised his fists in self-defense mode.

Nate gathered her into his arms. His heart beat wildly under her ear. His chest pumped up and down. She pressed closer as he kissed the top of her head, rocking back and forth.

"Oh. My. God," he murmured into her hair.

"It's over, and we're okay." She relaxed, loving the feel of his arms wrapped around her.

"Well, I'm not. Fighting in Afghanistan didn't scare me this bad."

Kay flinched as blows were exchanged and bodies tumbled to the floor. It was two against one, and soon, Jake lay facedown. Marcus's foot pressed against the back of his neck while Jake struggled to free himself.

"Holly?" Jake called from his position on the floor. "Are you okay?"

Holly slid the broken bed part through the handcuff, scrambled off the bed, and crawled to Jake's side. Tears streamed down her face. "I'm fine."

"Get away from him." Tyrell's words were thick and harsh. Worry lines on his face seemingly had aged him years. "He killed a man right in front of you."

"No. He saved my life. Now get off him," Holly protested, her blue eyes sparking anger. She sent a searing glance at Marcus and slapped his leg. "You're hurting him."

Marcus stepped back, lifted Jake's head, and applied pressure to his neck.

Relief Holly was alive hadn't stopped Kay's tremors, but she reluctantly extracted herself from Nate's warm embrace and went to her sobbing friend. Maybe talking would help. "It's over."

"Make them stop," Holly begged.

Jake's eyes rolled upward, and he went limp. Marcus released the chokehold and slid the unconscious Jake to the floor. "There. He'll be out for a minute or two."

"You didn't have to do that," Holly protested. "He's not a bad person."

"He kidnapped you. And would've killed us both." Kay understood her friend had suffered a great deal of pain and trauma. Holly's reaction was probably the result of shock.

"No. He wouldn't have ..." Holly's gaze drifted down the front of Kay's blouse. Small hands gripped Kay's shoulders. "You're bleeding."

"No, I'm not." Her lungs emptied themselves of air when she looked down to find blood on the front of her blouse. She'd been caught up in the moment and hadn't noticed her chest was wet and sticky.

"Nate?" She whirled toward him. Her heart went into free fall. His hand covered what had to be a bullet wound. Not even getting shot had stopped him from reaching her.

She rushed to him just as sirens blared through the silent countryside. He pushed himself further onto the bed and leaned back, using the wall as a brace. His face was pale, and his eyes were dull. She didn't know how the police knew to come, but she was grateful help was close by. She pulled off a pillowcase and stuck it under his hand. Then she wrapped her arm around him and gathered him to her chest.

"Sorry, sweetheart." He coughed, sucking in a deep breath. Pain deepened the lines around his mouth. His lips were drawn into a thin line. "I had to call my FBI contact. We were about to break too many laws."

Tyrell strolled over as if they were at a picnic in the park. His actions didn't fool Kay. His caramel skin had a pallor to it. Fear, something she'd never seen him display, oozed from his every pore and sent her heart into a spiral. If he was scared, she was terrified.

"Getting shot hurts like a bitch, don't it," he joked, pulling Nate's hand and the pillowcase away. Kay's temporary bandage was already soaked with blood. Tyrell sat on the other side of Nate and gently lifted him off the wall. Kay helped lay him down so Tyrell could check the wound. He folded the hem of Nate's bloody T-shirt in his giant hands and ripped. "Let's have a better look."

"Oh, God," Kay barely found her voice. Blood flowed from a wound in Nate's shoulder. She tried to swallow, but her mouth couldn't produce one drop of saliva. This could not be happening. Please, don't die, she prayed.

"Muscle," Nate said in a whisper. One corner of his mouth lifted in a sad attempt at a smile. "Not bad."

"Little Mama," Tyrell said. "Find me a clean towel or rag."

She ran around Holly, who appeared to be in shock. Kay

grabbed a dishtowel from the counter, and hurried back to Tyrell.

"I hope that's clean." Nate's wisecrack was replaced with a groan when Tyrell pressed the towel hard against the wound.

Kay clamped her hand around Nate's and squeezed. The ache in her heart almost doubled her over. She plastered a fake smile on her face, trying to be strong for him.

"Marcus has gone back up the road to lead the locals and feds in." Tyrell spoke as if administering aid to a wounded friend happened every day. "I'm hoping they brought an EMT, because you're bleeding all over the fucking place."

Nate blinked slowly. His eyes fluttered closed.

"Stay awake," Kay patted his cheek, her heart lodged in her throat. "Don't leave me."

"I'm not going anywhere," he said with a ghost of a smile. Then he went limp.

"No!" Kay screamed.

Chapter Twenty Six

Nate opened his eyes to narrow slits, tried to unscramble his brain. What the hell was going on? His arm hurt like a son of a bitch. Shifting his shoulders sent excruciating pain to every nerve ending. Damn, he'd been shot and was in the hospital.

Voices came from every direction and in surround sound. The room had turned into Grand Central Station. A couple of men talked about him as if he weren't there. His favorite female voice gave him a reason to wake. Kaycie's soft tone always stirred him and made waking worthwhile.

He rolled over. Sharp pain brought his memory better into focus. That asshole Hank got off a lucky shot, and a bullet wound up in Nate's shoulder. Which probably explained why he'd reached into the recesses of his memory and dredged up the worst day of his life.

Hell, last thing he remembered was Kaycie's frightened face before she'd faded from his vision. At least he'd made it to her before he blacked out.

A cool hand brushed his hair off his forehead. He expected soft lips to follow. Then he'd open his eyes and surprise her.

"Let him rest. Come on, we'll buy you lunch."

Why were Wayne and Tomas in Oklahoma?

"I'm not leaving until he wakes," she protested.

Good girl. Nate kept his eyes closed and remained still. Listening.

"It's important that we talk with you." Wayne sounded official. "And you need to eat."

"He's right, Kay. Finish up with DPD. I'll stay here with the patient."

Nate's eyes snapped open at the sound of Dalton Murphy's voice. What the hell was the FBI doing in the room?

"Welcome back." Kaycie's face loomed over Nate. Damn, his heart lurched. The dark circles under her eyes meant she hadn't rested in a while. Her refusal to leave his side gave him hope.

His throat was dry, but he had to try to speak to her. "It's good to be back."

"You scared us." Tears rimmed her eyes.

"She's right." Tomas stepped up beside her. "I was afraid you'd die and leave this mess on Kay's shoulders."

Shit. Nate had no doubt there was a lot to explain, but why had the Dallas detectives come to Oklahoma? What else was going on?

Nate had asked Dalton to call Dallas PD at the last minute. What Nate hadn't expected was the two detectives and the agent himself to show.

"Hello, Tomas," Nate growled. "Happy not to have disappointed you."

Tomas's lips curved into a sneer. "After the Oklahoma authorities are finished, I'll be talking to the Dallas DA about an obstructing justice arrest warrant for you and your men."

Nate opened his mouth to argue, but Dalton stepped forward. He dropped a hand on the bedrail. Nate got the subtle message and shut up.

"Kay," Dalton said, his tone that of authority. "You guys go to lunch. I need to speak with Nate in private."

Wayne crossed the room and shook Dalton's hand. "Next time DPD would appreciate a heads up you're running an operation in our backyard."

"Sure thing." Dalton delivered a grin that made Nate bite back a laugh. The agent turned toward Kaycie, and this time his smile appeared to be genuine.

Before Nate could speak, Kaycie was whisked from the hospital room and out of his sight. He tried to sit up, causing shards of fire to shoot across his chest and shoulder. Dalton lifted an eyebrow, picked up the control, and raised the head of the bed.

"Thanks," Nate grunted. He waited for the pain to subside while sweat soaked through the thin hospital gown

"Nobody ever said getting shot was fun." Dalton passed Nate a glass of water, which he gratefully drained and then handed back.

"No shit." A couple of deep breaths and the discomfort eased.

It wasn't just his shoulder that ached, his head was spinning like a top. How upset was the Dallas Police Department? How much trouble would they cause? The last thing Nate wanted was to cause Kaycie trouble.

He nodded toward the empty doorway. "Is he bluffing?"

"Yeah. Big talk in front of the pretty lady. You've had a couple of lucky breaks over the past few days. Biggest one was me coming down."

"I'm glad you did. What are you doing here? Rumor has it you never leave Atlanta."

"I travel occasionally. Besides I was getting tired of that desk." Dalton, easily as big as Tyrell, dressed in the typical dark suit and white shirt, moved a pile of newspaper from a chair and sat. "Don't thank me yet. I want something."

"I figured." Nate squinted to read the headline on the paper. "Is that Sunday's? Last thing I remember it was Friday. I've been out for two days?"

"Yeah. Doctor said the slug wasn't hard to remove, but you had lost a lot of blood. Luckily, there's no permanent damage." Dalton tossed the front section of the paper on the bed. "And it was damn tough keeping your picture off the front page. If your face, name, and background had leaked, you'd be useless to the FBI."

"And I appreciate you handling things."

"DPD wanted you for a number of charges. You and your lady friend lied more than once to Wayne and his partner."

"So now you've lectured me and I'm appropriately contrite, bottom line it. What's coming?"

"Nothing. I convinced them you were working on contract for me. Which, if they figure out I lied, I'm on the DPD shit list forever."

"Is your lie going to backfire on you?"

"No. But there's a price for my help. When you're on your feet, I need you on the Colombian assignment we talked about."

Nate sank deeper into the pillows.

Was this where he and Kaycie ended? Wasn't his job for her over? Time to move on to the next one. She'd been upfront with him. Told him the sex was going to be a temporary thing.

"Hey." Dalton snapped his fingers in front of Nate's face. "Did you hear anything I said?"

"Sorry. I heard." Nate shoved his emotions down deep where they belonged. "I appreciate everything you've done, especially for Tyrell and Marcus. They were just helping me. I owe you one."

"Damn right." Dawson laughed. It eased the stern scowl he always wore. "And as soon as you're strong enough to travel, I'll send you the intel, and we'll get started laying the groundwork."

"On what?" Damn, Nate's mind kept drifting. He really hadn't been listening.

"Colombia? The drug cartel? I know you're still groggy, but I need to know you're in."

"That's a tough one, Dalton. Things are still unsettled here. The guy who killed Hank? He's not who he says he is." Nate paused when Dalton held his hands in the timeout position.

"I heard all about it from Tyrell and Marcus. Donovan's fingerprints confirmed their claim. Johnny Darling doesn't exist. However, Jake Donovan has been missing from the neurosurgical ward at Walter Reed for over a year. He's got a piece of shrapnel embedded in his brain, right above the amygdala."

"His what?"

"I'd never heard of it before either. The amygdala controls your emotions. The file I read said Donovan might be the worst case of traumatic brain injury to come out of the war."

"Can they fix him?" Nate's troubles shifted to the background. Nothing going on in his life could compare with what Jake must've gone through.

"I don't know. The shrapnel has to come out. If not, it will eventually kill him. The file was full of medical mumbo-jumbo." He set his briefcase on the foot of the bed, removed a folder and read from it. "The amygdala sits in the brain's medial temporal lobe, right above your ears. Only surgery, therapy, and time will tell how badly the nerves were damaged."

"And if they remove it?"

"Operation might kill him. Leave it alone, and he dies for sure. Take it out and he has a chance."

"Not much of a choice. What about his memory?"

"Report says the odds are not in his favor. Maybe some of his past life will surface. Who knows?" Dalton tossed the file back inside the briefcase and locked it. "One way or the other, we don't have long to get him to talk. We need to know everything about Hank and his organization."

"Get me in to see Jake. He might talk to me."

"Not sure I can make that happen. You're pretty much persona non grata with the Dallas Police Department."

"They may be pissed, but at least we interrupted the operations of the human-trafficking ring. We shouldn't stop trying to end this group." Nate dragged his fingers through tangled hair. Damn, he was stopping at the first barbershop and getting a haircut. "Seriously, I need you to flex your muscles. Jake used to be one of the good guys. I want to see him."

Dalton audibly sighed. "Your friend's in good hands. Confused as hell. But no harm will come to him. After the police question him, the military will pick him up in Dallas and transport him to the hospital. They take care of their own."

Nate hit the call button.

"What do you need, Mr. Wolfe?" a female voice asked.

"I'm checking myself out. Send someone in to remove this IV." He ignored the rockets exploding in his shoulder, pushed himself to an upright position and waited for the burn to cool.

The expected answer came back. "That's not a good idea, Mr. Wolfe."

"Good idea or not, I'm leaving." Only way to test his strength was to put some weight on his feet. A couple of seconds standing, and the room spun off its axis. Darkness engulfed his vision. His legs turned to rubber.

Dalton grabbed him and helped him lay back down. Nate hated feeling helpless.

"Remember the loss of blood thing?" Dalton loomed over the bed, staring at Nate as if he were a complete fool. "Give it another day. If you like to get up, I'm happy to help."

"Gonna help me when I need to take a leak?" Nate grumbled, pissed royally at needing help.

"I'll help you to the door, after that my friend, you're on your own."

Nate waved off the nurse when she bustled into the room. He'd have sworn he heard her snicker.

"So tell me about this drug cartel. If I'm stuck in this bed, the least I can do is use my brain."

"I have a file full of information on Colombia, the major players and your contacts. These are nasty bastards, and they're copying the Mexicans and killing off the competition. While that's not totally bad, a lot of innocent people are getting caught in the middle. Too many have died. Which needs to stop."

"I have approval to do what it takes to stay alive?"

Dalton's head moved forward slightly. "Of course. We'll disrupt their production, then the Colombian government will take control.

****

The sound of Nate's voice sent waves of relief through Kay. She'd paused outside his hospital room and let his baritone warm her soul.

She'd almost lost her mind when he'd collapsed in the cabin. The long ride through the dusty, barren countryside to the hospital had been agony. She'd worried that she'd never get to tell him how much she loved him.

Even with the doctor's assurance Nate would be fine, hearing him have a coherent conversation was better than opening presents Christmas morning.

An icy hand slid inside her chest when she heard the topic of their conversation. They were discussing the job opportunity in Colombia. Her skin crawled. He and the FBI agent chatted about people dying as easily as if they'd been discussing Sunday's football game.

She stepped backward and sagged against the wall. After all she and Nate had been through, she'd hoped he would turn down the assignment. She hadn't expected him to be this quick to run. Their time together had meant nothing to him.

She'd spent the past day and a half being grilled by the Oklahoma authorities. Then DPD and the FBI had questioned her, Marcus and Tyrell for hours. All that time, she'd pleaded to be allowed to go to Nate. To sit beside his bed.

She'd rushed back from lunch full of excitement. According to

Wayne, no charges were going to be filed. Not against her or the guys. Apparently, Nate having a friend with the FBI had come in handy. But it was clear, Nate didn't need her or her news.

The thought of him skulking around Colombia undercover rolled her stomach into a knot. What if his cover were blown? He could be killed. Or tortured and then killed. She clutched her stomach as if pressure would stop the churning.

She'd already lost her brother, and she'd almost lost her best friend. Nate disappearing into the jungle and perhaps never being heard from again was more than she could bear.

Damn him. He hadn't changed one bit. At the first opportunity, he was leaving on a mission. Running toward danger, putting his life in jeopardy would always be his first love. She could never fill his need for excitement.

But she'd known that all along.

Kay laughed at her own stupidity. She gathered what little pride she had left, and this time, she knocked before entering.

Chapter Twenty Seven

Shoulders back, head held high, Kay pretended she hadn't heard Nate and Dalton's discussion. Pretended Nate's leaving again wouldn't deliver a crushing blow to her heart. Pretended losing him wouldn't suck the joy from her life.

Her presence brought complete silence to the room. The void was deafening for a few minutes. Then as if a covert mission hadn't been their topic, the two men started discussing the events of the past few days. Their behavior added insult to injury.

She couldn't blame the FBI or Dalton for Nate's decision. But she bit her tongue more than once to keep from blurting out what she'd overheard. She waited, hoping Nate would bring her up to speed, but neither man mentioned the upcoming assignment. The longer she waited for the truth, the wider the hole in her heart became.

Dalton extended his hand to Nate. Thank God. The FBI was leaving. Maybe now Nate would give her the bad news.

"How will you manage your PI business with you laid up?" Dalton asked.

"I'm offering Tyrell and Marcus full-time work."

"With their military backgrounds, I can see it happening." Dalton turned to Kay. "Walk out with me?" His handsome face belied the fact he was hard-core government, making her wary.

"Sure." She leaned over and kissed Nate's forehead, searching for the connection she'd felt when he'd held her in his arms at the cabin. He loved her. She knew it, but did he? "Be right back. Can I bring you anything?"

Nate barely looked at her when he said, "Ask the nurse when the doctor makes his rounds. I've got to get back to Dallas."

She and Dalton stopped by the nurses' station, learned the

doctor wouldn't be back until Monday and then strolled out into the heat. The wind had shifted. A slight breeze out of the North reminded her a break from the high temperature was close.

"I've never been to Atlanta. If it gets cold, I may have to move." Small talk seemed easier than asking him directly what he wanted.

"Not all that different than Texas. Snows but it's rare. Black ice almost shuts the city down," he said, tossing his briefcase into the backseat of a rental.

"I'll make this easy for you," she said. "I overheard. He's leaving the country on a job for you as soon as he's fit to travel, and I shouldn't get attached to him because who knows when or if he'll come back to me. Well, you're too late."

She shifted from one foot to the other, uncomfortable because he stared down at her as if she'd grown a third eye.

"I would never violate a confidence. Only Nate can tell you if he's accepted an assignment. Nor do I know him well enough to speak to matters of the heart. I wanted to suggest you think through your decisions next time before you break the law. You were damn lucky. If the hostage had been killed ... well, we won't talk about the charges you could've faced."

"I appreciate everything you've done," she said, feeling thoroughly but politely dressed down.

"You're welcome."

With that said, he shook her hand, slid behind the wheel, and departed. Obviously, the men in black really were all business.

She made her way back inside, hoping Nate's blue eyes would darken with need at the sight of her. Then she'd know he cared. But his eyes were unreadable, giving nothing away and sending her heart into a free fall.

"Dalton seemed like an okay guy," she said, willing Nate to broach the subject of Colombia.

"I guess. How's Holly?"

"Her outside injuries will heal, but she's traumatized. I'm worried about her. Marcus is driving her home today."

"Where is she?"

"One floor up. She keeps insisting Jake saved her. That he would never harm her."

"I'd like to believe he wouldn't." Nate shook his head. "War does weird things to some people. Dalton says Jake's injuries are pretty bad. You heard he needs surgery?"

"Yes. And we have to stand by him, but right now I'm more concerned about Holly. She's put on a brave front, but she went through a lot." Kay couldn't close her eyes without seeing flashes of her friend's bruises. "It's just not fair."

"Kaycie." His voice mellowed to the soft tone she'd come to love, and her cheeks heated. "Come here. Please."

She shoved the tray table aside, lowered the bed rail, and then bent over him. She carefully rested her head on his uninjured shoulder.

Nate hooked a finger under her chin and lifted her head. He touched his lips to her forehead, her nose, and then her cheeks. When he leaned back and looked at her, the smile in his eyes had returned.

"If you'll help me brush my teeth, I'll give you a proper kiss."

His prim manner of speech sent a chuckle bubbling to the surface, and for the first time in days Kay relaxed a little. She blocked out the part where he'd be leaving soon and shoved the hurt to the back of her mind.

And for making her laugh, she kissed him anyway.

"That wasn't bad." She finger-combed his hair.

"Hmm," he moaned. "Feels good. I'd promised myself I'd get this mop cut off as soon as I got out of here."

Thank God, he was going to talk about the assignment. He'd probably leave his hair long to go undercover. She closed her eyes and braced for the news.

"Let me scoot over. I want all of you next to me." Through gritted teeth, he groaned and moved sideways, allowing her to lie beside him. He ran his hand across her arms, back, and neck. Wait. Was he committing her form to memory?

When he didn't mention the mission, she prompted, "But you're not getting it cut?"

His body tensed. "Not for a while."

"My mother always told me to never trust a man whose hair was prettier than mine." She gave him another opportunity to open up to her, but he laughed and held her tighter.

"I'm guessing Tyrell and Marcus returned the eighteen-wheeler and left my bike at my office. Will you drive me home?"

The lights went off in her soul. Snap. Pitched into total darkness, she worried she'd never find the way out. Her heart bled as if she'd been the one struck by the bullet. Nate hadn't actually lied, but he hadn't confided in her either. He'd simply changed the subject.

Kay dug deep, swallowed back the hurt. "The doctor won't be back until Monday."

He stroked up her rib cage, cupping her breast in his hand. "God, I never want to go through that kind of fear again. It took longer to reach you than we'd anticipated, and I was going nuts."

"Thankfully, it's over." Keeping her tone level required control. Control she felt slipping away. How could he carry on a conversation knowing he had to break the news?

"You were awesome. I'm damn proud of the way you held it together. You know, I could recover at your place for a few days. You don't happen to know where to get one of those sexy nurse's costumes. Do you?"

Self-pity vanished as the urge to choke him hit Kay. Did he really expect her to nursemaid him for a few days before he disappeared on his secret and deadly mission? How dare he be so flippant? Callous. Was she so unimportant he could make love to her one day and leave the next?

"Sorry. I have to go back to work Monday. Vacation's over." She tried to move to the edge of the bed. "One of the boys will drive you home. I need to check on Holly. Call if you need anything."

His hold tightened, almost as if he refused to let her go, and for a second, hope bloomed in her chest. Then his grip relaxed, and he released her. When she stood and faced him, the sparkle had left his eyes.

"Sure thing." His jaw muscle jerked then relaxed. He glanced around, located the remote, and then turned on the TV.

Battling the sob racing to the surface, Kay grabbed her purse and headed for the door. She knew it was pain lashing out but couldn't stop herself from taking a parting shot. "Send me a bill if my check didn't cover all your expenses."

****

Nate was ready to walk out of the hospital room on his own Monday when Tyrell arrived, pushing the wheelchair.

"Your chariot, my king." Tyrell bowed with a smirk. "You hear the cheer coming from the nurses' station? They were excited to send your bitchy-old-woman-ass home."

"I'll miss them, too. Who's gonna turn on the overhead light blinding me at six every morning?" Nate didn't defend himself. His behavior had been less than amicable after Kaycie had strolled out and hadn't returned or called. It didn't help that every damn time the door swung open, he'd expected her to come through.

She hadn't. What she'd done was give him plenty of time to think, and she wasn't getting away that easy.

She loved him. He could tell by the way she touched him as if he were a priceless treasure. She kissed him like she'd starve without him. By the way she made love. Kaycie wasn't the type to buy into the sex-with-a-friend thing. She loved him, and he intended to make her admit it.

Somewhere in the background, Tyrell droned on with his lecture about Nate taking it easy. He'd lied to the doctor and promised to rest. Big deal. He and dozens of other patients said whatever was necessary if it meant getting out of the hospital. Happened every day. If he hadn't lost so much blood, he'd have been cut loose two days ago.

Tyrell pointed at the wheelchair. "Sit."

"I can walk." Nate curled his lip at the thought of being wheeled out like an invalid.

"Get real. Use that snarl on somebody scared of you."

No use arguing against a lost cause. Sometimes a person had to accept the inevitable and keep their bitching to themselves. Nate sat and held his duffle bag on his lap. "Don't just stand there. Get me the hell out of here and take me home."

"I'll set your ass on the side of the freeway," Tyrell said on a chuckle, but he complied. "And I'm reconsidering my agreement to work with you full time."

Nate didn't comment because Tyrell was just mouthing off. He'd already committed to come aboard as had Marcus. Neither one of them would go back on their word.

"Dalton tell you Jake needs surgery?" Nate groaned when the wheelchair bumped onto the elevator.

"Yeah. He's got a long way to go. You'll keep track and let me and Marcus know how he's doing?"

"I will. He won't go through this alone."

The trip back to Dallas was spent strategizing. Tyrell's credentials as a Ranger had carried a lot of weight with the FBI and DEA, which was important, since both agencies were working the case. He'd been cleared to cover the Colombian assignment by both branches of the government. According to Dalton, Tyrell's background check couldn't have been better.

Nate read from the file. "I'd like this setup better if you were meeting someone other than a civilian."

"Ana María Vega Cisneros."

Tyrell's perfect pronunciation and knowledge of the language might save his life.

"You got a problem working with a woman?"

"I don't give a damn as long as she delivers the goods."

"She's got good credentials." Nate flipped through the pages. "Who is the contact with the Colombian government? I can't find his name in the file."

"Cisneros will introduce us. He's for emergencies only," Tyrell said, never taking his eyes off the highway. "He's supposed to cut through the red tape and provide a safe route out of the country if things blow up in my face."

"I'm not trusting your safety to anybody else. If you need out, contact me. Hang onto that satellite phone and stay in communication. I'll be your first call if you need help."

"Yes, Mutha."

Nate chuckled for the first time in days, detonating a blast of pain through his shoulder. "Careful how you pronounce mother, I might think you'd said half a word."

"And you might be right." The grin on Tyrell's face spread wide.

"You're looking forward to this mission."

"Hell, yeah. No more bodyguard work for me."

They fell into an easy silence. Nate understood that Tyrell was already running scenarios through his head. There was a real possibility this wasn't the first time he'd been tasked with covertly ending a life.

Nate ignored a pang of guilt racing through his system. He should be the one putting his life on the line. If this mission resulted in his friend coming home in a body bag, the blame would sit squarely on Nate's shoulders.

He didn't relish staying home. As a form of penance, he'd do something he hated. Rub elbows with the brass in a few government agencies. Dalton's help getting Nate some face time with a few government agencies would be one hell of a boost for business. With two extra on the payroll, the agency needed additional work. And they'd get more if ... no, not if, when Tyrell completed the op successfully.

As soon as Tyrell was squared away and on a plane, Nate had a mission of his own. Kaycie. He needed her to accept him and his vocation. This wasn't just his job. It was his calling. But one part of his life was incomplete. She was the missing piece.

****

Kay parked outside her apartment building. She was glad to have the first day back at work behind her. Nate had only crossed her mind a few dozen times, which turned out to be the bright spots of the day. Her heart had broken open once, forcing her to close her office door and pull herself together. Other times, she'd retreated to the restroom and hid in a stall until the desperation passed. Sheer willpower had kept her from calling Tyrell to ask if Nate had left the country.

The rest of her day hadn't been easy either. Her boss, the chief of police, her grandfather, and her mother had at one time or another taken delight in chewing Kay's butt out. A small jab to the heart came when she'd heard nothing from her father.

By afternoon, things had settled down. She'd been assigned new case files. Truth was, she was grateful she still had a job.

The FBI had semi-controlled the media by keeping her and the guys' names and pictures out of the paper. Dalton and the Dallas chief of police had smiled for the cameras and given a vague overview of what happened in Oklahoma.

Kay refused to second-guess her decision to keep the police in the dark. Holly was home safe, and Leann Vaughn's killer was dead. Jake's fate worried Kay, and she intended to follow his progress closely.

Eager to stretch out on the couch and put this day to rest, Kay dragged herself out of the car.

A man stepped in front of her, blocking her path. The pistol in his hand was aimed at her heart.

Chapter Twenty Eight

"Mr. Walsh. What are you doing here?" Kay's mind skittered in a dozen directions as she stared down the barrel of his gun.

"You killed my son." His hand trembled, and the pistol quivered. Chills rippled across her arms.

Kay stood very still, commanding her feet not to bolt. The wild gleam in Anthony Walsh's eyes iced the blood in her veins, and she scrambled to appear calm.

"I understand you're looking for someone to blame. I'm sure the police explained that Hank's accomplice, the man who calls himself Johnny Darling, killed your son." She scanned the parking lot, hoping one of her fellow tenants would drive up and call out to her.

"No. You meddling bitch, his death is your fault." He advanced one menacing step. The trembling in his hand ceased. "Move."

Unsure what he intended to do, Kay proceeded the direction he pointed. "Mr. Walsh, let me help. I can put you in touch with a grief counselor."

He jerked open the driver's side door to a dark sedan. "Get in and scoot over."

Her stomach dropped to her feet. Leaving with him in this agitated state would be a mistake.

"You don't really want to do this. If you harm me, you'll be no better than Hank. He kidnapped my friend. The FBI has only scratched the surface. Who knows what they'll uncover. But nobody has the right to sell another human being."

Anthony Walsh's face turned beet red. The vein between his eyes pulsed. She'd said the wrong thing about his son.

"Move." The gentle face of the silver-haired gentleman had morphed into a portrait of a cold-eyed, steel-jawed madman.

No way was she getting in the car with him. She'd been a cop long enough to know better. Steeling herself for a fight, she stepped in front of him.

Her skull exploded in pain, buckling her legs. She struggled to remain conscious, lacked the strength to resist being shoved into the car. She opened her mouth to scream. No sound came out.

****

Nate had studied maps of the terrain with Tyrell. They'd gone over drawings and satellite photographs of the jungle until both were comfortable with the plan.

Tyrell was to meet with Ms. Cisneros, who would then provide him with the equipment he'd need to penetrate a fortress built deep in the jungle and carry out the mission.

Nate left Tyrell at the office and drove straight to Kaycie's apartment. He parked next to her car, rolled his still-sore shoulder, and got out of his pickup. He appreciated that the pain was diminishing. He might be stiff, but it wasn't enough to prevent him from getting back to life.

He wished he'd prepared his speech as well as he'd planned the Colombian op. But here, facing Kaycie, was where he had to start. Or end. He'd have his say, and the rest would be up to her.

For the first time in a long while, he actually felt deserving of happiness. Kaycie had looked into his soul, held his heart in her hand and found a worthwhile person. Somehow, she'd lightened his burden of survivor guilt. He wanted to do the same for her. She'd suggested he'd lived for a reason. Maybe she was why.

She'd also said *send me a bill* and then marched right out of his life. Had she turned her back on him as a punishment? Or had she been telling the truth when she said he was past history?

Could it be fear he'd hurt her again? Of course, she didn't trust him. It was a hundred percent his fault she was skeptical.

The cool evening breeze blew across Nate's bare neck, sending a chill up his spine and a laugh from deep in his chest. He almost hadn't recognized himself in the mirror after the haircut. Kaycie was sure to be surprised. Maybe even pleased.

He knocked on her door and moved back, prepared to surprise her. Surely, she'd take his short hair as a sign of good faith. He waited and then knocked again.

"Please talk to me." He waited a few heartbeats and knocked harder. "I know you're in there. I parked next to your car."

He waited in the hall for what seemed like hours, knocking and talking to the peephole. Tired of speaking to the closed door, he dialed her cell and got her voice mail, so he left a message.

Maybe she'd gone down to Holly's. In a couple of strides, he was knocking on her door.

The purple and green bruises on Holly's face had faded, but her appearance kicked him in the gut. She really was as tough as Tyrell said. According to Marcus, she'd resigned her position at Child Protective Services. Wanted nothing more than to rest, go to therapy, and forget the kidnapping and beating.

"Nate," she said, backing up to allow him entrance. "I hoped to get a chance to thank you."

"Not necessary." He followed her to her living room.

"Still. I'm grateful." She slanted her head and stared up at him. "Nice haircut."

"Thanks." She motioned him to a chair, but he stood. "I'm looking for Kaycie. Is she here with you?"

"No, I'm guessing you already tried her apartment."

"Yes. She's not answering the door or her phone." Nate's guts twisted. "And her car's in the parking lot."

"She called when she left work and headed home." Holly blinked rapidly, her gaze darted around the room. "She's really not friends with anyone else in the complex. Maybe she stopped by the manager's office."

"I'll check." Nate hated to frighten her, but his nerve endings were screaming trouble, and he didn't know why.

"Wait. I can call." A minute later, she hung up. "The manger saw Kay leaving with a man about an hour ago. Didn't see much more, but she seemed to know him."

Nate checked in with Marcus while Holly called Tyrell. Kaycie wasn't with either one of them, and neither had spoken with her.

Nate returned to the parking lot to check Kaycie's car. He hadn't looked closely before, now he noticed the driver's-side door was ajar. Other than that, he found no signs of foul play.

He'd worried when Holly went missing, but this was Kaycie.

Fear gripped him by the throat, squeezing tightly.

As he jogged back to Holly's, his blood pumped rapidly through his veins. With every step, his shoulder throbbed. He blocked out the pain. Now wasn't the time to feel sorry for himself. Not until he was sure Kaycie was safe and he'd told her he loved her.

Holly waited in her open doorway.

"No luck?" Nate knew the answer before Holly spoke. Tears pooled in her eyes, threatening to spill. Her facial expression telegraphed her fear and shook him to the core.

"No one's heard from her."

After getting Marcus and Tyrell en route to Kaycie's apartment, Nate got Tomas on the phone and explained she was missing. Nate would've talked with the devil himself to find her.

When he hung up, he turned to Holly. "Call the manager again. Ask if she noticed anything about the man. What kind of car they drove off in."

"You think this is related to the human-trafficking ring. Don't you?" Holly wrapped her arms around her middle.

"Yeah. I do."

"You're scaring me. I had a hard enough time coming back into this apartment. Now I'm afraid of being alone."

"I understand. Tyrell and Marcus will be here soon. They'll stay with you." Seconds later, Nate had Dalton on the line.

"Has Jake Donovan been moved?"

"No. DPD wanted a few days to question him before letting him leave Texas. Why?"

"I have to see him."

"He's in a holding cell at the Lew Sterrett jail. Scheduled to be moved tomorrow. Again, why?"

Nate gave a down-and-dirty update. It was critical Dalton buy into the theory that Kaycie's disappearance was related to Hank Walsh. Nate's popularity with DPD sucked. It would take the FBI to get Nate clearance to speak with Jake.

"Call those two detectives and get them involved," Dalton said without hesitation.

"Already called them."

"I'm not making any promises." Dalton fell quiet for a minute.

"I'll contact the DPD Chief."

****

The cold seeped through Kay's thin blouse. She woke to find herself in the dark, shivering and chilled to the bone. The image of Anthony Walsh and the gun snapped her awake and sent her heart jackhammering against her ribs.

For the second time in weeks, the movement kicked off a pain in her head and sent the room spinning. Her wrists and ankles were so tightly bound the circulation had been cut off. Her hands and feet stung painfully.

Her lungs filled with a paralyzing fear. She opened her mouth to scream. Her vocal chords closed and nothing happened.

The familiar scent of bleach on cement hit her nostrils. Terror raced through her thoughts. Was this the Walsh warehouse where she'd been held the first time?

Walsh. Hank's father blamed her for his son's death.

The sound of a door scraping the cement sent shivers across her scalp. Her skin crawled. An overhead light came on, temporarily blinding her. A sudden burst of fire in her side knocked the wind from her. Her ribs burned.

"That's just a sample of what I have planned for you." Anthony Walsh leaned close enough for her to get a good look at his face. "You will not die as quickly as my son. I may leave you like this for days. I hear water deprivation is a horrible way to go."

A second blast of white-hot pain hit her rib cage, compliments of the toe of his shoe. She screamed, releasing the pent-up terror. The sound reverberating in her ears. "Please, don't do this."

"Please," he mimicked with a long whine. Then he laughed a maniacal sound that ricocheted through her brain and lodged forever in her memory.

A piece of hope withered in Kay's heart.

"I'm scheduled to attend a fundraiser for the district attorney. I'll make a big campaign donation, and then I'll be back." He put his foot on her stomach, mashed and laughed when she cried out.

"The rats will keep you company."

The small room fell dark and silent.

Kay fought to catch her breath. She rolled to her side, hoping the pain would ease.

Her imagination ran in a thousand directions. Would he really leave her here to die? Rape her? Put the gun to her head and pull the trigger?

She'd read case studies of extreme cruelty, and his irrational behavior painted gory images in her mind. Alone and shivering more from fear than the cold, Kay refused to give in to blind terror. She'd escaped before and she'd do it again.

No one knew she was missing, so no one was searching. When she didn't show up for work, somebody would call. Eventually they'd GPS her phone and come free her. Until then, she'd have to deal with the crazed father alone.

But where was her purse? Her cell? She could tell by the absence of weight her Glock was gone. Damn, she'd removed the tracer from her holster.

She pulled her wrists to her mouth. The small rope was securely knotted. She wouldn't rip the restraints with her teeth this time.

As the long night wore on, she faced the possibility of her own death. Kay questioned her own stubbornness. Her past mistakes. So many regrets. So many hurts unresolved. So many truths unspoken. She'd allowed her father to blame her for her brother's death way too long. Should she have come clean after he died? Would it have mattered?

The worst rip in her aching heart was Nate. She'd wanted him to stop her from walking away that day at the hospital, but he hadn't. So why hadn't she fought for him? Forced him to admit he loved her?

Instead of wondering where she was right now, her real-life superhero was probably deep in the jungle where he, too, might die.

The motorcycle-riding ninja who'd saved her wouldn't magically show up to rescue her. Not this time.

She sobbed out his name and whispered, "I love you."

Chapter Twenty Nine

Tomas and Wayne escorted Nate through the security checkpoint at the city jail. The group followed a broad-backed uniformed guard down the drab gray hall.

Nate's jaw ached from grinding his teeth. His shoulder throbbed, but he mentally forced the pain out of his mind.

Trying to pound answers out of Jake probably wouldn't accomplish a thing. Didn't mean the urge to try wasn't strong.

A guard led the way to a small interview room and motioned them inside where Jake Donovan, wrists handcuffed and ankles shackled, waited.

The guard spread his feet and folded his arms over his chest.

"You got zilch from him, right?" Nate wouldn't put it past the cops to hold back information.

Wayne gave his head a slight shake. "Other than denying he's Jake Donovan? We got nothing."

Tomas's hand was on the doorknob when Nate stopped him. "Let me talk to Jake alone. If he wouldn't open up to you before he sure won't if he feels like we're ganging up on him."

Tomas glanced over his shoulder, his expression stone cold. "No. If he sees three of us, he'll know we mean business."

"You've got ten minutes." Wayne clamped a hand on his partner's shoulder. "If you get nothing, then we'll try a group run at Donovan."

Tomas stepped aside.

Nate's palms itched when he entered the interrogation room. He turned the chair around and straddled it, facing Jake, who stared at the top of the table.

"Look, it doesn't matter if you remember me or not. Just listen."

Nate forced himself not to rush. It was agony to talk about the past, explaining how they'd been friends. He pulled the chain from under his shirt and over his head.

"Take a look." He slid his hand with his dog tags and the Saint Jude medal resting on his palm across the table. "Somebody gave you one of these. Do you remember who?"

Nate's blood pressure freaked when Jake lifted his head. His gaze was blank as it locked with Nate's.

"No."

Shit. He'd hoped for some kind of recognition. "Kaycie Taylor gave one to you, me, Marcus, and Tyrell over ten years ago. She had some foolish notion it would keep us safe."

"Seems to have worked for you."

Nate bit back his simmering anger. "Kaycie used to be your friend. And she's missing. I believe her abduction is tied to your case, and you can help me find her."

For the first time, Jake's expression brightened, and a smile tugged at his mouth. "I'd like to see Holly."

"After what you put her through, what makes you think she'd agree to be in the same room with you?"

Jake's shoulders sagged, and his gaze dropped back to the top of the table.

Damn it. Holly had suffered a lot. Asking her to confront her captor might be too much. Nate gripped the back of the chair until his knuckles turned white. Jake's silences stretched his self-control to the limit. Nate had to reach deep inside the silent man's subconscious.

"You and I have a lot of history. Out of Wolfe's Pack, as Kaycie nicknamed us, you and I were the tightest. Tyrell and Marcus were good football players, but you were great. You could read my mind from anywhere on the field. If I got into trouble, you were the one who broke free and came back to pull off the catch of the game."

Jake lifted his head and quirked one eyebrow. His lips might as well have been glued shut. Nate accepted that Holly was the key.

"I'll ask Holly. But if she refuses, I expect answers."

Jake's eyes locked with his. Nate swallowed. What if medical science couldn't help Jake? What had he endured that brought him to this place?

"I'll only talk to her."

Nate bolted from the room.

****

Kay's screams vibrated off the walls in the empty room. Her calls for help had gone unheard. All she'd accomplished was a dry and raw throat.

Flat on her back, she used her feet to shove her body through the darkness. Each time she applied pressure to her soles, the stinging from lack of blood burned worse. Convinced she'd been here and knew her way around, she struggled until she rose to her knees. Her bound extremities made moving difficult and exhausting. Still, she had to try to get outside.

The sound of footsteps brought both hope and fear. Maybe somebody was looking for her. Maybe a security guard was making his rounds. Maybe Anthony Walsh had returned to inflict more misguided punishment for his son's death.

Too close to the door, she turned her body, trying to get out of the way, but something slammed her in the back and sent her sprawling facedown. She landed hard on the cement floor.

For a second time, the overhead light came on, blinding her. She kept her focus on the figure's feet, recognizing Walsh's shoes immediately.

He dragged a chair into the room, sat beside her, and rolled her over. He was the picture of calm, but his brown eyes were cold and cruel. He poked the toe of his shoe against her and then administered a series of kicks to her ribs.

Kay gasped for air but refused to beg. It had only angered him earlier.

"Trying to leave before the party started?"

"Take me home and we'll forget this happened." She lied, and he knew it. "You're not thinking rationally. It's grief talking."

"You could be right. I did have a hard time concentrating tonight because of you. In fact, I made my excuses and withdrew early. I never understood some men's enjoyment inflicting suffering on a female. Until now." His gaze slid down her body, making her feel stripped naked. "First, I'd planned on having the pleasure of killing you. During the first course, I had a better idea."

"Kill me, and you're no better than Hank."

Walsh laughed through a sneer. "Stupid bitch. You haven't figured it out yet. You will soon enough."

He reached down, dragged her to her feet, and then he released his hold. He made no effort to catch her, allowing her to fall. The crack of her shoulder reverberated inside her head, and waves of nausea washed over her.

"Why?" she asked. "This is way past revenge." If he wanted to kill her, why hadn't he shot her in the parking lot? This was more. Torture?

"This isn't revenge. It's justice."

She closed her eyes away from the ugliness and pictured Nate. Prayed he knew she cared for him. If given the chance, she'd tell him how much she loved him. Always had. Always would.

She startled when something sharp pricked her leg. Walsh had a knife pressed into her skin. Grinning, he leaned down and cut her ankles loose. Blood rushed to her feet, sending electric tingles and shocks straight to her toes.

"Get up," he commanded. "We've got business to take care of."

Kay scooted to the chair. Using it for balance, she leveraged herself upright. She recognized the room. Just as she'd thought, she'd escaped from here once before. Could she do it again?

The knife blade came to her neck. The cool steel sent a shiver through her. Walsh had obviously gone crazy.

He half-dragged her out of the warehouse. He shoved her in a car, slid the knife into his coat pocket, and pulled out a gun, which he aimed at her as he moved around to the driver's side.

"Where are you taking me?" She glanced around the car, hoping to find her purse. If someone had noticed her missing, they could track her using the GPS on her cell.

"You won't find anything that belongs to you. That fancy smartphone's battery has been removed, and all your things have been disposed of."

After a few blocks, he drove around behind a different warehouse and parked. Using a key card, he swiped the lock and forced her inside. Kay moved slowly while her mind raced. Her head, ribs, and shoulder throbbed. Her hands had lost all feeling, and they were pale from loss of blood.

No time for pain. No time for tears. No time for fear.

He pushed her down the hall to a room where a post stood in the middle of a small platform. Handcuffs were welded to the top. Kay stomach roiled. She stared at the man standing beside her. The truth sent blood racing from her head.

"Hank wasn't the monster behind the kidnappings and human trafficking. You are."

The elder Walsh had come across so kind and concerned about his son, they hadn't considered him a suspect. She realized now it was all an act. He was as evil as Hank. Maybe more so.

"I said you'd understand soon." His lips curled into a smirk.

In a dangerous move, he stabbed the knife between the rope binding her wrists and cut her free. Blood rushed to her hands, sending a burning sensation all the way to the tips of her fingers. She clutched her hands to her chest, rubbing life back into her skin.

"Get up there." With his hand between her shoulder blades, he shoved her onto the platform.

"You're a sick bastard. A son of a bitch who preys on unsuspecting young women!" she screamed. "Well, I'm not one of them. I'll see you on death row for Leann's murder."

"Such brave words." His lips curved into a cruel smile. "It won't take long for you to lose that fake bravado."

The feeling had returned to Kay's hands and feet. So she searched for a way to take advantage of her freedom. She forced herself to wait and pick the right time to move. Anger fired heated rockets throughout her body and blinded her to the danger of making him mad.

"Don't you want to know what's about to happen?"

"And spoil your fun? I'm sure you'll tell me." She gathered all her resolve and tried to sound brave while every nerve cell quivered.

Wait. Keep him talking until he stepped from behind the post. When he moved into the clear, she'd rush him. If he expected her to go quietly, he was in for one hell of a surprise. She'd fight for her life with every breath in her body.

"You're right. Given some time to think about your death, I decided killing you was too easy. Wouldn't satisfy me. I came up with something more appropriate." His tone was as gleeful as a kid's on Christmas morning.

"More appropriate?"

"Yes. You were so interested in the business, I think you should learn about it firsthand. You're older than my usual stock, but you'll still fetch a decent price. The two bidders will teach you everything you ever wanted to know." His tongue slid out, snaked across his lips as he ran his fingers down her cheek. "Too bad I won't be there to witness."

"You wouldn't dare." Her voice cracked, belying her bravado. Frissons of tiny quakes zipped through her body.

"Oh, I would. You're a bit old for their liking, so I'm reducing the price for a quick sale. They get off inflicting excruciating pain, so I'm betting they will keep you alive for a long time. They each have an underground room chock full of fun devices. Death will be a blessing by the time they're finished." He pointed at two computer screens.

"Dear God," she cried when her gaze landed on two men. Lurid grins across fat greasy faces leered at her. She gagged.

Walsh moved to the side and said, with a wave of his hand, "Let the bidding begin."

Kay ducked her head and charged like a linebacker. Weak and unsteady on her feet, she stumbled forward. Walsh sidestepped her, and she fell on her shoulder again. He grabbed her by the hair, dragged her back onto the platform and clamped a handcuff around one wrist. His hand tangled in her hair and smashed her head against the post. A dark void softened the exploding pain by pulling her under.

****

For the first time tonight, Nate was glad he'd contacted Tomas and Wayne. With lights and sirens blasting, they'd made record time getting across Dallas to Holly's apartment.

"We'll wait here," Tomas said.

Nate sprinted up the stairs. He'd raised his hand to knock when the door opened. Tyrell and Marcus were there with her.

"What's happened?" Holly's hand gripped Nate's bicep, pulling down on the sore shoulder. "Sit," she commanded. "You're white as a ghost."

"Can't," he refused, rubbing his forehead to stave off the headache. He studied her bruised face. How strong was she? Was he about to ask too much of her? Facing the man who'd held her hostage would take balls.

"I need your help." He led her to her couch. Only after she'd joined him, Nate continued. "I wouldn't ask if I didn't believe Kaycie's life is in danger, but Jake refuses to speak with anyone except you."

Tyrell shook his head. "She's been through enough. I'll talk to Jake."

"No, you won't," Nate snapped. "I'm asking Holly if she's up to facing him."

Tyrell's eyes were ablaze with anger, but Nate wasn't budging. He needed Holly's help.

"Tyrell," Marcus barked out the name. "It's Holly's decision. Let her make it."

"There has to be another way." Tyrell's voice bounced off the walls.

"Stop," Holly said, raising her voice. "I want to see Joh ... Jake. Deep inside, he's a good man. If he can help, he will."

Tyrell towered over her. "He used to be a good man. We don't know that person sitting in jail."

Her jaw tightened, thinning her lips. "Don't you dare judge him." She grabbed a jacket from the hall closet and stormed to the front door, where she stopped and glared back at Nate. "Get your ass in gear."

****

"Does he have to be chained like some dangerous criminal?" Holly protested. The anguish on her face worried Nate. She'd gotten too close to Jake.

"I'm afraid so." Tomas rolled his eyes.

They watched Jake through the two-way mirror.

"Keep him on topic," Nate cautioned before leading her around to the door. "We're running out of time. I feel it in my gut."

She straightened her shoulders and nodded once. "Let's pray your gut is wrong."

When Jake saw Holly, his face relaxed, smoothing out the frown lines between his eyes. For all practical purposes, Nate might as well have been invisible. He didn't care if it got Jake talking.

"Are you all right?" Jake asked, his gaze drifting across her face.

Her hand brushed across the discoloration on her face as if she could dust the bruises away. "Thanks to you, I'm well." She eased down in the chair across from Jake, and Nate moved to stand directly behind her. "They'll help you get well, Jake. You have to cooperate."

"I overheard them talking. The operation might kill me."

"But the surgery might save your life. Please let them try. And please help us find my friend." Holly's tone was urgent yet soothing. "A man kidnapped Kay in broad daylight. Nobody can ID him. The cops are searching, digging into who else was associated with Hank."

Jake snorted a sound Nate assumed meant disgust. Nate capitalized on it by jumping into the conversation.

"So Hank wasn't the brains. You did the world a favor by killing him. Although, I'd preferred to have done it myself."

Holly stretched her hand across the table, almost touching Jake. "Who told you to kidnap me?"

"I followed orders."

"But who issued them?" she prompted.

"Mr. A is the only person allowed to give me direct commands. His business is very important to him. He has customers who depend on him for good product."

Nate clamped his hand on Holly's shoulder when she recoiled in her chair. Damn, Jake's condition was worse than Nate imagined.

"And you were charged with taking care of Mr. A's business. How did you dispose of the," Holly swallowed, "ah, merchandise."

"Video auction. There would've been one tonight."

Nate took a calming breath and dragged over a chair. He sat, casually leaned back, and rested one ankle over the opposite knee as if two old friends were talking. "Oh yeah? Gotta have a private location for that."

Nate sat quietly while Jake described where the auction went down and how the girls were transported.

Holly asked, "You think Kay might be at the warehouse where the sales are held?"

"She could be. It's secure." Jake's mouth lifted into a smile. "Hidden behind a fake wall."

"Really?" Holly feigned interest. "That's the building I was in, right? Where is that?"

Jake spilled the address easily. Nate wanted to bolt from the room but had one more thing to ask.

"Can you describe Mr. A?"

Jake remained silent, the tendons in his jaw flexed. Nate opened his mouth, but a glance from Holly silenced him.

"Tell us. Please," she whispered, her tone calm and patient.

Nate held his breath as Jake's gaze swept across her face. "Tall, thin, gray hair. Distinguished. Sharp dresser."

"Oh, shit." Nate sprang from the chair, sending it tumbling backward.

Chapter Thirty

Nate's sanity hung by a thread. Why hadn't they realized the bastard wasn't the fragile, elderly gentleman he pretended to be? With his standing in the community, Anthony Walsh had the perfect cover. Jesus. No one had suspected him.

All the pieces fell into place. Old man Walsh was the brains behind the entire disgusting organization. How many teenage girls were in captivity because of him? How many were dead?

"One more question. Why was getting Hank's ring back so important?" Nate righted the chair. The bullet wound in his shoulder burned from the tensed muscles. He steadied himself and moved to the door. Turning, he waited for the answer.

"It's a signet ring and identical to one Mr. A had to quit wearing when Hank lost his. The last present Mr. A's wife gave them before she died. Somebody could've recognized it and then tied the Walshes to Leann Vaughn's death."

"You killed her, didn't you?" Nate had already guessed the answer.

"I followed orders."

"Let's go," Nate said to Holly.

She leaned across the table closer to Jake. "Take care of yourself. Let the doctors make you well. Okay?"

"They'll probably kill me. Is that what you want?"

"No. I want you to promise me you'll let people help you."

Jake nodded. "I'm sorry you were dragged into this mess. That's why I insisted on talking with you. So I could apologize." The corners of his mouth lifted briefly, and then he turned his gaze away from her.

"Holly." Nate opened the door. His patience was gone.

"Wait," Jake called out.

Nate spun, his impatience boiling over. "What?"

"Were you lying to get answers, or am I really Jake Donovan?"

"I don't lie. You're Jake." Nate's anger subsided at the bewildered expression on Jake's face. "And you have friends who won't turn their backs on you. We'll be around, and we'll be there when you get well. But right now, we have to go."

Wayne waited just outside, blocking the hallway. "Tomas is getting a verbal warrant for Walsh's warehouse."

Nate stepped around Wayne, pulling Holly along behind. "I'm not standing around doing nothing while Kaycie's in danger."

"Neither are we. By the time we get to the parking lot, we'll have the judge's okay on the warrant. This bust has to be legal."

Nate hurried Holly outside. Tyrell and Marcus had followed. They'd parked and waited.

"Wolfe," Wayne spoke from behind. His tone commanded attention. "You'll agree to do this the right way, or I'll have you arrested for obstruction."

Nate placed Holly's hand in Tyrell's. "Take her home. She can fill you in. Old man Walsh has Kaycie."

Turning to Wayne, Nate said, "Then I'm riding with you."

****

The raid almost resulted in Nate's arrest. He'd wanted to go in with the first wave. Damn police procedures. As soon as SWAT gave the all-clear sign, Wayne made Nate surrender his weapon before he could go inside. He didn't get through the door before a group of black-clad, Kevlar-vest wearing officers confronted him. Wayne waved Nate on past the blockade.

They went straight to the back wall and down the now open secret passageway.

Wayne reached out and grabbed Nate's right arm.

Nate clutched his shoulder, and growled, "Get off me. I'm going back there."

"With me." Wayne's gaze was icy. "Or I'll have these guys haul you out and handcuff you to my steering wheel."

A SWAT member stepped into view. He slid his helmet off and shook his head. "No female found, sir. The suspect is in the fourth office on the right. No one has questioned him."

"Thanks." Wayne clapped the man on his shoulder. "I'll kill him."

"Not on my watch," Wayne commented firmly.

Nate couldn't hold back any longer. He ran down the hall. The doors to rooms were splintered and hanging off the hinges. SWAT must've put their boot to each lock and kicked. Guards stood on either side of the door. Nate and Wayne stepped into the office.

"Mr. Walsh." Wayne wasted no time. "We know you abducted Kay Taylor. Where is she?"

Walsh sat straight-backed in a chair, hands in his lap. His lips curved downward in a sick sneer. The dignified appearance he'd presented to Nate and Kaycie was replaced by pure evil.

The hair on the back of Nate's neck rose. For the first time, he feared they were too late.

"Like my son, she's gone. Unlike my son, she'll suffer great pain before she dies."

"You scumbag." Wayne leaned forward. "How do you sleep nights?"

"Very well, thank you. I grew up being passed around like garbage. Do you know the price for a little boy sixty years ago?" He held a finger up as if issuing instructions not to interrupt him. "Not much. It didn't take me long to learn the value of human life. The fate of other people means zero to me."

The calm demeanor the old man displayed sent Nate's rage to explosion level. "You sick bastard. Tell us what you've done with her."

"She's gone. And you'll never find so much as a remnant of her."

In one motion, Walsh pulled a gun from under the desk, pressed the barrel into the underside of his chin, and fired.

Hair, blood, and brains exploded out the top of the old man's head, splattering pieces of him on everything and every person standing nearby.

Memories of war flooded Nate. He'd seen a man's head explode before. Hell, he'd pulled the trigger more than once. But never from this close range and never a suicide.

"Son. Of. A. Bitch," Wayne drawled out his words calmly as if that shit happened right in front of him every day. "Never had a suspect off himself before."

Tomas ran in with gun drawn. "Holy shit." He signed the cross before taking another step. "Nobody checked Walsh for a weapon?"

The young cop standing in the door swallowed a couple of times. The color drained from his face, leaving behind a ghastly pall. "I searched Mr. Walsh's person before ordering him to sit in that chair. I don't know where the gun came from."

Wayne shrugged and held his hand out to end the conversation. "Get out of here before you pass out," he said to the guard, whose face had paled to a ghastly white "We'll worry about those details later." He stepped to the door and spoke to a member of SWAT. "Get the techs in here to go over the computers. And keep those night-shift workers separated from each other until we talk to them. Then get a bus out here. We'll haul the lot downtown. Those bastards knew what was going on back here."

Wayne's calm, all-business demeanor said he'd seen death before. "What the hell was Walsh talking about?" Nate asked nobody in particular.

"Don't know yet." Wayne shrugged off his jacket and handed it to one of the cops close by. "Nate, he'll need your jacket, too. Looks like you've got brain matter and bone fragments on your collar."

Nate removed his coat and carefully handed it over. Damn old man Walsh. They needed him alive. Not fragments of him scattered across the wall.

His best chance of finding Kaycie had taken the coward's way out. Nate's lungs seized, wouldn't pull in a breath. He stormed out of the room and headed outside for fresh air. He turned a corner and spotted a cop at the other end of the hall. The officer's eyes were wide as saucers, and his jaw hung slack.

Nate forgot needing air. Instead, he hurried to the man. Nate stepped into a doorway. His fingers curled around the facing and squeezed.

Smack in the middle of the room was a small platform with an iron post cemented dead center. His gaze came to rest on a blood smear next to the handcuffs mounted on the post. He swept the room, taking in the camera and computer setup.

Son of a bitch.

Had the last act of old man Walsh's sorry life been to sell Kaycie? She'd probably been consigned into the hands of some sick bastard with no conscience. One who'd torture and inflict horrible pain without so much as a second thought. How long did they have to find her alive?

"Fuck," Tomas said from behind Nate. "Officer Ross, get the techs on these computers first. I want to know exactly where the last transmission came from. See if we can get an address."

Nate's head was about to explode. "Somebody provided transportation. We need the destination of every truck dispatched from this facility in the last twenty-four hours."

Tomas's face was rigid. Did he believe they'd lost her for good? No way was Nate ready to give up hope. He'd spend the rest of his life looking for her and the man who had her.

Before he took his last breath, he'd kill the bastard who bought her.

Chapter Thirty One

Kay jerked awake. The last thing she remembered was Anthony Walsh talking with the two fat slobs who were about to bid on her. Walsh must have knocked her out cold.

The auction. What had happened?

Her chest seized. She couldn't force enough air into her lungs. Tried to swallow, but her mouth was dry. She couldn't muster enough saliva to moisten her lips.

She tried to decipher the noises and motion around her. She was in the sleeper of an eighteen-wheeler being taken somewhere. The odor of stale cigarettes, old sweat, and ashtrays sent her queasy stomach into turmoil. Country music droned in the background.

Darkness surrounded her. Fear crawled through her like a snake through wet grass. Tears slid from the corners of her eyes.

She was going to die.

She wiggled her hands and feet. No bindings?

Gingerly, her hand swept across various throbbing body parts, and she sighed with relief. She still wore her clothes. So far, the pounding in her head was the worst thing that had happened.

She fingered the dried blood caked in her hair. How many blows could her skull take?

A male baritone coughed, hacking like a lung was about to come up. From the sound and the odor, his hacking and spitting were the result of too many cigarettes.

The rumble. The movement. The man.

Kay's heart rate quickened, climbing out of the stratosphere. Kay had been sold and was being shipped. Some sorry excuse for a human being had bought her.

Light flooded the area. She blinked against the glare. A seed of hope bloomed.

An unshaven, yellow-toothed man, reeking of sweat, grease, and tobacco leered over his shoulder. Kay refused to blink or flinch.

"You're awake. The drug wore off quicker than I expected." He patted his denim shirt pocket and focused on the highway. "Got your next dose right here."

"Please don't. I won't cause any trouble," Kay lied. "Really. I'll be good."

He glanced back again. Every muscle in her body tensed when his bloodshot eyes drifted across her body, and his tongue darted across his lips.

He coughed, leaned over to spit in a beer can, and then cleared his throat. "I'll bet you could be good."

How far would she go to stay alive?

"What's in the syringe?" She wanted to know how long she had been out but wouldn't ask. Her watch was gone, so she scanned the dash for a clock. Twelve-thirty and still dark. They couldn't have gone too far.

"You're a fighter. So the boss fixed you a shot. This is more than enough juice to keep you under control."

Right. Nothing would stop the fire racing through her blood. Or keep her from escaping.

"If you leave the sleeper open, we can talk."

"You got nothing I need to hear. The boss would have me gutted if you got away."

"He's about to be arrested."

He laughed, lit a cigarette, filling the cab with foul-smelling smoke. "That so? He didn't come off as too worried to me."

"His son's dead, and his head honcho is in custody. Who do you think will be next? I'm glad we won't be there when the raid goes down."

"You sound like a cop." His tone turned edgy and distrustful.

"Not a cop. An officer of the court. I'm a child protective agency investigator."

His head whipped around. His gaze narrowed. Had she said too much? "Well, you just upped the ante. The price for hauling you just went up."

Kay had agitated him. Maybe she could get under his skin.

"Now would be a good time to turn state's evidence. The FBI is involved. The feds come down hard on the interstate transportation of young girls." She had to bring him to her side. Convince him he could trust her. Or cause him to make a judgment error. Either way, she'd be free.

"Can't help you. This was my last run anyway. I heard about the killing from another trucker. The world didn't lose nothing when Hank died."

"He liked to hurt women," she said, using a timid tone.

"What he done ain't none of my business. I do my job and keep my mouth shut."

She gazed into the darkness. How much longer would she have to work on him? The absence of traffic struck her as odd. Why weren't they using the freeway?

"What are you hauling?"

"Dishwashers. I gotta drop you off first." He coughed and spit again. The odor wafted to the back of the cab and in her face.

Kay shivered at the matter-of-fact manner in which he'd delivered that piece of news. How many times had he made this same run? He delivered drugged, helpless, young women to monsters. He turned his head and looked the other way for money. The jerk was as guilty as one of those sick bastards.

She did a visual scan of the cab, searching for anything to use as a weapon. Other than the beer can, a carton of cigarettes, and paperback book, she found nothing.

"How far are we going?" She held her breath and leaned closer to him. Maybe if she let him think her mind was still dulled because of the drug, he'd be talkative.

"You ain't going far at all. Soon as I dump you, I'm headed for Ohio."

"I'm not one of your dishwashers. I'm a caring, feeling person. My name is Kay Taylor. And I can help you."

"You must think I'm stupid. I'm not fucking with that old man. I'm making my delivery, collecting my money, and then getting lost for a while. Now shut up."

Anxiety raced through Kay. Her stomach churned. Now was not the time to lose control. She rested her hand over her midsection and scooted as far back in the sleeper as she could get. Forcing her eyes to slits, she pretended to doze.

****

Running on black coffee, hate, and fear, Nate wadded the paper cup and dropped it in the trash. He dragged his hands through his hair, wishing it were still long enough for him to rip it out by the roots. Anything to pull him out of the abyss he'd fallen into.

"It's taking too long." Nate scrubbed a hand over his forearm. Shit, had millions of stinging ants burrowed under his skin? He could not stand still. Kaycie needed him, and he was doing nothing.

"We're doing everything we can." Wayne spoke, pulling Nate out of his pit.

"Well, it's not enough," Nate snapped. If the anger in his voice bothered Wayne, he didn't show it.

The warehouse had dispatched over twenty trailer loads to all corners of the US before SWAT had busted down the secret door. DPD had pulled out the stops to find Kaycie. The license plate numbers of each truck had been issued across the country.

Tomas had contacted the FBI for their assistance in the search across state lines.

Nothing minimized the guilt riding high in Nate's chest. He'd failed to protect her.

"I want Holly to talk with Jake again." Nate hovered over Wayne's desk.

"Why?"

"He knows more. Maybe he'll tell her which drivers haul the girls. That alone will narrow down the possibilities."

"If he tells you the truth." Wayne lifted a shoulder.

He dashed off a phone number. "Give me thirty minutes to get to Holly's and then you call us. Put a speakerphone in front of Jake, and I'll talk her through what to say."

Wayne called the jail and explained the plan. He ended the call with a hint of a smile.

"Donovan finally broke and gave us a little information. Seems he dated the file clerk in our office. She won't be supplying him with answers any longer."

"All the more reason to try and learn more from him."

"The feds are moving him this morning. You have about an hour before he's out of DPD's custody."

Wayne had a cruiser drop Nate off at his office. He pushed the bike into the alley, slung a leg over, and then turned the key. The big bike roared to life, and Nate sped toward Holly's apartment.

Tyrell answered on the first knock. Just as Nate had expected, nobody in her apartment was asleep.

"Give us some good news."

"None to give. The cops and feds put out a BOLO. They'll stop and search all the trucks recently dispatched from Walsh's warehouse as they locate them."

Nate moved into the room and tried to gauge Holly's mental condition. Red, swollen eyes said she'd been crying. He dropped down on one knee and wrapped her small hand with his.

"This hide and seek with the truck drivers isn't the way to find Kaycie. Too easy to miss the one rig she's in. If she's in one. Jake's the key, and we have to get him to open up." Nate was prepared to beg Holly if necessary. "I won't ask you to face him again, but will you talk to him over the phone?"

"Absolutely," she answered without hesitation. "I want to help."

Nate understood why she and Kaycie were such good friends. Loyalty had always been important to her. When he got her to safety, if she'd give him the chance, he'd prove just how faithful he could be.

****

Kay's bladder was about to pop. She'd waited a long time to mention it, giving the truck driver time to cool down. He was smarter than she'd anticipated, and she'd insulted him with small talk. She'd be more careful this time.

The driver changed gears. The big rig lurched and slowed down. The methodical *click-click-click* said he'd turned on his blinkers.

She slowly slid to the side of the bed. "I need to use the bathroom."

"I don't know what to tell you." He turned his head toward her and chuckled.

"Can I ask where we are?"

"You can." The cigarette hanging from the corner of his mouth filled the sleeper compartment full of smoke. "Don't mean you're gonna get an answer."

Kay fanned the air. "Really, I have to pee."

"Your timing couldn't be better." He downshifted, changing gears again. The truck slowed to a crawl.

Judging from what she could see, they were on a dirt road in the middle of nowhere. This time of the year, the weeds and trees were dead, but it was pitch black, and she couldn't even tell if they were still in Texas.

The air brakes groaned, and the rig came to a complete stop. The driver reached down to the floor and came up with a rope. He tossed the end with a loop back to her.

"This goes around your neck."

"What? Like a leash?" Kay's jaw dropped. He thought to walk her as if she were a dog. No way. She'd pee right there in his truck first. So what if he killed her? At least her death would be on her terms.

"Where you're going the least of your worries will be getting treated like an animal. Put it on, get out, and meet your master."

"No," she screamed.

The driver grabbed a handful of her hair and pulled her into the front of the cab. She fell, sprawled on the seat. Something hard pressed against her side. The syringe! She wrapped her fingers around what could be her freedom.

The truck's passenger-side door opened and hands gripped her ankles. Who had joined the struggle? Within seconds, Kay was facedown in the dirt.

"What's the hell's going on here?" a male voice demanded. He sounded angry.

"Help me!" She struggled to sit up.

"Shut up," the voice said. He shoved her flat on the ground with his foot.

"She wanted to pee but refused to put on the rope."

"Then she can hold it."

Damn, she'd dropped the syringe. Her chances of escape faded more with each second.

"Get her up. Let's get a good look at her."

Yeah. Get her up on her feet. They'd made a mistake by not

binding her ankles.

Chapter Thirty Two

"Jake had better be right." Nate accepted the earbud from Marcus. Staying in contact would be critical. "I need a gun."

"Where's yours?" Tyrell's fingers stopped pounding the keyboard on Holly's computer. He slid a knife from his boot and passed it to Nate. "Take care of this."

"Thanks. The cops made me surrender my weapon before I went into Walsh's warehouse. All hell broke loose, and I didn't get it back," Nate grumbled. "They were afraid I'd kill the bastard."

"Would you?" Holly picked up her purse, making Nate nervous that she might want to go with them. He couldn't allow her to put herself in jeopardy. "Would you have killed him?"

"Without blinking an eye." He left out the part where he'd have been happy to do it.

"Then take mine." She hauled a 45-caliber Glock from her purse and handed it to him.

The sight of this short, barefoot blond holding a weapon of that size would've been comical under different circumstances. Tonight, he was grateful.

"Shit, that's a cannon," Marcus commented after he pulled his chin off his chest. "Is it legal?"

"Like I told Kay, God and Texas know I carry."

The medallion on Nate's chest grew heavy. He absentmindedly removed the chain from under his shirt and rubbed the medal between his fingers. Marcus moved next to him, studying the Saint Jude.

"You've really got it bad. Don't you?" Marcus stated, a smile creeping across his face.

"No," Nate snapped.

"So why do you still wear it?" Marcus's eyebrows rose,

punctuating his question.

"Don't make something out of nothing," Nate answered. "Where's yours?"

"Who knows?"

"Where's what?" Tyrell growled, apparently not happy with the chatter.

"Nate's still wearing the Saint Jude medal Kay gave us."

"Ain't that sweet?" Tyrell made a sound like a muffled chuckle. "Although it doesn't surprise me."

Ready to change the subject, Nate stood behind Tyrell, checking if he'd found locations and pictures of the men Jake had suggested they look up. According to him, the two guys were long-standing customers of Anthony Walsh's. They'd eagerly taken problem girls off the old man's hands in the past.

It made sense Walsh would have wanted to get her out of sight fast. Maybe he had sold her to somebody out of state. These two men were in Texas and close by. This was one hell of a long shot, but Nate couldn't wait while all those big rigs were hunted down, stopped, and then searched.

The printer kicked into high gear, and Nate hovered until the documents rolled onto the tray. He retrieved and read carefully, committing the information to memory. The coffee in his belly rebelled just looking at the pictures of the sick sons of bitches.

Both men were masquerading as upstanding citizens. Stephens was a veterinarian. His home and office were in the country outside of Fort Worth, and the other twisted bastard owned Duncan's used car lot in a small town fifteen miles east of Dallas.

"Jake had better be right," Tyrell grumbled, handing copies to Marcus.

Nate understood Tyrell's concern, but Jake had been adamant. These two bastards were Walsh's go-to buyers when a female was too hard to sell because of bad behavior. Sick motherfuckers should be tortured themselves.

Holly handed Nate a cup of fresh coffee. Without thinking, he drank. The hot liquid burned the back of his throat. For some odd reason, experiencing a little pain was comforting.

What was Kaycie enduring right this second? Was she suffering?

Frightened? His fingers flexed. Palms itched. The gun felt good in his hand.

"You're sure we shouldn't wait for the cops?" Marcus asked.

"Hell, no. I'm not waiting for anybody. They'd want to put a plan together while they tried to get a warrant. I'm not holding their hands. You and Marcus take Duncan, he's the closest. I'll take Stephens."

Tyrell slid on his old-fashioned shoulder harness. A leftover from his bodyguard days. "Let's get to it."

Nate was bouncing on the balls of his feet. Adrenaline pumped through his veins at supersonic speeds as he slid the Glock into his empty holster.

"This is right. I feel it." He turned to Holly. "I owe you. Big. I won't forget everything you've done."

"Just bring Kay home."

Nate stuffed a piece of paper in Holly's hand. "Give us forty-five minutes then call this number. Tell Tomas I know he listened to your conversation with Jake. Tell him we've gone ahead to check out these two perverts."

Tyrell and Marcus followed Nate down the stairs. No further discussion or planning was needed. They simply separated in the parking lot to carry out their assignment. No words were spoken. Nobody gave a rah-rah speech to tell them how important this was. Each man loved Kaycie in his own way and wanted to bring her home. Nate refused to believe they'd accomplish anything less.

The motorcycle moved under Nate as if it understood the urgency. When he hit the on-ramp to the freeway, he pushed the bike faster until billboards, speed-limit signs, and light posts blurred, looking like toothpicks. Air swirled under his visor while his heart twisted inside his chest. For the first time in years, Nate prayed. Prayed for her safety. Prayed he'd get to her in time.

Kaycie was alive. Every pulse of his racing heart said she was close. He felt it. Tasted it. Wore it like a shield as he raced into the night.

The Saint Jude medal scorched his determination into his chest. He would find her. He had to.

****

"Master," the monster said, while tightening the rope around Kay's neck. "You're to address me as Master. And keep your gaze and head pointed to the ground. Punishment will be severe if you look me in the face."

Kay swallowed, fighting for a breath. By slipping the rope over her head before allowing her to stand, they'd effectively ended her plan to run. She clamped her lips shut, grinding her back teeth. If this sleazebag expected her to play his game, he was crazy.

She glared at him, openly defiant. She memorized every peak and valley on his face. She'd never forget how his eyes were set too close together or the pencil-thin scar that bisected his left brow. When she escaped, she'd remember every detail and easily describe him to a police forensic artist.

Around five-feet-nine, with a pork jowl, the overweight, middle-aged man might have appeared benign to a stranger, but to Kay, he reminded her of the deadly copperhead. The one snake that dared humans to cross its path. It didn't slither away if given the chance—it would come after you.

He shrugged his shoulders. "I've dealt with arrogant bitches who tried to escape. Fought me. Disobeyed me. After a few lessons, they learned just as you will. I won't tolerate disrespect."

His gaze raked across her. With a disgusting gleam in his eyes, he gripped her tattered blouse, ripped it off, and inspected her like a prize hog. He poked at her flesh. His fingers clamped down on her nipples and twisted.

She screamed in agony. The truck driver laughed, tightening the rope around her neck.

The monster smiled. "Yell all you want. Nobody will hear you." He leaned in close and stuck his face close to hers. "Except me. And the louder you are the better I like it."

Suddenly, all of the females he'd stripped of their dignity, tortured and killed, gathered and filled her with rage. She collected what saliva she could and spit in his face.

He wiped his face with her blouse, tossed it to the ground, and then rammed his fist into her abdomen. The blow struck with such force, her bladder released, soaking through her underwear and jeans. When he realized she'd wet herself, he laughed in her face and then hit her again. Kay gagged and collapsed against the noose.

Despair drained every ounce of strength out of her. Nobody was coming for her.

The trucker's voice seemed far away when he spoke. "You want her in the trailer?"

"Yeah," the monster said. He stepped to the back of a horse trailer and opened the side walk-through door.

Each man grabbed an arm and jerked her up and forward. Kay surprised herself. Hell, yes, she still had fight left, and she proved it by struggling against them while they pulled her along. She dug in her feet and made them drag her. Her shoes came off so she fought for purchase with her toes.

She wrestled with every ounce of strength she had left while they fastened metal clamps around her ankles and wrists.

When the two men were finished, she was standing spread-eagle in the nose of the enclosed trailer. She strained against the binding only to have the metal cut into her skin. She was trapped like a wild animal. Still, she thrashed and tried to free herself.

The stench in her new prison was overwhelming, causing her eyes and nose to burn. The walls were a dark gray, and she stood on black rubber mats that were used to help a horse or cow to keep their hooves under them.

So the bastard actually hauled animals in this contraption when he wasn't carrying helpless girls to their doom?

Where the strength came from, she didn't know. But she whipped her head back and slung her matted hair off her face. She lifted her gaze, locking onto the man's who'd bought her.

"You will die for what you're doing. Maybe not while I'm alive, but a man will come. He'll hunt you down like the vermin you are. And I promise, come hell or high water, you will suffer wrath like you've never known."

"Stop. You're scaring me," he said in a high-pitched, mocking tone. He jerked a rag from his back pocket, stuffed it in her mouth, and then tied one around her head to secure the gag in place. "That should silence your smart mouth until we get home."

"Want me to give her this last shot before you go?" the truck driver asked.

"No. I want her fully awake. Let her spend some time thinking about the gadgets and fun items waiting for her."

She ignored the razor-like pain and bucked against the metal braces. Apparently satisfied she couldn't get away, the two men exited without looking back.

On her chest, the Saint Jude medal rested between her breasts. Knowing one other person wore its mate eased her fear.

Nate. Saying his name inside her head gave her comfort. Comfort knowing when he came home from Colombia and learned of her fate, he'd search until he found the bastard who'd killed her. Comfort that the punishment he'd administer would be fatal.

Soon the trailer started moving. Her wrists and ankles were shackled, but her head and body jerked and swayed with the movement. The road was bumpy, leaving her to believe they were taking a back or deserted road to their destination. With each rough spot, Kay's appendages were stretched by the restraints, cutting grooves into her skin. The burn in her shoulders felt as if they'd slipped the sockets. Maybe they had.

This kind of hate and cold fear was alien to Kay. She'd never wanted to kill a person with her bare hands. But then her future had never been this bleak.

She tried again and again to spit out the gag. The trailer bumped to a stop. Then the pickup's engine died and a door opened and closed. Not a sliver of light could get inside.

Kay was frantic. She could only imagine the horrors that the pervert had in store for her. To retain her sanity, she refused to stop struggling. Had to believe she could break free. She lunged forward. Again and again, she battled her restraints. The pain in her joints intensified. She used it. Got madder. More determined to find a way out.

Even as the cold night air numbed her skin, her self-preservation instinct refused to let her give up. Until, exhausted, she collapsed. A dead weight, supported only by the shackles, she listened to the quiet. No human sounds. Nothing but her heaving while she fought to breathe through her nose. Her lungs demanded oxygen.

She waited. The bastard would have to drag her outside. Where had he taken her?

Chapter Thirty Three

Nate killed the bike at the beginning of the dirt road and stowed it out of sight in nearby bushes.

A hint of a breeze stirred. The sky was clear and full of stars. Using the almost-full moon, he traveled the rest of the way on foot.

Every nerve was taut as he moved silently through the darkness. Kaycie had to be here. Had to be alive. He prayed he hadn't made a mistake by going straight to Stephen's house. The veterinary clinic seemed an unlikely place to hide a torture chamber. It faced a busy highway and the traffic was heavy even late at night.

The residence, however, was secluded in the country away from curious people and the law.

His gaze swept over the property. A brick house with detached garage and a barn sat in the middle of a wooded area. No outside lights were on, which suited his plan. He whistled low, fully expecting to find a couple of dogs wandering loose. Nothing. He stepped into the open and went straight to the house.

He'd put all his military training to work tonight. Control was the key. Mentally, he slowed his racing heart to a nice normal rate. Regulated his breathing.

He wasn't going to waste time covertly searching in the dark. If Kaycie was here, Stephens could get his ass up and take Nate to her.

Opening the back door was a snap. He eased inside then glanced around to get his bearings. This was a big house with room for more than one man, but Tyrell's intel indicated Stephens had never married and lived alone.

A dim light shone from the front room. Nate moved closer, keeping his body flush against the wall. A Budweiser clock that looked like it belonged behind a bar hung over a rock fireplace. It provided enough light he could see his way around. A couch, a couple of chairs and a flat-screen TV gave the place a homey look. Nice cover.

Nate quickly moved down the hall. The first and second bedrooms were empty. The third, he hit pay dirt. They were alone.

He slid the knife Tyrell had lent him from his boot. In one motion, Nate jerked the figure in the bed to the floor and pressed the razor-sharp blade against soft flesh.

"Nod if you're Carl Stephens."

The bastard moved his head in admission.

"Where is she?"

Nate's sense of right and wrong had vanished long before he entered the house. The pain he wanted to inflict on this sorry excuse for a human being almost consumed him. He eased the pressure, reached up, and flipped on the bedside lamp.

The man lay very still. That he didn't struggle or fight sent warning flags waving in Nate's head.

"I don't know what you're talking about," the weasel croaked out.

"Tell me, or I'll cut your fucking balls off and stuff them down your throat," Nate growled. His confidence Kaycie was here grew when Stephens refused to look at him.

"Who are you?" The fear in Stephens's eyes didn't sway Nate one bit.

"Your executioner. And you're closer to death than you realize. Where. Is. She?"

"You can't break in here like this. If you're the law, where's your warrant?"

"Pressed against your neck."

Stephens's body tensed. His gaze narrowed. "If you're not a cop, you're breaking the law."

Nate's lips curled in disgust. The pervert had nerve. "Which means I have no boundaries or restrictions on my behavior. I kill you and nobody ever knows I was here. You brought a woman home with you. Where is she?"

"Look around. There's nobody here but me."

Nate dragged the overweight man to his feet and threw him in the corner. "Don't you move."

He searched the room. Looked under the bed, dug through the closet and found nothing. His frustration built with each failure. He stomped his boots on the floor, looked for loose boards. Tossed the rugs, checked for secret rooms. Found nothing.

He wrapped his fingers around Stephens's shirt collar and pushed him from room to room where Nate repeated the search.

"Listen you scumbag, I know all about how you get off torturing women. But you picked the wrong woman. For every pain you've inflicted on her, you'll suffer three."

"You're crazy." Stephens tried to look defiant, but the flicker of panic behind his eyes had given him away. "Get off my property."

"Outside." Nate threw the bastard onto the porch when he moved too slow. "Don't you move a hair."

Pulling a penlight from his back pocket, he searched around the porch. Frustration built when he came up empty. Stephens's refusal to tell the truth drove Nate to the edge of snapping.

The barn sat a few hundred feet behind the house, and he marched Stephens down the drive to the big double doors. Nate's heart rate jumped. No padlock, something most people who lived out in the country didn't use, made him fear she wasn't inside. He kicked open the doors, dragged the vet inside and unceremoniously tossed him to the dirt floor.

Nate stuffed the flashlight into his pocket and then stabbed his fingers through his hair. The urge to beat the shit out of Stephens was getting hard to resist. Fear for Kaycie ate at Nate's insides, churning his guts into knots. He tightened his hands into fists then relaxed them again and again, forcing his muscles and tendons to unwind.

He was nowhere near finished looking. He shoved bales of hay and sacks of feed out of his way. He searched a storage room full of medical supplies. The more frustrated he became, the more he tossed the place. He found no trace of Kaycie or any other female.

"You son of a bitch." He stalked back to Stephens. "I'll kill you if you've hurt her."

Stephens's lips narrowed to a thin line. He didn't speak. The look in his eyes had shifted to cold and defiant. Way too cocky.

"Tyrell." He and Marcus hadn't checked in since heading to the other suspect. "Talk to me."

"Sorry, bro. Been busy. We found a girl." Tyrell's voice came through Nate's earbud. "Alive and hysterical. Fucking torture devices everywhere."

"No sign of Kaycie?" Nate rocked back on his heels, barely controlling his urge to lash out at the vet.

"Not that we can see. The young woman was naked, cut, burned, and barely coherent. Marcus unchained her, wrapped her in a blanket, and carried her outside into the fresh air. We asked if she'd seen another female. She shook her head. Cops and paramedics are on the way."

"Then Kaycie's here." Nate turned his gaze toward the vet. Pounding the sick bastard into the ground was getting closer to a reality.

"We're heading your way when the EMTs arrive. Kay has to be there," Tyrell said.

Nate stuffed his cell in his pocket. He jerked Stephens to a standing position, pulled him close.

"I'm about to cut your sorry throat. Which means you're seconds away from death." Nate pressed the blade into the man's flabby neck hard enough to draw blood. "I'll find her while you bleed out."

"Wait. I know what you're searching for. I'll show you," the slimeball said, his self-confidence apparently reversing itself. "But the person you're looking for isn't there."

Ignoring the stab of pain in his shoulder, Nate dragged Stephens outside the barn and tossed him in the dirt.

"Where?" Nate's mind couldn't imagine what might be in such a torture chamber. Besides, Stephens was too quick to give up his hiding place. If this was a trick, it was about to be his last.

Stephens scrambled to his feet, and Nate took his flashlight from his pocket. Illuminating a small path, he escorted Stephens through the trees to a clearing. Nate sucked in a breath when he spotted the cellar door.

"Open it." A deadly calm washed over him. Stephens would die underground if she was down in that dark hole.

The stench of urine and fear burned his eyes as he followed the man down the steps to a man-made hell. A flip of a switch flooded the chamber of horrors with light. Nate's mind took a second to wrap around the disgusting scene.

He shoved Stephens against the wall, bouncing his head off a shelf and rattling chains suspended from the ceiling. "Move one inch, please. There's only one thing I want more than seeing you dead."

"I told you," Stephens whined. "No one is down here."

Nate's experience in the war had taught him about the cruelties of man. But as his gaze swept the area, he realized the horrors he'd witnessed in Afghanistan were nothing compared to what had been endured down here. And by how many young women?

A metal table was surrounded by leather whips of every size. Chains with handcuffs were suspended from the ceiling along with branding irons and cattle prods. He turned away from the razor-sharp instruments scattered around the small room and searched. He found no hidden chambers and no Kaycie.

"You sick son of a bitch, you'll sleep with the devil tonight."

"I'm a collector," the vet said. "I would never use any of these things on another human being."

"Keep lying, and I'll suspend you from the ceiling and leave your sorry ass down here to rot. You can die with your collection." Nate herded Stephens back outside. "Get your disgusting ass back to the barn."

Nate shoved Stephens across the yard and through the barn doors. A low whinny drew his attention.

"Get halters on those two horses. Release them into the corral out back."

Stephens followed the instructions while Nate watched. Then he turned off the flashlight, returned it to his pocket, and then flipped on the interior lights. He grabbed a pitchfork and carefully pushed through the dirt floor of the stalls, hoping to hit a fake bottom. He prayed to hear the dull thud of the tines striking a hidden door. His efforts were fruitless.

His temples pounded, and the tenuous hold he had on his sanity faded. Stephens sat slumped against a bale of hay, watching. His smug expression had returned.

"You have ten seconds to tell me where she is." Nate advanced, ready to snap the bastard's neck.

A noise stopped him midstep. He froze, listening. A sliver of hope filled his heart, and sweat beaded his face in the cool air.

"I have another storeroom." Stephens shuffled to his feet. Animated and full of life, he waved enthusiastically toward the back of the barn.

"Shut up," Nate commanded. "Kaycie," he yelled and then listened.

"No, really. Come this way." Stephens was all of a sudden willing to help. Or was he trying to distract Nate?

Again, Nate heard a noise. A thump. Then another. From behind him. He whirled and ran toward a pickup sitting out back with a horse trailer still hitched to the bumper.

Nate jerked open the cab door, looked in the backseat. His heart dropped when she wasn't there. A quick check proved the truck bed was empty, and the storage box full of vet supplies.

"You sick bastard. You heal animals and torture humans." He spit on the ground. "Get against the barn and sit."

Nate stood back, focusing on every sound.

"Kaycie!" he shouted. "Kaycie." A level of helplessness he'd never experienced almost drove him to his knees. "Help me," he called as he started to the back of the rig.

Nate came to a stop. The walk-through door and the rear trailer gate were padlocked. He stuffed the knife in his boot, drew the Glock, aimed at the side of the lock, and pulled the trigger.

A barely discernible sound came from inside. Please, God, let it be her. He swung open the gate. The sight brought a roar up from deep in his chest. He holstered the weapon and closed the gap between them.

Her body hung limp against metal shackles. A rag had been tied around her mouth. Dear God, she looked like she'd been nailed to an invisible cross.

"I'm here, sweetheart. You're safe." He stroked her face and removed the rag then tugged the gag from her mouth.

She gasped for air, her lungs rising and falling as if she'd almost smothered. His undivided attention was on the woman he loved.

"Nate." Her voice was so weak he prayed he hadn't imagined it.

"Shh. Don't try to talk." He wrapped his arms around her, taking her weight off her bindings for a minute. "I can't take a chance on firing a gun inside this trailer. I have to get something to free you."

"No," she whimpered. "Don't leave me."

"Count to thirty. I'll be back before you finish." He reluctantly released her. Her moan of pain and protest cut through him like a knife.

He ran to the barn where he'd noticed a rack of tools, slowing when he realized Stephens was nowhere to be seen. Kaycie was Nate's priority. He'd track Stephens down later.

Nate skidded to a stop. The slot where he'd seen the ax was empty. He sensed a presence behind him. He dove to the dirt floor just as the steel point slammed past his head. He rolled, drew the Glock, and fired. The bullet struck Stephens dead in the heart. The strong buck of the gun in Nate's hand was the second most satisfying feeling he'd had today. Stephens dropped. Eyes open. Blood seeping from the hole in his chest.

Nate jerked the axe from the dead man's hand and ran to free Kaycie. He managed to pry the chain from the side of the trailer and unbound her hands. Her body draped across his back while he struggled for enough leverage to free her feet. He pulled her up where he could look into her unblinking eyes. The agony in them tore through his soul.

He patted her down, checking for broken bones. She'd been through hell, but he couldn't find anything life threatening. Her body would ache for a long time, and no doubt, he'd hold her in his arms through some nightmares, but she was alive.

"The gunshot?" she asked.

"That bastard's dead."

"Good."

Nate removed his shirt and slipped it over her head. Her teeth chattered from shock. He rubbed her arms and back, trying to warm her.

"Cops are on their way. Let's wait right here."

"Outside." Her voice, even weak and pleading, gave him hope. "Take me out of this thing."

"My pleasure." Cradling her limp body as if she were a child, he carried her to the open driveway and sat with her on his lap. His chest felt as if it would burst when she curled around him. She released a soft cry, her breath warm on his neck.

He rocked her while the sun painted the sky with gold and orange streaks. He'd never seen a more beautiful dawn.

She lifted her gaze to his face. "Are those tears for me?"

Jesus. His cheeks were wet. He'd been ten years old the last time he'd cried, after learning his parents had died in a boating accident.

"Looks like it." He brushed her dark tangled hair off her forehead. "I love you. You know that, don't you?"

Crashing from an adrenaline high, his body and mind ached while he waited for a response. He might be holding her in his arms, but she held his heart in her hands.

"You saved me. Again."

"I'm not so sure about that," he whispered. "You said maybe I'd survived Afghanistan for a reason. Maybe you were right. Maybe I was meant to be here when you needed me. Maybe you saved me."

The silence of the early morning sunrise was shattered by sirens. Judging from the sounds, more than a few cops and EMTs were about to descend on this chamber of horrors.

"Nate," she said, soft as the breeze sliding through the cold morning. Her eyes closed and her body went limp.

This time he did cry out to the heavens.

Chapter Thirty Four

Nate's scent, clean, woodsy and all man, tickled Kay's senses. True to his word, he'd taken a quick shower and returned to her.

"Hello, gorgeous." His baritone words sent tingles across her skin. He leaned over her bed and kissed her forehead.

"Hello, yourself." Stiff, bandaged wrists didn't prevent her from reaching up to slide her fingers through his short hair. "You do clean up nice."

She marveled at her handsome hero. His tailored navy shirt set off his blue eyes and broad shoulders. Crisp starched jeans highlighted his narrow hips. Yep. She was definitely feeling better.

Her heart fluttered when he grunted and ignored her compliment. With his dark shaggy locks cut and bad-boy day-old beard shaven, his blue eyes sparkled even brighter. When his lips lifted into a smile, the cold, clinical feel of her sterile environment vanished. His presence diminished any residual aches and pains. He'd sat through the nights with her to keep the nightmares at bay.

"Between the two of us, we're spending way too much time in hospitals."

"And not even in the same bed." She patted the mattress. "You could join me."

He arched one eyebrow. "Don't tempt me."

His finger ran along her jawline, and his thumb brushed her lip. She relaxed into his hand, enjoying the warmth of his touch.

"I have plans for you later today." Her hand drifted down the front of his shirt to his waistband.

"Stop that." He glanced at the open door. "Your mom and dad could walk in any minute."

"There you go ruining the mood. Besides, I'm not sure I can talk to my dad about the accident."

"You'll be fine," he chided. "You confided in me, and the world didn't end. Your dad needs to know the truth."

"What truth?" Her father's cold voice sent Kay's determination into free fall.

Nate crossed the room and extended his arm. "Nice to meet you, sir." He turned to Kay's mother. "And you too, ma'am."

Her dad's jaw was set and his eyes unreadable as he accepted Nate's handshake. "I understand you saved Kay's life."

Kay's resolve sank even lower.

"She's a fighter. I just got there before she freed herself."

"So you're still on the payroll. What are you protecting her from now?"

"Dad." Kay was stunned at his question. She swallowed the hurt. Her father hadn't bothered to thank Nate.

As if he knew she needed him near, Nate moved to her side. The nerves in his jaw twitched. He reached behind himself, pulled out his wallet, and then took out the check she'd written him. He held it up for everyone to see. She had no idea he hadn't deposited her retainer. When he tore it into small pieces and placed it in her hand, tears sprang to her eyes.

"I'm not on the payroll anymore, sir." His gaze locked on her dad's. "But she's important to me, and I'll protect her from anyone who wants to hurt her."

She wiped away a runaway tear, refusing to show any weakness.

Nate had removed all obstacles blocking her trust. Except one. Why hadn't he told her that he'd accepted the FBI assignment? Every time he'd stepped into her hospital room, she'd hoped he'd come clean.

If today was about truth, she had to call him out.

"You can't protect me if you're in Colombia." She hated that she sounded bitter after everything he'd done to save her life.

Damn him for saying he loved her. And damn him for not saying it since. That old niggle of doubt resurfaced.

"Tyrell flew out this morning." His hurt expression cut right through her. "I told you I wouldn't leave."

The air whooshed from her lungs. They'd talked a lot over the past few days, but Kay realized there was still more to say, later when they were alone.

"And I didn't believe you. I'm sorry." Guilt washed over her. Wasn't it time to trust him? Time to let go of the past?

"Dad, there's something I need to tell you."

****

Nate sent Kaycie an occasional encouraging wink while she relived the night of her brother's death with her folks.

Nate rolled his sore shoulder. Funny how before it felt like a hot poker stabbed into his flesh. He'd completely forgotten the injury when he'd learned she was missing.

Since getting things straight with both Fort Worth and Dallas police, he'd spent every available minute next to her hospital bed. They'd talked for long hours. Not Nate's favorite thing to do, but emptying and tossing out old baggage was for the best. Cleaning house so to speak.

She'd told Nate about the accident that had killed her brother. She'd agreed in order to move forward, she had to tell her parents the truth. Her mother had promised to ensure her father came today, if she had to drag him.

So far, Charles Taylor had remained stone-faced. His head was turned, directing his gaze out the window instead of at his daughter.

Nate swallowed the urge to twist the asshole's head off and send him home without it. He twined her fingers through his, while cursing her father for turning away from her.

"Go on, sweetheart. Finish this." Nate hoped his words of encouragement would give her the strength to set the record straight once and for all. She gave his hand a squeeze, and Nate loved this strong, remarkable woman even more.

"It's the truth, Dad." Her voice grew steady. "I was in the car behind Kevin. He was drunk and refused to give me the keys. When we pulled him from the wreckage, he was still conscious. A DUI and a wreck would've cost him his scholarship, so he begged me to say I was driving. When the cops arrived, I lied."

Kaycie's mother moved closer. "Oh, baby. Why didn't you tell us?"

"After Kevin died, you two were in such agony. What good would it have done?" Kaycie leveled her gaze on her father. "Would it have made any difference in the way you felt, Dad?"

"I don't know." Her father turned to face Kaycie, and chills raced up Nate's spine.

"You wished it had been me."

The pain reflecting from Kaycie's eyes ripped Nate's insides to shreds.

"Honey, that's not true. Why would you think such a thing?" Kaycie's mother's tone was incredulous.

"I remember the exact words." Kaycie's gaze never moved from her dad. "'If God had to take one of my children, why did it have to be Kevin.' That's what you said, wasn't it, Dad?"

Kaycie's mother whirled on her husband. "You didn't."

"I was distraught." He turned away. Not denying nor apologizing.

Nate's palms itched. Between him and her father, it was no wonder she didn't trust men.

"Kaycie's been through enough for one day," a deep voice said from behind. "You two clear out and let her young man take her home."

"Papa." Kaycie held her hand out to the older gentleman. Nate willingly stepped back to let him closer.

Her grandfather kissed her cheek. "I stopped by the nurse's station. They tell me you're going home."

"Yep. They've pumped me so full of fluids my veins slosh." She wiggled her arm as if to demonstrate.

"Dehydration is nothing to fool with." Her grandfather pulled his glasses from the top of his head, seated them on the bridge of his nose, and inspected her abrasions.

"Quit that," Kaycie grumbled. "I'm not one of your cadavers. You've probably got better preserved bodies waiting for you at the morgue." She smiled, and Nate recognized the playful look.

Apparently satisfied, Mr. Taylor turned to Nate.

"Thank you again for bringing my granddaughter home safely."

"No thanks necessary."

The older man lifted a shoulder. "I'm afraid you'll have to get used to it. I can't seem to say it enough."

Kaycie's father moved one step toward her, and Nate hoped he was coming forward to bridge the gap. He didn't.

Her grandfather leveled his gaze on her father. "Go home, Charles, and think about the harm you've caused. Then come up with a plan to get your daughter to forgive you."

****

"Your dad will come around," Holly said in her typical bossy manner, prompting Kay to pull her friend in for a hug.

"Who knows? At least it's out in the open." She'd promised Papa that she'd try to reconnect with her dad. So Sunday she and Nate were having lunch at her parents' house.

"You're sure I can't stay and do the dishes?" Holly asked.

"No way. You've done enough for me." Kay linked her arm in Holly's, escorting her to the door. "Go."

"Good to see you bossing people around again," Marcus said, bending to drop a kiss on Kay's cheek before stepping into the hallway. He grinned, which was something he didn't do often and cast a glance at Nate. "You'll let me know when you hear from Tyrell?"

"You bet," Nate promised. "We're in this as a team."

His hand on her waist separated her and Holly, and he gently pulled Kay back inside the apartment. Snuggled against his hip, she listened as he continued to discuss the new agency with Marcus.

She was getting close to hero worship, and she couldn't seem to stop herself. The relationship she wanted with Nate didn't depend on his heroics. His strength, honesty, and loyalty set him apart from a lot of men. Her pride in the man he'd become filled her with love.

His warmth wrapped around her like a blanket and sent her woman parts throbbing. She tried to get even closer. What she had in mind after the door closed sent a shudder of anticipation coursing through her. He'd make love with her even if she had to seduce him. A prospect she rather enjoyed.

She dragged her mind back to Marcus and Holly, who with any luck were leaving soon. Heat flashed up her cheeks when she realized Holly was watching with interest. The twinkle in her friend's eyes said she knew where Kay's mind had been.

"Enough talk. See you tomorrow." Holly took charge, wrapping her hand around Marcus's sizable bicep.

Kay worried about Holly. She hadn't returned to her lively, mouthy self. She'd resigned from the agency even though she'd had no direct contact with the cases. As systems manager, she'd read and heard a lot of sad stories. She'd said she simply couldn't cope anymore. Kay hoped counseling would help.

"Goodnight," Kay said fondly before closing the door.

She sighed and realized Nate had done the same thing. It brought a chuckle from them both. They were alone for the first time today.

She looped her fingers through his and led him into the kitchen. They cleaned up the supper mess, which really consisted of paper sacks, a bucket of chicken bones, and four glasses.

"I wish I'd been coherent enough to watch the Fort Worth cops handcuff you," she said, having trouble keeping her mind on anything other than the sensual nearness of his body.

"Nothing to see. As long as they were taking care of you, I went peacefully."

He tilted his head and studied her. His lips lifted into that sexy, heart-stopping Cheshire cat grin. The one he had to know turned her knees to rubber. The one that said he was close to giving in. The one that he hadn't used last night when she'd tried to get him in her bed. No way was she still too weak for sex.

He handed her a dirty glass, which she stared at until her brain started working again. She recovered and placed it in the dishwasher.

"Seriously. Are you square with the law?"

"Yeah. Thanks to Dalton having vouched for me with DPD earlier. Tyrell taking the Colombia assignment made my employment with the FBI more official."

"Will you have enough work for all three of you?"

"I'll have to get busy. Drum up enough business. We'll lean heavily on Dalton for introductions and recommendations, but, yeah we'll make it."

"Is that the reason for the haircut and shave?" she asked.

"I think it had more to do with my mental state than anything."

Smack, he hit her with the smile again. Cleaned up and in a business, he'd have women falling over him.

"You'll be the front man for your detective agency."

"Until we're established. I don't think you can call what we do detective work. We'll be more in the business of problem solving."

"For the government," she added.

"Sometimes. The money's good."

"And the work's dangerous." She wished she could take the statement back. She loved the whole package and this was part of it.

"You're right on both counts. Think of it this way. The pay's enough to allow us to help regular people find solutions. I'd like to continue finding lost or missing people."

"Lost and Found, Inc. has a nice ring to it."

His hand went to his head. His fingers seemed to hunt for the long hair no longer there.

"You looking for a job?"

"I have a job." She paused. "At least, I think I do." She again noticed the tattoo on the inside of his bicep. The SEAL markings over his right breast made sense, but this one was a mystery. She stroked a finger down his arm. "You never explained the tattoo. It's a word, isn't it?" His raised eyebrows prompted her to press harder. "It's my name, isn't it?"

His laugh stirred heat through her veins, coiling low in her stomach. "Aren't you the conceited one?" He tried to sound stern, but the edges of his mouth quivered.

"Well? Am I right?"

"No. As a matter of fact, you're wrong."

"Then tell me." She stalked him, and he moved to the living room, avoiding her.

If he continued to handle her as if she were a piece of fragile glass, Kay might just tackle him.

"You didn't give me a definitive answer. Do you want to work with us?"

His question floored her. "You're serious."

"Hell, yeah. Why not? You're smart and trained. Besides, if you're involved, maybe you won't freak out every time I take a job that's the least bit dangerous."

She placed her hands on his chest and stroked up to his neck, kneading her fingers as she went. His gaze darkened for a second, then he tried to escape.

Kay pressed against him. The length of their bodies touching, she rested her head on his shoulder and breathed in his essence. Warmth rushed south when his large, strong hands caressed her back.

"Don't push your luck. It was all I could do to resist your moves last night."

She moved back a step and slid her hands under his T-shirt, up the trail of hair to his nipples. Lord, heat boiled from his body, soaking through her clothes and deep into her skin.

She stood on her tiptoes and nibbled her way around his jaw to his ear. She pulled the lobe between her teeth and then gently sucked. His groan sent flames licking through her nervous system.

"I won't break. I promise," she whispered, staring up into eyes full of desire. Waves of need rolled through her.

"There's nothing I'd like better than to set you on that countertop and ravage that sexy body of yours. But you've had a rough few days. The doctor said bed rest."

His chest rose and fell rapidly against her. From the size and hardness of the erection pressing against her, he was struggling. She wasn't about to let him get away.

She kissed him, a soft and gentle touch of the lips that quickly exploded to a round of simulated sex as his tongue dove in and out. She willing surrendered as he plundered her mouth.

He tugged her shirt over her head.

"Shit," he muttered. "I wish I could kill him again." His head snapped back and studied her injuries. He lowered his head and placed feathery kisses on her collarbone.

"Nate." She tugged his face to hers. "Don't see the bruises. Don't treat me as if I'll break. Make love to me."

The air crackled around them as his gaze filled with concern. "You're sure?"

"Positive."

He tilted his head and captured her lips again. Hard, hungry and demanding.

She jerked his shirt up, and he finished by tossing it and his jeans across the room. She followed by kicking her yoga pants and panties off.

His gaze drifted down her naked body, searing her skin as he went. He cupped her breasts with those large hands.

"You are incredibly beautiful."

His encouragement gave her strength and power. She sank to her knees in front of him, dropping small nips and kisses on the way down. She licked the satin skin of his erection with the tip of her tongue, circled him before taking him in her mouth.

"Oh, God," he moaned. His tone urged her on. His hands tunneled deep in her hair.

She placed her hands on his butt, pulling him closer, deeper inside her mouth, feeling him grow larger still.

Nate hissed through his teeth. Ha. She had him.

"Tell me." She took one more swirl with her tongue and then looked up from her kneeling position. "The tattoo."

"You cheat. It's nothing romantic. It says, One Shot One Kill."

She stood, running her hands up his body as she rose. She placed her hand over his racing heart before continuing her trek down to his hips and back to his stomach. She kneaded, smoothed, and relished the perfection of his body as he stood still, barely breathing. Standing on tiptoes, she kissed his cheek and then the other.

"Make love to me."

"My pleasure. There's one particular thing I'm looking forward to. But we need the bed for this."

She relaxed and let him take control. He wrapped his hand around hers and led her down the hall. As if she were a piece of fine china, he helped her to sit on the side of the bed. Kneeling in front of her, he tongued her nipple. Of its own accord, her back bowed, offering her body, her mind and her soul to him.

He lay down, and rolled her on top of him. "Sit right here." He patted his chest.

She hesitated before putting one knee on either side of his belly and sliding up his body. She settled herself, the apex of her thighs resting against his upper chest.

"You okay? Not hurting?"

"I'm fine. I swear."

"Then don't get too comfortable. I need you to lift up for a second."

"Do what?" A sizzle of excitement raced across her skin.

"Kaycie. Up on your knees, okay?" His eyebrow arched as if to say "don't question me."

He'd said her full name in the same throaty way he had when they were young and in love. It rolled off his tongue, seeped into her pores. He always could seduce her with his voice. She willingly complied.

He held her thighs still and slid down the bed between them. Kept sliding until his face lay directly under her most private parts.

"Nate?" she questioned, feeling way too vulnerable and exposed.

He answered with a slide of his tongue. Spreading her layers open with his fingers, he provided himself access to her very core.

She gasped out loud, her last remnant of shyness evaporated, leaving nothing behind but a glorious need. Her passion dominated her every thought, demanding more.

"You say something?" he asked, his breath warming her moist folds.

"No. Nothing," she choked out. She struggled for balance, couldn't find anything to hang onto until she leaned forward and placed her hands on the wall above his head. Then she surrendered to the luxury of his mouth.

He explored, probed, and licked, bringing her to the very edge of a climax, before backing away to nibble on the insides of her thighs.

She moaned his name as his tongue returned and set a blistering pace, holding her to him with his hands dug into her hips. She abandoned all reason as her orgasm rushed to the surface, and she lowered herself closer to his magical mouth. Stars exploded inside her head. She cried out as her body vibrated, pulsated, throbbed when his teeth gently pulled at her. Spent, she slumped forward, trying desperately to catch her breath.

When he slid out from under her and laid her down to face him, she was sated and exhausted.

"Sex like that should be illegal." For a second, she considered purring.

"Then I'd happily become a criminal."

He trailed kisses around her belly button. Slowly worked his way up to her face, setting every nerve ending on fire. Desire spread to her core like lava flowing to the sea. He moved away for a condom, and she instantly missed his warmth.

He rolled to his back, placing her astride him once more. Her body, still melted into the mattress, found strength in that desire.

"This way I know I won't hurt you."

His tender concern for her bruises touched a place deep in her heart. Emotion welled in her chest, and she slid sideways and then onto her back.

"No. You drive," she whispered.

"You're the boss." His Cheshire cat grin lit his face.

"Not anymore." Opening for him, her hand slid down, guiding him to her opening.

"At last," he said as he drove himself deep. "Inside you, this is where I belong."

His thrusts grew in intensity. Their Saint Jude medallions clicked against each other, playing the tune of lovers. His eyes turned midnight blue, and she lost herself completely. The fullness, the belonging, the love swept her to a new dimension of sensation. She went to the very edge with him, until in one breath, she cried out his name, and together they surged into a realm reserved for lovers.

"Kaycie?" His face was burrowed into the pillow next to her head, muffling his voice.

"Nate?" She answered from inside a dream. Still strolling around in the clouds, her mind seemed reluctant to return to earth.

"I love you," he said.

"I know." It was all she could say, words of joy stuck in her throat.

****

Nate hesitated. His heart jackhammered against his rib cage. He was pretty sure his climax had blown the top of his head off. Yet she'd ignored his announcement.

A satisfied, contented and confusing smile lit her face. "You're amazing."

"No. We're amazing." He rolled to his side and disposed of the condom. Returning to her, he held her snugly against him. "We keep this up and one of us will have to be wheeled down the aisle."

She lifted her head and locked gazes with him, a question written across her features.

"What?" he asked. "You don't think we should get married?"

The light from the nightstand reflected off her eyes. Did he read doubt in her gaze?

"Never mind," he said, trying to sound blasé. Instead, his tone came across as that of a hurt teenager.

"No." She smiled and stroked her fingers up and down his arm, generating an instant reaction from his body.

"No what?" He braced for her refusal.

"No, you're not backing out. You asked. I accept." She reached up and wound her fingers through his hair. "I love you. Always have. Always will. So, no. You're stuck with me."

"Thank God. You scared the crap out of me." The weight on his shoulders lifted.

Together they'd work through anything life could throw at them.

"You do have more than one condom?"

"Yes, ma'am." He wasted no time in taking care of the situation.

She slid on top, and he found his way back inside her warm body. Where he felt whole.

"See, I told you I wasn't too injured to make love."

"Point taken." Then with a slide of her hips, she rendered him almost speechless. This chocolate-eyed woman, beautiful, brave and his.

"About that job."

"It's yours."

Whatever she wanted, he'd figure it out. Together they'd build a business, stay close to their friends and help Jake get well. At the same time, they'd make the world a safer place.

Read COLD DAY IN HELL

Book two in the Lost and Found, Inc. series.

Ty Castillo shook his boot and flicked a tarantula larger than his hand to the jungle floor. The arachnid crawled away uninjured, disappearing into the constantly undulating ground cover. Poor bastard was probably looking for relief from the heat.

His original orders were to meet his Colombian contact in Bogota, meet his contact, pick up the necessary explosives, and use them to blow up Manuel Ortega's drug-manufacturing compound.

Lost and Found, Inc. had taken this supposedly simple assignment to pay the rent. Slip in, obliterate the place, and then get the hell out. The plan fell apart when that contact, Ana Cisneros, failed to show. She'd left Ty scrambling for supplies.

Then the FBI added the task of locating and rescuing her. After some digging, he'd learned she was being held at the very site he intended to obliterate off the map.

A minimal number of guards were on duty tonight. The rest had bedded down for the night. Various birds and nocturnal animals squealed and squawked, providing him with good noise cover.

One of the guards spotted the fire Ty had started in a small clearing four-hundred meters from the compound. The warista yelled at the top of his lungs and fired two rounds into the air.

Half a dozen men ran from three buildings, some struggling to get their pants fastened. They barreled into the jungle with nothing to fight the fire with except the AK-47s they carried over their shoulders.

Ty knelt behind a row of palm fronds. A perimeter guard came into view. He continued his patrol, ignoring the shouting and the fire. The oversized gorilla at the back door hadn't budged either.

It would be a deadly mistake.

Ty waited five minutes to allow the men to reach the fire. Then he pushed the button on a radio frequency timer and blew the C-4 he'd placed on the diesel-powered generator. The compound fell into total darkness, leaving the remaining guards at a loss for which fire to fight first.

Chaos was a good thing.

He had a lot to accomplish and no time to waste. His plan didn't allow for a lot of interruptions. He stepped out of the darkness and directly behind the guard. His neck snapped easily, and Ty dragged him into the dense growth. Now to get inside to Ana Cisneros.

He ran across the open area. Hugging the exterior wall, he circled to the back to find Gorilla Guy's attention turned toward the blaze. By the time the guard realized he was in danger, it was too late. Ty drove the SOG up through the diaphragm, through the lung, and into the man's heart. He retrieved his knife, wiped it clean on the man's shirt and entered the back door.

Thanks to his surveillance of the compound over the past few days, he knew where he'd find the woman. He moved through the large kitchen and headed up the stairs. He paused at the landing. Shit. Gorilla Guy's twin stood outside the hostage's door. Ty stepped into the hall and cleared his throat. Before the man turned, the SOG was airborne. It seated in the man's chest with a soft thump. The last person between the target and freedom slid to the floor.

Ty retrieved his knife, dragged the heavy body away from the door, and quickly moved to the figure handcuffed to the metal headboard. She stood as close to the window as the restraints allowed. Craning her neck to see outside, she was unaware he'd entered the room. With no time for introduction, he reached around and clamped his hand over her mouth.

As expected, he'd startled her. She fought, slinging her body back and forth like a wet dog. She kicked at him, so he whirled her around and jerked her body snug against his.

"Quit struggling. I'm here to help you," he whispered, trying to sound reassuring. No doubt, with the flames outside casting an eerie glow, he looked like an alien. The night-vision goggles would scare most anybody. "Do you understand?"

He took the slight movement of her head as a yes and relaxed the pressure off her lips. His reward? She bit his finger and pummeled his chest with her free fist.

What the hell? The lamb had attacked the lion.

"Stop that," he commanded, holding back a chuckle at her bravado. He reapplied the pressure while keeping one eye on the door.

Even through the lens on the goggles, he spotted a bruise on her cheek. Anger sizzled up his spine at the bastard who'd hit her.

He'd expected fear or panic to be oozing from her every pore, but didn't sense either emotion from her. Waves of rage rolled off her instead.

"Do you understand?" he repeated. She nodded slightly, relaxed her tense muscles, and then tried to kick him in the nuts.

He didn't have time to reason with her. And from what he'd seen so far, sweet talking her was out. "I'm going to remove my hand. If you fight me, I'll tie and gag you. Got it?"

This time he got a full nod. The expression behind her eyes made him doubt her honesty.

"I don't have time to argue, so you'll have to trust that I'm the contact you were supposed to meet in Bogota." Cautiously, he lifted two fingers from her lips and waited to see if she complied.

"I know who you are," she hissed. "And you've ruined everything."

"Me? I think you've cornered the market on screw-ups." He made quick work of the handcuff and pulled her to her feet. Long dark hair fell around her shoulders. She wore jeans and a T-shirt. All she needed was shoes, preferably a good pair of boots.

Damn, she was a little thing. Beautiful, bruised, and boiling mad. It was bad enough the jungle was sweltering. This woman was going to make the next few days a living hell.

"Get something on your feet. The rest of this place is going to blow soon, and we're going to be clear when it happens."

Her eyes went wide. "Did you make sure Ortega's on the property?" Her tone hinted at panic.

"Haven't seen him. He—"

"I have to know." She curled her fingers around Ty's bicep. He ignored the holes her nails dug. "Promise me that he'll die in the explosion."

That piece of information caught his curiosity and slowed him for a second. Under different circumstances ... nope, he'd been tasked with bringing her out alive. He didn't have the time to help her with whatever wrong she thought she needed to right.

"I'd advise against going barefoot. With or without shoes, you're leaving with me."

Never taking her eyes off him, she jerked a pair of leather ankle boots from under the bed and quickly pulled them on. Good. They were running out of time.

"You don't understand." Her voice dripped with anger.

"Let's go." She didn't move. He shoved the goggles to his forehead and leaned down inches from her face. Standing this close, the bruise on her cheek was even more noticeable. She'd been treated like shit, and he hated to add to her troubles, but he didn't have time to argue.

"You'll walk, or I'll haul your ass out of here like a sack of potatoes."

She set her jaw and didn't budge, so he did what any smart man would've done. He tossed her over his shoulder firefighter style. She was light as a feather. He'd bet she didn't weigh much more than his backpack.

"Oh. Hell. No. You are not carrying me anywhere."

He stopped at the door, checking his watch to ensure he wouldn't run into one of the perimeter guards. He reached up and patted her on the leg.

"Were you not listening? This entire compound is about to disappear from the face of the earth. And you want to stay?"

"Wait," she muttered.

"No talking."

"Put me down. We'll move faster." She sounded defeated, but had she really surrendered?

Ty glanced at her bottom, which currently rested on top of his shoulder. It was a great ass but not much of a gauge to use when testing for the truth. "If you run, I'll catch you. Traveling hog-tied and slung over my shoulder will get old fast. At least for you."

"I get it," she spit the words out as if they tasted bitter.

He slid the goggles into place. "Stay close."

An inappropriate shiver shot up his spine when her fingers gripped his shirt.

She nodded toward the jungle. "I hope you know what you're getting us into."

"I do." He ignored that she doubted his ability. Once outside, they hugged the house until another perimeter guard walked close enough to spot them. He opened his mouth but was silenced by a bullet from Ty's suppressed .22. The man fell right on the path. Time was the bigger enemy, so Ty dragged the body close to the house and left him.

He glanced down and found the woman's gaze locked on his face. One quick nod and they sprinted across the open space and into the dense cover of jungle.

He pushed hard, watching for movement on every leaf. The ferns, grasses, small plants and dead matter provided the perfect cover for hungry creatures of all species. No way was he letting her get bitten, stung or eaten. Losing her wasn't an option.

A sound coming from behind stopped him. He recognized the steady swoosh, swoosh, swoosh of a machete. Someone was coming fast. He'd hoped they would have more time, but expected the guards to be hunting the person who disrupted their drug production.

Judging from her quick intake of air, she'd heard the noise, too. Ty spun to face her and placed his finger to her lips. Silently, he pulled her into the thick bush. A quick scan of the surroundings didn't reveal any obvious hazards. Leaving her alone was dangerous but a calculated risk he had to take. If he wound up in hand-to-hand combat with more than a couple of men, protecting her would be difficult at best. He leaned close to her ear and whispered, "Stay here."

"I can't see." She tightened her grip on his arm.

"Right now they're focused on me. I can fix this easier and faster without you along." He slipped his Beretta into her hand, hoping it would give her a measure of security. "Do you know how to use this?"

"Probably better than you."

Any other situation and he'd have laughed at her assumption that she could out-shoot him. Now wasn't the time. He wrapped the fingers of her free hand around a small tree limb. "Listen to the sounds around you and shoot if you have to. I'll identify myself when I get back."

"Go ahead. I'm not going anywhere." She stood perfectly still. Even through the goggles, he saw determination in the way she held her head. The lady had guts.

Ty moved silently in the direction of the rhythmic sound of the swinging machete. Whoever it was, he was hacking at vines, widening the path and getting closer.

The flapping wings of frightened birds and chatter of spooked monkeys stopped so fast the quiet was startling. The night turned as still as a church during prayer. Through the trees, a single flashlight beam caught his eye. Moving quick and soundless, Ty looped around behind the man. Just as Ty had expected, it was one of the guards he'd monitored over the past few days. Stupid to have come alone.

Ty eased the .22 pistol from the holster strapped to his leg. One shot and the warista crumpled like a piece of wet paper. He dragged the body into the bushes. Ty picked up the AK-47 and took it with him. He saw no advantage in leaving it behind.

He backtracked to Ana. She stood right where he'd left her. Judging from the way she held the gun, she'd told the truth and knew how to handle one. "I'm right behind you."

Lowering the Beretta, she turned toward the sound of his voice. "Who was it?"

"One of Ortega's guards," he said, closing his hand over hers and relieving her of the weapon.

"You killed him?"

"Yeah. We have to move."

He took her hand in his, slid his arm behind his back, and headed out. She stayed right with him, allowing them to move fast. The lady might be small in stature, but she had the stamina of a soldier, which was going to prove to be an asset. Over the next few days, she'd need it.

Once they reached the small hideaway he'd carved out for storage, she could rest until daylight. First thing in the morning, they'd start across the thickest and roughest terrain of their trek.

About the Author

Author of <u>The Green-Eyed Doll</u>, <u>The Last Execution</u>, and <u>Someone To Watch Over Me</u>, my husband and I live in Texas with our rescue dog,
Buddy. I write alpha males and kick-ass women who weave their way through death and fear to emerge stronger because of, and on occasion in spite of, their love for each other.

Get up to date information on new releases. Sign up for my newsletter at <u>http://www.JerrieAlexander.com</u> and connect with me on <u>Facebook</u> and <u>Twitter</u>.

If you enjoyed this book, please help me spread the word. Facebook and tweet your approval. A review on Amazon and or GoodReads would be greatly appreciate. Send me an email if you post a review, I'll want to thank you personally.

PRAISE FOR THE GREEN-EYED DOLL

"Jerrie Alexander's debut novel THE GREEN-EYED DOLL is a gritty, thrilling can't put it down romantic suspense. I'm looking forward to seeing what she has for us next."

-<u>Fresh Fiction</u>

"Two lonely people meet at a routine traffic stop, a woman with a sad, violent past, and a man on the good side of the law. Add a crazed serial killer to the mix, and you have the makings for a gripping romantic suspense read!"

-<u>InD'tale Magazine</u>

PRAISE FOR THE LAST EXECUTION

"I stumbled across The Last Execution book, so glad I did as thoroughly enjoyed it. I searched the author then also read "The Green-Eyed Doll" in record time. They both get you hooked from the start, and had me reading till the wee hours of the morning! If you like thrillers, with a bit of romance on the side, you will love both Jerrie Alexander books. I just hope she is writing more...and soon!"
Amazon Reader Review

Made in the USA
Lexington, KY
18 September 2013